"Lauren Brandenburg tells a d... redemption with playful twists... that draw you through a story o. ....g.... to something more valuable than riches. This story weaves lessons of simplicity and hope through the tale of Charlie Price, the warring Blackwells and Tofts of Coraloo and their mystical market, where some trinkets carry greater value than their cost."
David Rawlings, author of *The Baggage Handler* and *The Camera Never Lies*

"Charming, eccentric, and truly heart-warming, *The Death of Mungo Blackwell* is a breath of fresh air. From laugh out loud hilarity to deeply authentic moments of fear and anxiety in the wake of devastating financial loss, Brandenburg weaves a lush, entertaining story. A delightful tale about family, marriage, friendship, and macarons... you can't go wrong, and I can't wait for the sequel!"
A.C. Williams, author of *Finding Fireflies*

"A cast of delightful and eccentric characters bring to life this heartfelt story about discovering real friendship and what's truly important in life. If only Coraloo were a real place we could all visit!"
Claire Wong, author of *A Map of the Sky*

"They say there's nothing new under the sun – oh yes, there is! Fun, quirky, and totally original!"
Amy Willoughby-Burle, author of *The Lemonade Year*

"Lauren H. Brandenburg has created a classic. She's woven a story that mixes real life with mystery. Her witty unassuming demeanor and personality come to life on the pages. You instantly fall in love with the characters and her."

Gigi Butler, founder of Gigi's Cupcakes, speaker, and author of *The Secret Ingredient*

"Hilarious and entertaining, a fantastic story for anyone who has had a hiccup in life."

Danny Gokey, recording artist and author of *Hope in Front of Me*

"Lauren's characters are relatable, lovable, and engaging, captivating the reader's interest immediately. You'll find yourself thinking about them without the book in hand, wondering what turn the story takes next!"

Nina Roesner, Executive Director of Greater Impact Ministries and author of *The Respect Dare*

THE DEATH OF MUNGO BLACKWELL

LAUREN H. BRANDENBURG

Illustrations by Sarah J. Coleman

LION FICTION

Published by
Lion Hudson Limited
Wilkinson House, Jordan Hill Business Park
Banbury Road, Oxford OX2 8DR, England
www.lionhudson.com

ISBN 978 1 78264 291 6
e-ISBN 978 1 78264 292 3

First edition 2019

A catalogue record for this book is available from the British Library

For Jamie
How boring my life would be without you. I love you.

CHAPTER 1

Tofts were not welcome at the renowned Coraloo Flea Market. The Blackwells made certain of that. On the brick wall, the sign outside the once prosperous shoe factory proclaimed, NO DOGS OR TOFTS – GRANNY BITES! Reading these words, Charlie Price scratched his thinning blond hair, musing over the long-standing rivalry he had read about between the Tofts and the Blackwells. Today was Thursday; the market was closed, but there was nothing stopping Charlie from exploring. The scent of old leather and lavender lured him – as it did countless others – through the stone archway into the still, quiet building, carrying with it the promise of unearthing a hidden treasure or memorable trinket. Inside, the shops, each specific to their wares – antique books, hand-dyed ribbons, flowers, freshly pressed olive oils, leather goods, and an occasional antique dealer – lined the perimeter like tiny homes. These, Charlie knew, belonged to the Blackwells. The center, reserved for paying vendors and hungry shoppers dining on Granny's delicacies at hand-hewn tables, was empty today.

He peered through one of the storefront windowpanes. In front of a faux mantel, two armchairs were arranged in such a way the shop almost looked livable. Charlie moved on. The next shop appeared promising – less orderly, no décor. He spotted a French horn, dented and in need of a polish. *Music is money* – a mantra he heeded when considering a purchase. He'd come back and make an offer in the morning, but he would have to arrive early if he wanted to turn a profit – especially at the Coraloo. Pickers arrive early.

Nestled at the top of a rolling green hill in a picturesque town with stone inlaid streets, overlooking curving rows of carefully maintained cedar-shingled rooftops not yet touched by the deluge of tourists or modern construction trends, sat the Coraloo Flea Market. *Wayfaring* magazine called the market one of the country's hidden wonders – known for its charm, history, food, and peculiar owners. The writer described it as a place where peace and simplicity dine with the eccentric – a trove for modern-day treasure hunters – keeping watch over a quaint commonality held together by deep ancestral roots and rivalries.

It's why Charlie entertained the thought of moving his family two hours and forty-one minutes southeast of the big city – to start over, to live simply, to shop the Coraloo. He shined his flashlight into the shop – an antique globe perched on a wooden pedestal caught his eye. He doubted they would take less than the asking price, but it was worth a try. Beside it, sitting on top of a pile of yellowing maps, a gold rimmed teacup sat chipped and out of place. It wasn't valuable anymore. Somebody had probably tossed it out during a spring clean, along with broken picture frames and melted candles. But regardless of its worth, it had a story. The cup once had an owner – possibly a fan of Ceylon orange pekoe or Earl Grey. Had the vessel been a gift or a souvenir from an unplanned road trip? Had the owner been forced to part with this fragment of everyday life to make room for simplicity?

No... that was his story. With his hands in the pockets of his slacks, Charlie slumped down on an old church pew outside the market shop. Had life really come to this? Had four years at university and a career with a six-figure income dwindled down to sorting through the discarded wares of others? He had been good at his job and never doubted his instincts. He was meticulous, thorough – except on the day the proposal landed on his desk.

A balmy August breeze crept into the brick edifice, bringing with it the sweet aroma of freshly hung tobacco from a farm on the other side of the hill. Charlie closed his eyes and inhaled distant days – memories of a life absorbed by legality and expectation, before the whirlwind of the past year wreaked devastation on his once predictable life.

He remembered the loan. How could he forget? An equipment loan three times what the proprietor needed. His university roommate and colleague, Carl Rogers, had pulled him aside. "This guy is a pal of mine. Everything's here. Just sign and you're done." That should have been his first red flag – slow down, look closer. The plan seemed solid, the client a chef and former restaurant owner. It was a lapse in judgment. A missing document. He should have caught it. With the fragile state of the financial world, there was no room for error. On a wider scale, the newspapers swarmed with rumors of a crumbling economy in response to banks' overlending to house-hungry newlyweds. Pair that with this class-action lawsuit of press-worthy proportions, and the bank would take a healthy loss, leading to some very unhappy shareholders.

He had called Velveteen. She had said she was mid-foil at the salon and could not meet him for another two hours. He had packed up his office and walked out the front doors of Heritage Financial without looking back. He had needed time to strategize, to carefully word how he was going to tell his wife of eleven years that he was unemployed – not just unemployed, but most likely blackballed from every bank, accounting firm, and food truck in the city.

Stupid food trucks. Charlie let his head fall into his hands, vowing to never eat at a food truck again. The fragmented events leading up to this moment entered his mind, overshadowing the potential of Coraloo.

His rear end was sore from sitting for so long, and he wasn't sure he could swim in his own guilt and self-loathing much longer. He raised his eyes at the click clack of high heels.

Velveteen Price arrived with the latest Melba DuMont novel peeking cautiously over the edge of her handbag. He stood and kissed her – a quick peck on the lips. Whenever he kissed her in public, he pretended all of the other men around were jealous. He loved every inch of her, inside and out, and dreaded telling her their life would drastically change. He sensed she already knew something – regardless, Charlie had wanted her to hear it from him, so explained every detail, from how Carl, despite being a known idiot, had insisted his street food truck client was an easy underwrite to the fact that when it fell apart, Charlie took the fall. At this Velveteen informed him her friendship with Carl's wife, Mary Beth Rogers, was over.

"I'm done with that woman. I really am!"

Charlie had laughed – he used to laugh more.

"But I'm proud of you, Charlie Price."

"For what? Losing my job?"

"No, for making it this far. It's not over, you know. You'll find something better. You were almost VP of the country's largest bank! Somebody will see the value in that… Somebody will see your value! What about Standard? I'm sure they would hire you. I'll call Rebecca, her husband is pres –"

"I've already started putting in applications." He held up two fingers.

"Two applications already! See! You're a fighter, Charlie!"

"Two rejections."

"Today?"

"I applied and they denied. Two, right after I left the office. Nobody's hiring in this economy. Homes, cars, anything financeable – banks are calling in notes left and right. They're losing money. There's not a chance they'll take a risk on a man deemed responsible for a hunk of the city's employees being forced to take sick leave."

"They can't blame you for poor immune systems, Charlie. Besides, God never intended for us to eat from a truck." She cringed.

He brushed a lock of hair away from her dark eyes. "What about the truffle truck or the cupcake truck on 7th?"

"Dessert is always an exception, Charlie." She glanced down at her heels – most likely a recent purchase. Even with the added two inches, the top of her newly quaffed hair barely reached Charlie's chin. "Charlie, are you trying to tell me we will lose everything?"

"Not everything. We have each other and Gideon. There's enough in savings and a few side investments to get us by until I can find work, but we might need to cut back… to be safe."

"Will we have to cancel the Christmas party? I think we should appear as if life is carrying on as normal, don't you agree? If we cancel the party, everyone will start talking, and before long, Jennifer will be telling that gossip Mary Beth we are headed for the poor house. If we can swing it, we must have the party."

Velveteen started planning in July for their annual Christmas Party – lining up caterers, researching tree farms, and spending hours at the stationery shop on the corner of 9th and Canary picking out invitations. Hospitality was her gift, her art form. She studied it, practiced it, and paid so much attention to every detail of her craft he was quite sure she even prayed about it. The party was her event, her personal year-end final examination – a night culminating in the glitz, greenery, and glamour at the invitation of his best friend and wife, Velveteen Price. He couldn't have denied her.

"Only if we invite the Rogers," he joked.

He used to joke more too.

"You've got to be kidding, Charlie!"

"You were friends with her this morning."

"Be serious! This is important. If we don't have the party, I'll need to work on our excuse, or our guests will think we've abandoned them! That would be horrible, Charlie! Maybe we can make up a story about an aunt who passed away or tell everyone the Duke of Such and Such has invited us to spend Christmas in Europe."

"You're related to a duke?"

"I wish!"

"We can have the party, if..."

"If what, Charlie?"

"If you invite your long-lost relative the duke."

That year was the last party in the townhouse. There was nothing he could have done to stop their downfall. Without his six-figure salary, their savings were quickly depleted, and with that, the lifestyle Charlie's job had afforded them slowly slipped away as the funds disappeared from his bank account. He feared he might even lose his sanity. The word *failure* loomed over him, a dark cloud so heavy he no longer heard his wife sobbing in the closet.

Velveteen's car had been repossessed on a Wednesday. As she very rarely drove the vehicle, it took them until Friday to realize it was gone. Their ten-year-old son, Gideon Price, had found his mother in the closet crying that day. Except for the loss of the car, however, Charlie took on any work he could find to make sure Velveteen's life carried on as close to normal as finances would permit. And Velveteen did her part as well. She had her long brown tresses highlighted and trimmed every four weeks instead of two and learned to shop online using coupon codes. But her small sacrifices were not enough.

Charlie had cancelled his membership at the Gentleman's Hall and the gym – working out twice a week did not appear to help his middle-aged middle anyway. He had refused to buy a new suit even when Velveteen insisted he have one for an interview. And when his personal finder had called to tell him he had located the elusive 1894 leather-bound first edition of Rudyard Kipling's *The Jungle Book* that had occupied his every spare thought, Charlie had declined the purchase. Velveteen had nearly fainted with disbelief. He loved books and read often – at least until *The Rooning*, after which time seemed to speed up and a veil of debt collectors and fear masked the joys they tried to find in their everyday.

Charlie shook his head. Coraloo would not know what hit them when Velveteen Price graced the door. She could hold her own, of that he was certain.

Four months after the Christmas party, during Velveteen's Tuesday book club, the doorbell rang and she was served the foreclosure papers on her five thousand square foot dream home. Before the foreclosure agent exited, Velveteen had asked him if he would like a macaron. He had no idea that his answer – a baffled "Yes, please" – would incite such rage in his wife as to go down in Price family history as *The Rooning*. She had sauntered her petite frame back to the ladies, grabbed the sterling silver tray of brilliantly colored treats and began throwing the meringue confections at the man's forehead. The man scrambled for the door, fumbling to pull it open. But Velveteen didn't stop. Another one hit him on the back of the neck. He turned and faced her. "Crazy woman! I'll take your house and your stupid *macaroons*!"

At this, the fire already stoked in Velveteen turned into a full-on inferno. She gritted her teeth, arm cocked with the delight in hand. "They're *macarons*, not *macaroons*, you imbecile! One 'o', not two." The man was gone before she had fully settled on throwing the tray. From that day forward, the family of three had nicknamed their financial misfortune *The Rooning*.

"Before *The Rooning*" became such a common phrase in their house they often forgot its dark implications. But Charlie knew the truth. It was just an easier way to say, "Before we lost everything." Following *The Rooning* things had moved quickly.

On his way home from his seventh interview – desperate and knowing any day they would receive notice their home was going to auction – Charlie had spied a royal blue fountain pen – a Waterman – in the window of a pawnshop. He had two just like it at home and was certain he was reading the price incorrectly. He had stepped inside and confirmed the briarwood pen was rare and grossly under-priced. At that moment an idea took root. If it worked, he could double his money. If it didn't, they would be eating bacon and eggs for dinner for the rest of the week. He purchased the pen, did a bit of research on selling over the Internet, listed the pen for a three-day auction or best offer, and waited.

Before the day was over, the interested party had offered him twice what he had paid for it. That night Charlie Price listed his collection of fountain pens and took the family out to dinner. The rush of the deal made him feel powerful and in control, like during his days working at the bank. The next day he had listed everything he could think of that might make an easy profit – gold cufflinks, a vintage telescope he had never used, calculators, three watches, and a pair of binoculars. Soon, almost every object in their home promised an easy dollar. But he wanted the thrill of the Waterman. He started spending his days scouring pawnshops and digging through donated goods at church rummage sales. In the evenings, he diligently researched asking prices and resale values before listing every purchased item on the online auction site.

Gideon had been the first to jump into the project. Seeing his father's excitement and fearful *The Rooning* had squashed his chances of owning the latest edition of *Pirates of the Cosmos*, he had plopped a stack of old comic books down on his father's desk and said, "Dad, I'll split the profit with you fifty-fifty."

It took Velveteen a little longer. Charlie would never forget the look on her face the day she walked into his home office to find his latest pickings.

*She gasped and slapped her hand over her pink lips –
eyes wide, shaking her head in disbelief. "Oh, Charlie!
Are these truly our belongings? It all looks like piles of
cheap junk!"*

*"Funny, isn't it? I guess we can be thankful we have
enough junk to sell."*

*"I have to hand it to you, Charlie Price. You're keeping the
lights on." She shot a glance down at her chipping Flamingo
Fiesta nail polish.*

He saw her.

"How much longer do you think we have?"

"Before we starve?" He tried to make a joke.

She frowned.

*Charlie took a deep breath. "We have at least three
months before the house goes to auction."*

"I see."

Charlie had nearly been hit in the face by a flying Lucetta Vacher clutch after a series of thuds sent him sprinting to their bedroom. Just outside her closet lay four purses, a pair of boots, two pairs of designer blue jeans, and a mink shrug Charlie had given her on their tenth anniversary.

*"Outdated! Out of style, and useless! I won't wear a piece of
it. It's closet filler. All of it! Sell it all, Charlie."*

Charlie had listed her "useless" items, covering their groceries for the next month, and insisted Velveteen have her nails done. He had created this lifestyle for her, given her more than her modest upbringing had ever allowed her to dream, and no matter what, he was going to take care of his family.

It wasn't long before the Price family had become reclusive – avoiding social events and close encounters with country club companions. Velveteen had sent word to the ladies that she would not be hosting book club the following month as their Maltese, Barnaby, was ill. Fortunately the ladies were too wrapped up in their own concerns to recall that the Prices didn't own a Maltese.

They sold everything that had resale value – even stripping the walls and cleaning out the cupboards – and did quite a number on Velveteen's jewelry boxes as Charlie continued to unearth bargains in the darker corners of the city.

What came next was the hardest.

Charlie had received word their house was going to auction mid-June, the day before his birthday. They would barely have two months to move out. He had dreaded the conversation with Velveteen – he purposefully put it off – partly because of her prior antics with the foreclosure agent. The idea of being whacked in the head with a macaron – or worse – haunted him. He had known she hoped their days of picking up random objects for resale would produce enough income to save the house, but it wasn't enough. He had planned to tell her, suggest they lease a modest house in a nearby suburb. He could continue looking for work in the city. So many times he had wanted to suggest she join one of those home-based network-marketing companies – sell plant-based facial products or imported jewelry. But she hadn't worked since Gideon was born – he didn't want to ask her. He couldn't ask her. It was not the life he promised her, no matter how bad things had gotten.

He had prepared his speech, researched affordable properties in the suburbs, and practiced ways to embellish them by calling the pantry "the butler's closet" and the family room "the hearth room". He jotted down words like "charming", "quaint", and "chef's kitchen". But the conversation had never happened.

On his way back from his weekly Friday pawnshop visit, the cover of *Wayfaring* magazine had caught his eye. In brilliant blue letters it read: "Shop the Coraloo". Charlie had heard of Coraloo. Not too far from the city. He had thumbed quickly through the article – hidden wonders… treasure hunters – and used what little gas he had in his car to make the trip to find out for himself what the place had to offer.

Charlie Price raised his head, looked out upon the historic market, and tried to replace the memories of a regret-filled past with hope of life in the town at the bottom of the hill. They would find a new house. It would be the adventure of a lifetime. It was a long shot, but what other choice did he have? Living in the city was not an option. The Prices would make this work. *Unless… What if…? Another Rooning? Failure.*

He breathed in the cool air of the open market and listened to the gentle silence – the peace of Coraloo settled him, replacing doubt with possibility. *This could be it – our fresh start. What was it Velveteen had said they needed? A "quelque chose de nouveau"?*

A something new.

CHAPTER 2

Velveteen Price gazed out the window at the passing homes – sprawling manor-style estates bordered by rolling green hills and limestone walls. Last month's issue of *Country Life* magazine lay open in her lap, flaunting images of brilliantly colored canned fruits sitting on a table with auburn vials of homemade oils surrounded by shiplap-covered walls and freshly picked flowers. She sighed.

Charlie had visited Coraloo once more before he'd sat her down and proposed the drastic move.

"Vee, I want to be completely honest with you about Coraloo. No surprises. I didn't see a salon, and I think the hardware store might be the grocery. But I've done some research, and if what the articles say is true, their market is going to turn that little town into the country's next hot spot. They'll line the streets to draw in tourists – high-end stores, those retro barbershops that are popping up all over the place, and most likely a restaurant or two. We'll have to wait for it, but it will come."

Velveteen watched her husband's eyes dart from one magazine to the next. He held up images of the picturesque town, pointing out the stone church and rows of historic brick homes with gated courtyards. She could envision it.

"There is one restaurant already… it's more of a tavern." *He pointed to a two-story building with red shutters and a heavy wooden door. "The locals call it The Beaver's Beard. And get this, their specialty – deer meat nachos, but only*

if it's deer season." He chuckled. She gagged. "See here – it's surrounded by farmland and woods. And on the hill, that's the market. I'll pick there. I've seen it in action, Vee. The place is packed. I could find something to flip every weekend if I wanted. Those people don't know how much money they have sitting right in front of their noses, but I do."

She hated it when he used those words: *pick* and *flip*. Velveteen had no intention of digging through piles of junk and had already informed Charlie she would rather not partake in his financial dealings at the Coraloo. If her mother were alive, she would have forbidden it, saying, "I worked too hard cleaning Mrs Vanderschmidt's toilets for you to go rifling through rubbish. That woman made you a debutant!" Velveteen missed her mother, but was thankful she wasn't around to witness their *Rooning*.

They sat in silence, Charlie watching her every breath, Velveteen's mind whirring as she tried to absorb Charlie's excitement – deer meat nachos, tavern, old, vintage... his grandmother's Christmas ornaments...

"Vee, are you okay? Tell me what you're thinking."

Velveteen pulled from her musings. "I'm thinking about Christmas, Charlie."

"Christmas?"

"Wouldn't a vintage Christmas be absolutely lovely?"

"What's Christmas have to do with Coraloo?"

"Surely we will still celebrate Christmas in Coraloo, won't we Charlie?"

Charlie shot up from the upholstered wingback chair and nearly slid into the marble fireplace. "So you're okay with it?"

"Of course! Oh, Charlie! Don't you know? It's absolutely fabulous. It will be an adventure. Just like Melba DuMont!"

18

"You mean Melba from your book?"

"Of course, Charlie. Who else?" She took pride in the fact she had read The Countess of DuMont *more than sixteen times. "Are there sheep, Charlie?"*

"Are you looking for your sheepherder?" he joked.

"Charlie Price, you know you are my one and only. Besides, Melba only ran off with him because of what that evil Count Horace did to her. Oh, Charlie! This is it. You found our quelque chose de nouveau." She threw her arms around his neck. "But Charlie, I'd rather not… " – she chose her words carefully – "go to the market. It's just that…"

"But it's so much more –"

"No thank you, Charlie. I've tried my hand at it. You know I have, but there's something so… Oh I don't know, what if those items belonged to a dead person?"

"Then I guess they won't mind me selling them, will they?" He laughed at his cleverness.

Velveteen did not.

She said yes to Coraloo. She'd warm up to the market when she was ready.

"Okay, no market."

She squealed. "I can't wait to tell the ladies! Mary Beth will be absolutely green over it. Who would have thought it, Charlie? The Prices are moving to the country!"

In that moment, the quest for the light of simplicity brightened the darkness surrounding *The Rooning*. Velveteen embraced their oncoming move like it was her new life mission. The feelings of defeat and fear surrounding Charlie in the days after the food truck debacle were now replaced by a sense of purpose – a mission – and a new family motto: "Simplicity." They would start over, this time living with much less. Not just because they had to, but because they wanted to. They would drastically downsize their lifestyle – living on what Coraloo could provide without looking back on life in the city. And they would be happy.

Velveteen twirled a string of pearls around her pointer finger, pulling them closer to her neck, and glanced back down at the staged scene gracing the glossy pages. *Simplicity.* She could live like this; surely it wouldn't be that hard. She and the book club had talked about it often. The ladies were entertained by her obsession with the tragic life of Melba DuMont – the heiress driven to servitude who falls madly in love with the prince disguised as a sheepherder. For Velveteen Melba's misfortunes represented a blissful escape from the constraints of their upper society life – though, she had to admit, she already missed the gourmet pastries from Francine's on 5th.

Maybe Coraloo will be good for all of us. She passed a glance back at Gideon whose head was jammed inside another one of his comic books. Maybe he would make some friends. Maybe *she* would make some friends. She hardly called the ladies in the city "friends" – "acquaintances" was a more suitable word.

As Charlie drove, Velveteen flipped through the pages of fresh white minimally decorated kitchens, herb-filled gardens, and articles on repurposing tool shed finds into home accessories. She imagined herself with her dark hair pulled neatly into a ponytail and a monogrammed linen apron wrapped around her waist as she waited for the homemade vanilla to ferment so she could use it to make her own bread. Her daydream was briefly interrupted as she tried to recall whether or not one would put vanilla into dough.

The warm sunlight wooed her back into thoughts of hand-painting her own greeting cards, drying herbs for homemade teas, and decorating their new home in Charlie's flea market finds – at one time she had liked doing her own decorating; she could do it again. And the all-natural cleaning products she would make – it would be much more affordable to make their own. She could see herself flitting across the pages. It would be lovely.

The car bumped. A gorgeous image of a rhubarb tarte Tatin with accompanying recipe scowled at her. She glared back, stuck out her tongue, and tossed the magazine onto the floorboard. Who was she kidding? She had not cleaned her own home in ten years, and the closest she had come to baking a pastry was opening the box from Francine's. And flea market finds? She would have to pass on those. There was no way Charlie could convince her to step foot in the flea market. She'd gone with him on one of his adventures before, and by the grace of God, narrowly escaped the flapping tongues and horde of phone calls that would have followed if Mary Beth Rogers figured out why she was really at the church rummage sale.

"Are you okay?" Charlie reached over and placed his hand on top of hers.

Velveteen forced a smile.

They had spent weeks sorting out the order of their new life – deciding what to sell and what to keep and scouring online real estate sites in search of a home that would not only fit their budget but would fit inside Velveteen's *workable* parameters.

Workable arrived on a Tuesday from a Coraloo real estate agent who referred to himself solely as "a Toft". The online image revealed a brick cottage nestled among other similar homes on a winding side street in Coraloo. Delicate vines grew around the front doorway, and a picket fence outlined the front flower garden. The description said, "Gilded by the morning sun, the historic cottage beckons lovers of simplicity with its Highland charm."

"Well… what do you think of the place?" It was their only option. The realtor had assured Charlie there were no other available residences in Coraloo.

Velveteen squealed. *Destiny.* Charlie signed the lease.

She glanced at the time on the dashboard and tried to re-enact a series of breathing techniques she had once learned in a yoga class. She laid her head against the headrest and closed her eyes. Despite her fears and self-doubt, Velveteen was giddy to enter a world she had only read about in her novels. She had even taken comfort in bragging about their new residence to the acquaintances.

"In Coraloo? My decorator says the place is a riot!" The acquaintance had gone on: "I think it is absolutely fabulous! How on earth did you convince Charlie to move?"

"Simplicity," Velveteen had told the woman over the phone, knowing full well this one call would spread faster to the acquaintances than if she had phoned them herself. "I told him we needed simplicity."

"Just like Melba! Oh, Velveteen, I am entirely jealous! Who are you having do the remodel? Let me give you the name of my…"

Velveteen didn't listen. The woman on the other end of the phone had visions of a charming estate surrounded by gardens of lavish green grass and a handsome sheepherder at her beck and call. Velveteen purposely withheld explaining that their two bedroom, single toilet home in Coraloo was no bigger than the quarters occupied by most of their nannies.

"This is it!" Charlie Price pulled the car to a stop.

Velveteen sat up straight. *I can do this. This is what we want.* She slowly opened the car door and stepped into the presence of her new home. "Are you certain this is the right place, Charlie? I'm not quite sure this is correct because… well… it's *yellow*, Charlie."

"Yes, it is a tad yellow, isn't it?" Charlie laughed. "Not quite *gilded*."

"It looks like a baby puked on it," Gideon added.

"The realtor said the owners had made a few upgrades."

"It's yellow." Velveteen fought the emotion birthed by the bold color.

"You like yellow."

"I like Lemon Chiffon, Pineapple a la Mode, Meyer Spritz, and Optimistic Yellow," she muttered, reciting the paint swatch samples from memory. "This is –"

"Puke yellow." Gideon pushed past her.

"Puke yellow," she repeated.

The cottage that stood in front of the Price family was a far stretch from the Internet image. Not only was the brick structure painted a garish yellow, falling somewhere between brown and orange, but the mossy mold growing up the side appeared to have eaten and spit out what plant life had once accented the doorway and paned windows. The small front garden was overgrown with a stalky wheat-like plant and smelled as if someone's cat had relieved itself near the dying hydrangeas on more than one occasion.

Charlie reached for her hand and kissed her on the cheek. She had willingly agreed to start over in Coraloo – all for him – all so they could have a second chance at life, so he could have a second chance – a do over, an opportunity to live a different, less complicated life than the one they had led in the city.

"This cannot be it." She coughed. "Oh… the smell. It's horrid!"

Charlie let go of his breath and exhaled. "The mailbox says, '31 Odenbon'. This is definitely it. Let's go inside. You can't judge a book by its cover, right?"

"What about the smell?"

"I like the way books smell."

"You like books that smell like vinegar and death, Charlie?"

Velveteen crossed the threshold and took a look around. No sooner had her petal pink pump landed on the orange shag pile carpet, than a small, involuntary gasp escaped her and she fainted. Hitting her head on the doorframe, Velveteen landed face first on the mercifully fluffy, vertigo-inducing carpet.

The next thing she knew, she was waking up in the Coraloo County Hospital with two magnified eyeballs looking over her. She pulled the crunchy one-hundred thread count sheet up around her neck and yelled, "Charlie!"

A pair of nurses appeared at her side, followed by Charlie and Gideon – his nose in his fifty-third read through of *Pirates of the Cosmos*.

"It's okay, Vee. The car ride, dehydration, stress… nothing serious. It's just a bump." Charlie gently squeezed and then kissed the hand he was holding.

Velveteen reached up and felt the mass of taped gauze on the side of her head. "Flowers," she mumbled. "There were so many flowers."

"She'll be all right," the owner of the alarming eyeballs informed Mr Price. "Could have been worse."

"I know. She's a tough one." Charlie held his wife's hand.

Velveteen pulled her hair carefully to one side. "Charlie, how do I look?"

He kissed her on the forehead. "As beautiful as the day we met, but with less paint on you."

On the day they'd met he had backed into her while she was working on a display for the university's college of design. She loved the memory even if he had ruined her painting.

"Just a few papers to sign, and you will be on your way back to Mother's house." The doctor wiped a bead of sweat from his forehead while shining a light into her left eye.

"Mother's house? You mean *my* house." Velveteen pushed her hair behind her ears and wiped dripping mascara from underneath her eyes.

"Mother was alone when she passed there. Not real sure what had been cooking on the stove when she went. We got the smell out of the house for the most part. Don't worry – she won't haunt you."

The team of nurses tittered. Velveteen asked for a Valium.

The doctor laughed, those big eyeballs bouncing with each chuckle. Was he, Dr Whatever, laughing at her? She couldn't remember his name. Had he told them? She had a name for him: Doctor Eyeballs. That was a good fit.

"It's a sweet place," Doctor Eyeballs said. "Lots of memories. Any who, welcome to Coraloo, Price family."

On the car ride home, her insides shook and her head ached. She tried to close her eyes and imagine herself pulling a freshly baked pie from the oven, but when she did, all she could see was flowers – big orange dahlias and hot pink mums, covering every inch of the walls.

"I really think I should have stayed in the hospital a few more days… or weeks. Maybe a month."

Five minutes later they were back. "Let's try this again." Charlie helped Velveteen from the car.

She hooked her arm in his, hoping the gaudy wallpaper had been a nightmare, but one foot into the doorway and her knees went wobbly. The longhaired tangerine carpet seemed to pull the saucer-sized dahlias right off of the walls.

"It's not so bad." Charlie escorted her into the room that was no bigger than the laundry space in their townhouse. "Okay… it's bad. I don't think I've ever seen a room so ugly in my entire life. But at least it doesn't smell, right?"

Then they walked into the kitchen. The pea green cabinets and matching linoleum floor covering were nearly camouflaged by the coordinating green walls. Above the porcelain sink, a giant stained-glass bumblebee with illuminated wings swung back and forth casting eerie shadows across the ceiling. Velveteen surveyed the room, pulling open drawers and rubbing her hand down the Formica countertop.

Charlie was disappointed; so was she. How could she not be? He would have a talk with the realtor in the morning – who strangely enough had a profile picture very similar in appearance to the man Velveteen had them all calling Doctor Eyeballs. Charlie had no words of apology for his wife. He had said his fair share before *The Rooning*, but she wouldn't accept it – reminding him that if he truly were responsible for the claimed salmonella outbreak among the professionals of the city, the Price household would have been infected, and they were not.

Velveteen gasped as they stepped through the door of the master bedroom. It was black – black carpet, black walls, and what had possibly at one time been a black, but was now worn to a threadbare gray, cushion on the window seat. Charlie rushed to her side and tried again. "I'll call first thing in the morning. We'll find a new place –"

She walked to the window and looked out. Lamppost lighting illuminated the quiet, empty street and row of facing houses. "No. It's perfect. I can work with black." Then she laughed. She laughed so hard Charlie nearly took his turn at passing out. He did not know why she was laughing, but nonetheless, she was laughing, and it reminded him of the twenty-something interior design student he had fallen in love with.

Soon they were both laughing, lying on the black carpet, eyes glued to the rhinestone-bedazzled ceiling fan. Velveteen sat up and smiled at her husband. "Old lady Toft died in this room, you know."

Charlie pulled her back down to the ground and kissed her.

"I found my room!" Gideon called from the second floor. "My bed's built into the wall, and I have bookshelves. My carpet's all red and there are cowboys riding hippos all over the walls, but I can deal with it!"

With that, Charlie and Velveteen burst into another round of laughter. "Sweetheart… " He could barely get the words out, and his sides hurt. "I think the doctor might be our realtor."

Velveteen fashioned her fingers into circles over her eyes. "Mr Price, I'd like to sell you a house, not exactly a house, more like a shoebox. It's a lovely fixer-upper. But first, we must remove your appendix!"

Charlie brushed a loose strand of hair away from her face and kissed her again. If every night in Coraloo was to be like this one, then maybe, just maybe, *The Rooning* was worth it. Tomorrow he would go to the market.

CHAPTER 3

Gideon Price, thin like his mother and light-haired like his father, stood outside the stone archway rocking back and forth on the heels of his tennis shoes while Charlie sorted through a collection of old windows, rusted bicycles, and cracked flowerpots stacked by the entrance to the market.

"Dad, don't you think if there was something to be found, someone *else* would have found it?"

"Maybe, but if I don't check, I could be passing up on my greatest pick yet!"

Gideon sighed.

The sweet smells of cinnamon, yeasty breads, and spicy sausages rolled out the entrance.

Inside, the light from the grand chandeliers flicked on, illuminating the interior. Cars pulled into the small gravel lot, spraying a thin veil of dust on the outside wares of the market.

Charlie wiped his hands on his slacks. "Time to go!"

Gideon stepped through the doors and into the Coraloo Flea Market for the first time. Parallel rows of long folding tables filled the open brick structure, holding piles of previously unwanted goods. Eager vendors stood behind, waiting to strike a bargain. Gideon knew how this worked. He had watched his dad do it at the pawnshops in the city. Charlie would act uninterested, pick up the object of interest, turn it over in his hand, ask how much, shrug, and walk away. A few moments later, Charlie would have his phone out checking the possibility of resale against similar sold items. Then, he would casually return to the item and make his offer. The process made Gideon uncomfortable.

Gideon passed a glance at the discarded electronics and a basket of unmatched kitchen utensils – his mother would cringe – and to a stack of deteriorating comic books. This he found interesting. He flipped through the gritty stack. They smelled of stale cigarette smoke. *No thanks.*

"Here." Charlie handed Gideon a ten-dollar bill. "Go grab a bite to eat. Bring back the change."

Gideon happily took the offer to leave while his dad haggled over his next pick.

The further Gideon went into the Coraloo Flea Market, the warmer the air became and the thicker the hints of nutmeg and rosemary oozing from the back. It didn't make sense that a place with fancy shops would allow the temporary vendors and all of their junk to set up right in the middle of it all, but Gideon had seen stranger things – like the time his dad purchased a vintage drum set only to find the former owner had attempted to use it as an elaborate fish tank.

A crowd congregated under one of the grand antique chandeliers hanging from a wooden beam above the second-hand dealers. Curious, Gideon inched his way under the shoulders of expectant tourists to the front of the gathering.

At the center of the circle of spectators, a boy pretended to take something from his pocket and smear its contents onto a fake mustachio. The boy waved in Gideon's direction. Gideon looked over his shoulder, assuming the stranger was waving at someone else. Another boy entered the drama with a headdress of feathers wobbling from side to side on top of his head as he walked proudly to the center of the circle of onlookers. The audience laughed. A girl followed with a star painted on the bridge of her nose.

The boy with the mustachio knelt down on one knee in front of the one with the feathers. "I'll do anything to wed my true love."

"Anything?"

The crowd snickered. Gideon frowned. He was not a fan of love stories.

Mustachio boy confidently and overdramatically placed his hand on his hips. "Anything!"

The feathered one pointed at the shoes on the feet of the other as the girl appeared to swoon, with eyelashes blinking wildly. "Shoes!"

The other boy removed the shoes and handed them to the native chief. The girl wrapped her arms around the neck of the now barefoot boy as the audience followed with a chorus of "aahhs". Then suddenly a cry like a baby's rang out, and the native princess dropped to the ground with a thud, her arms spread, tongue lolling out the side of her mouth, eyes shut tightly.

"Cursed!" the chief shouted at the boy.

Then the three, plus a tiny child who appeared from behind a black sheet held up by two redheaded girls, bowed before the entertained audience. The pleased tourists clapped, cheered, and tossed coins into a work boot set aside for the purpose of collecting tips. Gideon shook his head. If this was how the children of Coraloo had fun, he wanted no part of it.

But as the aromas of the delicacies pulled him toward his destination, he hoped what his father had read to them from *Wayfaring* was true: "The delicacies mouth-watering and as interesting as the woman behind the counter..."

Gideon stood on tiptoes behind a line of breakfast-hungry patrons. Wooden shelves filled with sticky sweets, freshly baked muffins, and jars of apple butter framed the brick wall. The chalkboard above the case listed the prices of the treats, breakfast sandwiches, homemade sausages, and the morning's special: Moroccan wheat berry bread. A short, portly woman with silver hair pulled tightly into a bun on the top of her head moved hurriedly back and forth, occasionally wiping her hands on her white apron.

As interesting as the woman behind the counter.

Gideon finally inched up to the counter. "Excuse me?" The woman stopped and glared at him. His mother often told him he spoke too softly. He tried again. "Ma'am?" But she didn't answer. Why wasn't she asking him what he wanted?

There was a tap on his shoulder. Gideon turned quickly to face the gray-eyed, redheaded boy from the performance a few moments earlier.

"It's your first time, isn't it?"

Gideon nodded. A line of people formed behind him, sharing with one another phrases like "my favorite" and "best in the state". His mind waffled between the sticky bun and a trio of spiced doughnuts. He'd eat any of it, except for the purple pickled eggs housed in an oversized mason jar sitting by the cash register.

"She only responds to *Granny*. Give it a try."

With his stomach rumbling and his mouth salivating for any one of the delicious treats, he took the boy's advice. "Excuse me, Granny –"

"What!" the woman barked.

Gideon stumbled back. "I think I want the sticky bun."

"Well, do you want it or not? I don't have time for thinkers." She huffed. "It's got bourbon in it? Are you twenty-one?"

Terrified, he shook his head. "I'll have –"

"I'm just messing with your mind. The alcohol cooks out… most of it, I think. Are you good with that?"

Speechless, he nodded.

The woman reached for a square piece of brown parchment paper. She then removed the warm pastry from the case and bundled it in the paper. "Pay at the end."

Gideon scooted to the end of the case where a younger version of the old woman pushed buttons on an antique cash register.

"Three-fifty."

He paid the lady and took his pastry to the dining area of the market. The rich smells of caramel, cinnamon, and bourbon invaded his senses and fought with the earthy naturalness of the homegrown herbs sold in the shop across from him. He picked up the yeasty, sugar-drenched treat and was about to take a bite when the boy from a few minutes earlier plopped down beside him.

"Granny's are the best. I don't care for the bourbon one so much. My dad likes it though." The boy chomped down on an apple spice muffin and then motioned for Gideon to eat as well. There was silence as the boy forced every morsel of the delight into his mouth, chewed the hunk of muffin, and then gulped it down. "You're new, right? Live in the Toft house?"

Gideon didn't answer. He preferred to stick with Captain Turnlip and the crew from his comic book.

"It's okay if you're shy. I'm not shy. Blackwells aren't shy. We are people-people – born to walk the earth meeting people."

"I'm not shy," Gideon fibbed with a mouthful of pastry.

"I'm Danger. Danger Blackwell." He extended his sticky hand.

"Danger?"

"It's a family name."

"Oh."

"You like Coraloo?"

"It's okay. Different." *Different like this sticky bun.* The unique flavor created a sensation that burned his throat and came out of his nostrils.

Gideon did not know what else to say. Should he say it was weird the town physician and the realtor were one in the same? Or should he mention last night when the family tried to go out for dinner, the tavern had already run out of deer meat, and they had to eat pizza on their living room floor because the moving truck had gotten lost finding the town?

"Right," Danger mumbled. "I like your shirt."

Gideon glanced down at the logo of two pirate swords crossed over a shooting star. "Thanks."

"Pirates of the Cosmos?"

Gideon raised his eyebrows, hopeful for a fellow follower. "Do you read them?"

"No. Not much for comic books. Too short."

Gideon had a feeling the boy wasn't going to go away unless he engaged in the conversation. "Oh. I have them all."

"You're a collector?"

"No. I'm an expert." Gideon was not only president of the POTC fan club; he was also the founder.

"Me too."

"I thought you didn't read comic books."

"I don't. My mom says I'm an *expert* on the family."

"The Blackwells?" Gideon had heard his dad go on about their strange habits and odd customs.

"Of course! I know everything."

"Nobody knows everything." Gideon stuffed another bite of sticky bun into his mouth.

"I do! I know everything about the Blackwells... everything."

"That's good, I guess. I should probably get back to my dad." Gideon wasn't ready to make friends.

"I have to go to our shop anyway. You can come see me there, if you want. We're the second one on the left, across from the flower shop."

Gideon would rather hide inside his oversized sticky bun than visit with total strangers. He hated it when his parents had company back in the city. His mom would make him wear trousers and a bowtie, and his dad wouldn't let him read his comic books in front of the guests. It didn't make sense to put on fancy clothes to sit at your own table and act like you were interested in things like taxes and Derby hats.

He glanced up to see if he could spot his dad through the sea of people.

Charlie quickly sorted through the odds and ends of the temporary vendors. He knew what he was looking for. He had already acquired a vintage Rolodex, three pairs of reading spectacles, and a chrome mid-century stapler. The best deals came from the temporaries. He had learned that on his second trip to Coraloo. Most were eager to make a quick sell and would take a decent offer.

The corner of a flute case peeked out from under a stack of yellowing *National Geographic* magazines. Charlie hurried over. He had made the mistake of waiting once before and lost two silver, however badly tarnished, candlesticks to a decorator.

Charlie flipped open the case. The flute was in need of minor repair, but it would resell well. *Music is money.* After his victory with the Waterman, Charlie had spent hours online reading articles on the art of the pick by a man who made his fortune rummaging through backyard barns. The man even had his own television show. "How much?"

"Fifty."

He could get at least two hundred for it. "Will you take thirty-five?"

"Fifty." The vendor held firm.

Charlie closed the case. There were too many people. He could not chance walking off to double check the selling price on his phone. *Music is money.* "Fifty it is." The deal was done.

For the fun of it, Charlie ventured past a few of the shops. Velveteen would've loved the shops. Hopeful, but fully aware she would not, he had asked her to come along.

"I have work to do, Charlie."
    "I beg your pardon?"

"*The wallpaper has to come down, Charlie! I can't bear the sight of it. It makes my eyelids flip inside out. You go ahead. Stay as long as you like.*"

Charlie and Gideon stared at her with their mouths agape for a full minute. "I'll stay back and help." The offer was surface. He needed to go to the market. What little funds they had were quickly depleting. He would have to find items to flip quickly.

"*I've got this, Charlie.*"

When Velveteen said she wanted to do something, she did it. Charlie hoped she would still be alive when they returned home. As far as he knew, it had been years since she had so much as hammered a nail – not that he doubted whether or not she could, but it had been a while. Now she planned to remove vinyl wall covering. He smiled, imagining her lost among the dahlias with a pink posy glued to her bottom.

Charlie stopped in front of the bookshop's entrance. There was no need to go inside; haggling in the shops was unacceptable. Unlike the temporary vendors, the Blackwells did not haggle. The collector in him begged to go inside, to take a peek, but the man who had failed in business and could barely afford to house his family pushed back.

Hobbies don't make money. But a glimpse wouldn't hurt, just a peek at the myriad unseen adventures and dramas enclosed in battered leather bindings, wrinkled and worn from countless hands, like his own, eagerly clutching them with childlike fervor. It would be torture to step inside, knowing he had wiser ways to spend his money and his time.

Only a year ago, the words on the pages of fiction had flung him into the lives of other people's misfortunes. He read through their pain, laughed at their victories, and held closely to the moment when the protagonist made it safely to the other side of the plot line.

Not today. Now they were living sell to sell, barely scraping by. He paid the bills, but there was rarely extra. And when they did have extra, they felt guilty spending it. Even with a new drive, if he were to tell the truth, he did not feel he would ever find his happy ending.

Charlie turned to walk away but bumped straight into a boy who in appearance was about Gideon's age. His faded t-shirt and tattered blue jeans brought out the blue in his gray eyes, and his fiery red air was slightly disheveled, as if the boy had intentionally wanted it to be that way.

"Excuse me, sir." The boy passed through the entrance, easily, free of the hold of life's *Roonings*. The carefree child walked past the neatly organized rows of vintage books to the back of the store.

Charlie's eye caught a glint of light, a reflection off a case, and a flash of blue – cobalt blue. He knew the cover, had searched for it, and had paid his former finder handsomely to locate the highly valued rare first edition. It could have been his, had the timing been different. The cover was the screen saver on his laptop, but he had never held it. And here it was: the coveted Kipling.

The lure of the Kipling pulled him through the door. He inhaled the familiar scent of aged parchment and old leather. He ran his hand along the spines – many of which were familiar. Some were similar to ones he owned and had chosen not to sell, despite their value. His personal collection was carefully boxed, wrapped in acid free paper, and would remain there until, if ever, he had a place to put them. Here, he had stepped into his element, a piece of his past that was hidden deep within him. For a moment time stopped, as memories of Saturday morning trips downtown with Gideon flooded his mind.

He stepped closer, the Kipling in sight. At one time the book had absorbed his attention. He simply had to own it, to claim it belonged to him. It would be the highlight of his collection, until he found something new to purchase. But this book – it was more than a piece of literature; it was a part of him, a part of his childhood that had molded and shaped him into the man he had become.

"Are we selling books, Dad?"

Charlie whipped around, nearly dropping the flute. Gideon stood in front of him with a smidgeon of brown goo stuck to the corner of his mouth. Charlie suddenly felt as if he had been caught doing something immoral.

Gideon waved his hand in front of his father's face. "Hello! Earth to Dad!"

Charlie blinked. The hustle and bustle of the Coraloo outside the walls of the bookshop snapped him back to reality. He turned back around, wondering if it had been a dream, but the book was still there.

"Dad, are you all right?"

"Yah…" Charlie leaned in to his son, the strong smell of sweet liquor hovering in his general vicinity. "Have you been drinking?"

Gideon stared blankly at his dad.

"Never mind." Charlie shook his head. Did he just ask his ten-year-old son if he had been drinking? He changed the subject. "They have the first edition."

"Hey, it's you!" The redheaded boy slapped Gideon so hard on the back that Gideon nearly toppled into a shelf of local authors. "This is the shop I was telling you about. It's been in the family for thirty-three years. Well, longer than that really. The factory closed down in the late seventies and sat empty for four years. Papa had to run out the hooligans. He fixed it up and started selling off all the old equipment. They added the stores in '95, but they were no account until –"

"Nice to meet you. May I see the Kipling?" Charlie's mind was on the Kipling and far from the history of the Coraloo.

"It's not for sale." The voice emerged from behind a shelf of historical fiction. A man, a grown-up version of the redhead, extended his hand to Charlie. "Stephen Blackwell, fourth generation. This is my son, Danger. The others are around here somewhere."

"Charlie Price, and this is Gideon. We're new in town."

"Nice to meet you. I heard a family had leased the Toft house. It's cozy."

"Minuscule would be a better word," Gideon mumbled.

Stephen Blackwell laughed. "It may be small, but like everything around here, it has quite a story to tell."

"I'm a fan of stories." Charlie's attention drifted somewhere between Mr Blackwell and the Kipling. In his early online explorations of Coraloo, he had read the Blackwells were infamous for their overly exaggerated tales and public portrayals of the family's bizarre history.

"Then I'll tell you all about it. Supper it is! Our camper van is out back. You can't miss it."

"Ours is the biggest," Danger interjected.

"Tonight, six o'clock?"

Charlie passed another glance at the book. "Sure. Sounds great."

"Wait! I've got something for you!" Danger Blackwell disappeared for a few minutes, then returned with a stack of yellowing papers held together with a black spiral binding. "It's our history!"

Gideon shot a hesitant look at his dad. Charlie nodded. Gideon accepted the book.

"Thank you, Danger." Charlie patted his shy son on the back.

"You'll read it, won't you?"

Gideon nodded and followed Charlie back out into the Coraloo. "Dad, you better have Doctor Eyeballs on speed dial."

"Why is that, son?"

"Mom's gonna pass out when she hears where you're taking her to dinner."

"Oh, and why is that?" He vaguely recalled the Blackwell invitation.

"Dad, we're eating in a camper van!"

CHAPTER 4

1856

Mungo Blackwell's father, Mumford Blackwell, unintentionally stepped foot into the camp of the tribal Na-rts. He did not mind the cooler temperatures in this part of the country. In fact, it reminded him of winters back home. Mumford's parents, hardworking Scotch immigrants, had journeyed far and across the seas during the Highland potato famine, selling hand-cobbled shoes to whoever would pay or trade for them before settling. An explorer at heart and eager to traverse the lands to the west and south of his parents' new homestead, Mumford – with the blessing of his mother and father – set out into the world, surviving on his family trade.

As one cannot predict such things as a potato famine, one also cannot predict with whom they fall in love, but one look at the native princess and Mumford's heart was no longer his own. They called her Ipunistat for the mark of the star staining the bridge of her nose. Her hair hung long, plaited ornately down her back, and her smooth skin was darker than any Mumford had seen before. To the shock of the women in the village, who found their guest awkward and too pale, Ipunistat developed a fondness for the redheaded stranger. But a union was not to be; she was already promised to a great warrior of the tribe. However, Ipunistat did not love the warrior – for many reasons, but mostly because his crooked hooked nose dripped a constant stream of clear fluid, running faster than his legs.

Mumford was in love and desperate to spend the rest of his life with Ipunistat. He got down on his knee in front of the chief and pleaded, "I'll do anything to wed my true love."

"Anything?" the chief responded.

"Anything."

The warrior protested, raising his spear to Mumford's forehead. The tribe shouted and chanted for a challenge. The chief waved, silencing his people, and said one word: "Shoes."

The challenge had been set to the dismay of the warrior, for everyone was aware the chief's arthritic feet had brought him great pain for many years. A pair of shoes to ease his discomfort would undoubtedly win the hand of the Na-rt princess.

The betrothed warrior took off toward the East to track a family of shoe-wearing missionaries who had passed through the camp a month prior. Mumford, however, set out on his own in search of the rare heaken beaver, whose skin was known to bring strength, healing, and long life to the wearer. Before sunset he returned, and in his satchel there was a pair of handcrafted heaken beaver sandals.

Mumford placed the banded leather shoes on the feet of the chief. The tribe waited, anticipating the reaction.

The chief stood, wiggled his exposed toes, and cried, "Shoes!" He turned to Mumford. "Anything."

With eyes only for one anything, Mumford replied, "The Star."

Before the warrior returned, Mumford had married the native princess. For nine months he lived with the tribe as son-in-law to the chief. At the end of nine months, when the moon waned, Ipunistat began her three-day labor, gave birth to a son, and died.

The chief blamed the traveler and cursed the child, proclaiming the child's soul discontented and condemning him to roam the earth in search of peace. Mumford fled the country with his newborn son, hoping to rid his child from the curse. But the chief had been right: the child, Mungo Blackwell, was never content to be in one place too long.

On one occasion, Mungo Blackwell walked into the woods and did not stop walking until he found himself enslaved by a caravan of traveling gypsies – with whom he and his father lived for five months until Mumford had paid for his son in shoes. Mumford told people it was because Mungo had grown up without a mother that he wandered so, but in his heart, Mumford knew the truth: Mungo Blackwell was cursed.

So Mumford and Mungo traversed the far corners of the earth for eleven years, searching for the contentment his son would never find. Mumford taught his son to make shoes from the hides of whatever they could kill – pigs, cows, wildebeests – and trade them for shelter and food. Before long, father and son became famous for the craftsmanship of their shoes and were sought out by sheiks and kings. But once again the moon waned, and Mumford was struck by misfortune. The coughs began, followed by the night sweats and fever. Mumford Blackwell died measuring the foot of a Middle Eastern dancer, leaving Mungo to journey alone in search of his stolen contentment.

CHAPTER 5

Gideon was right: Velveteen nearly fainted when Charlie explained they would be dining with the Blackwells in a camper van.

"Are you sure he said *camper van*? Really, a camper van? Like a motor home, Charlie? And they live in it?"

Charlie nodded. Gideon stifled his laughter with the palm of his hand.

Standing among a pile of torn wall covering with her brown hair pulled into a messy bun on top of her head, Velveteen wiped wallpaper paste off her face with her forearm. "And what does one wear to such an event, Charlie? I mean seriously. They have that big market, and they want us to eat in a van?"

In the short time Charlie and Gideon were at the market, she had scraped away every inch of the dahlias, exposing the soft gray walls they had seen on the realtor's website.

"You did a good job on the walls. They look nice."

Velveteen gazed at her progress. "Thank you. They will need some paint, eventually, but it's better than losing my eyesight every time I walk into the living room." She turned around sharply and pointed a finger at her husband. "You're changing the subject, Charlie! That's not fair!"

"I imagine we'll eat outside. It'll be fun!"

"Break out the ponchos! The Prices are coming to dinner!" Velveteen wrapped a large piece of the former wall covering around her body. "How does this look, Charlie?"

"If you wear it, I'll stop asking you to go to the market."

"Tempting… but I would rather go naked."

Gideon's face twisted into a look of disgust. "Gross! I'm going to my room."

"You would eat naked in a camper van?" Charlie asked.

Sitting bare bottomed anywhere, thinking about who or what might have sat there before was a disturbing thought. "As long as you are there, I'll eat anywhere, Charlie Price… even in a camper van, but I'm wearing a dress. Now, do you really like the walls or were you trying to seduce me into eating with those people without me knowing it?"

"Are you saying that in order to *seduce* you all I have to do is compliment the walls?"

"Yes."

Two hours later, and a quick drive up the hill – Charlie suggested they walk, but Velveteen reminded him she was wearing heels – the Price family stared at the rolling homes in front of them. The long row of camper vans – short, colorful trailers once pulled behind some other vehicle and long, larger ones revealing their lengthy stay by the amount of grass growing up around the wheels – formed the Blackwell compound. Gideon was especially fond of the one painted like a rooster. An orchard of apple and lime trees, rows of suspended grape vines, and a large garden filled the space behind the campers.

The camper vans were ablaze with light fixtures crafted of everything from glass fizzy drink bottles and aluminum cans to plastic flowerpots turned upside-down, and embedded with colorful translucent beads. A scattering of Blackwells sat outside whittling away at their wares, while others sat by small fire pits as children and dogs entertained one another behind their backs. An unorchestrated mix of guitar, banjo, and possibly an accordion – Charlie wasn't sure – hung over the scene. It was like a kaleidoscopic circus, welcoming the Prices to the Blackwell show.

With one hand, Velveteen gripped her husband's hand so hard he feared his wedding band might become permanently embedded into his finger. In the other, she held a candle – unused, secured in its purple box, and neatly tied-up with a green satin bow. She adored its fragrance, a combination of bergamot and lavender. It had been the signature scent of their home in the city. Since *The Rooning*, she had determined that ordering candles from France was probably not on her road to simplicity. With only five – now four – cylindrical luminaries remaining in her possession, she rationed their burning to thirty minutes every other week. Regardless of her deficit, according to *Shmandervilt's New Guidebook for the Civilized Lady*, it is rude to arrive without a hostess gift.

Charlie knocked on the metal door of the largest camper van – a shiny silver Airstream that made Velveteen think of an elongated toaster. Danger had said to look for the biggest. She hoped Charlie had chosen wisely.

Stephen Blackwell opened the door. "Come on –"

"Out!" a voice shouted from within. "I was talking to you too, Fie!"

Partially frightened and partially relieved, Velveteen grabbed Gideon by the arm, planning to follow the stone road down the hill and back home – heels or no heels.

"Wait!" Stephen called.

Suddenly, a pile of teenagers, including the younger Danger, stumbled over one another to get down the metal steps and out of the narrow exit, followed by a moping girl, holding a book close to her chest. Velveteen watched hesitantly. The sight reminded her of a childhood trip to the Ringling Brother's Circus where twenty clowns, to the delight of a shocked audience, piled out of a car fitted for four.

"Sorry about the chaos, Price family. The gang was finishing up a project for school. School and sleep, that's about all we can do in here. Half the time we don't know where the kids are."

Velveteen pulled Gideon closer.

"Come on inside."

Charlie climbed in first, followed by Velveteen and then Gideon. He placed his arm around her waist, pulling her to him ever so slightly. "This is my wife Velveteen, and you've already met Gideon."

"A pleasure to meet you." Stephen leaned over and kissed her casually on the cheek.

Velveteen forced a smile and fought off the temptation to wipe away the awkwardness.

Inside, the recreational vehicle turned permanent living space was not only much larger than it had appeared from the outside, it was also updated and tastefully decorated. The kitchenette held a small stainless steel stovetop and oven nicer than the one in the Toft house. A miniature oil painting of a boy and girl at the ocean hung in a gilded frame over the sink, and the entire interior was fitted with white board and baton siding. The space was crisp but welcoming.

From behind a slim sliding reclaimed wood door stepped one of the loveliest women Velveteen had ever seen.

"This is my wife, Clover." Stephen kissed the woman on the cheek and gave her a loving wink. The mother of five's hair hung in loose strawberry blond ringlets around her face. She wore blue jeans, stylishly ripped at the knee, and a stark white button up shirt.

Velveteen glanced down at the woman's bare feet and then at her own red high heels. She suddenly wished she had worn her casual, but cute, strappy sandals instead.

The woman leaned over and kissed Velveteen as her husband had done. "You must be Velveteen."

"Yes. It's a pleasure to meet you. I brought a little something for your –" She was about to say home, then considered saying camper, but neither quite fit. Velveteen had a sudden revelation that a candle was quite possibly the wrong choice for this kind of living quarters. She imagined the flame of the candle igniting the gray striped curtains. The sofa would be the next to go and then the Berber carpet. Before long, the entire circus would be one big bonfire, and who would the Blackwells blame? The conversation played out in her mind: *It smelled like bergamot and lavender! I bet it was that Price woman!*

Clover stepped in, halting Velveteen's musings. "That's kind of you. Please, have a seat."

Charlie slid into the restaurant-style booth seating; Velveteen followed his lead.

"Danger is outside," Clover addressed Gideon. "Go on out; have him show you around the camp and introduce you to the others. We'll eat in a bit."

With everything in her, Velveteen wanted to keep her only child by her side. She didn't know these people. She didn't know why some of them slept in the same room where they ate. She didn't know why an old woman was running around outside chastising a chicken, and she didn't know why someone would choose to live this way if they didn't have to. Velveteen recalled the conversation she and Charlie had had while she coiffed for the evening. He had told her Stephen was a university graduate. *Educated people don't choose to live in camper vans*, she had argued while squinting to place her false eyelash.

Gideon sat on the steps of the traveling home, watching the children chase one another around the lot. He didn't know how to play with other children, so he opted to entertain himself by eavesdropping on his mother trying to make small talk with Clover. *How long have you been here? Where did you call home before Coraloo? What brings you to Coraloo? You have a lovely... home.* His mother's discomfort made him laugh. He halfway wanted to stick around and see what kind of mess she would find herself in.

Danger plopped down beside him, his hands filthy and his bare feet even worse. "That's Finella and Fiona – twins." He pointed to two girls sitting with a group of teens around the fire pit. "My older brother Fife, and the weird one is Fie." All four heads were as red as Danger's rumpled hair.

"I guess your mom ran out of 'F' names before she got to you."

"Mom says names are important. She didn't want to settle because of a letter, so I'm named after a traveling preacher. The doctor couldn't get here fast enough, so the preacher delivered me right in the middle of the market. Dad said the tip boot was full that day."

Gideon remembered watching shoppers at the market toss coins into the old work boot after the Blackwell performance. He shook his head; the Blackwells were definitely different. He stared at Fie, her nose stuck in a book. She didn't look weird; she looked immersed. He wished he were at home, in his room, hidden among the cowboys, immersed in *Pirates of the Cosmos*.

As Charlie had speculated, they ate dinner under the stars – roast beef, mashed potatoes, green beans, rolls, and for dessert, a blackberry cobbler prepared by Granny. Velveteen could not get her head around how such a large meal had been prepared in such a tiny kitchen. She wriggled on the wooden bench brought over from the market.

"You'll meet Granny later," Stephen informed them. "She'll be over for compliments. It's shotgun night."

Velveteen slowly lowered her plastic fork. "Shotgun night?"

"She cleans it once a week. It's the only night it sees any action. Most of the time it's hidden under the market counter."

"I will keep that in mind." Velveteen returned to her dinner with another reason to avoid the market.

Charlie and Stephen discussed the Kipling, while Clover and Velveteen did their best to connect the pieces of their very different lives. Velveteen fought to balance her plate of food on her lap and would have gladly wiped her greasy hands on her paper napkin had it not fallen to the ground, twice. Charlie and Stephen appeared to have hit it off with their common interest in dead authors. She watched him laugh and listen, talking more to the Blackwell than he'd ever talked to the spouses of the acquaintances. He was happy – that was what mattered, right? For him to be happy? Clover poured her another glass of the strong gingery fizzy drink – the carbonated beverage would be fine. Velveteen would detox in the morning.

"Clover, the food is delicious, and the room is lovely –" she caught herself, realizing *the room is lovely* was not the appropriate compliment. "The… um… setting is lovely." She blushed and wished she had brought her sunglasses; they were always a good place to hide. The younger Blackwells stared at her curiously and then returned to their conversation. Velveteen had rehearsed the encomium; it was what she said at every dinner party she and Charlie had ever been to. It's what *Debrett's* handbook on style and etiquette said to do; however, she had searched it – as well as her Emily Post – from cover to cover and it said nothing about camper van dining.

Embarrassed and completely out of place, she watched as Gideon sat quietly in a lawn chair on the other side of Charlie picking at his food, and then glanced over to a group of the Blackwell children who were playing some sort of game involving two boards and a handful of beanbags. Had she made Gideon this way? Had she put him in pre-school too early? She had followed the child-rearing book to the letter. But it hadn't worked. No matter how hard she had tried, he would decline her offers to set up play dates and refused organized sports. The point was to socialize him, to introduce him to other children at an early age so he would develop confidence in early adolescence. She wanted him to have the childhood she never had. Early education was a luxury her mother could not afford.

Velveteen gained her composure and cleared her throat. "Gideon, Mrs Blackwell homeschools her children. Did you know that?"

"Yes."

She had to be careful. She had no desire to be a homeschooling mother who made macaroni necklaces all day and dressed up like Mary Todd Lincoln to teach history. "Clover, what is Danger's favorite subject in homeschool?"

Danger rushed over from his game. "History! I'm an expert!"

"On his own family," Gideon mumbled.

"I know all about the pygmies and the pirates."

"Pygmies and pirates? Well, that sounds quite intriguing." Velveteen faked a laugh. Gideon laughed too. Velveteen eyed him curiously. He was paying attention.

"Did you get to that part in the book, Gideon? If not, I can tell you all about them, if you want."

Gideon nodded. Velveteen nearly cried at the thought of her son's classical education marred by this family's made-up history. She was tired, a bit bloated from the meal, and her Chanel No. 5 was quickly attracting a variety of biting insects. She did not feel like taking part in the legendary Blackwell tales; however, at this point, if it would get Gideon to communicate with someone his own age, she would stay all night. She shifted uncomfortably on the bench, catching Charlie's eye. She smiled pleasantly, honestly.

"It's getting late; we should go." Charlie stood, arching his back for a quick stretch.

Gideon tugged on Charlie's shirtsleeve. "Dad, I need to know about the pirates." Charlie and Velveteen stared at their antisocial son.

"Are you coming to the market in the morning?" Stephen asked.

"Can we, Dad?"

"Yes!" Velveteen jumped to her feet, squishing the heels of her shoes deeper into the grass. "Yes, you can." Even though the Blackwells were their polar opposites, to get Gideon doing something other than burying his head in his comic books must be a step in the right direction.

"Really?" Charlie asked, before he could stop himself. They had discussed it before and the plan was clear. He would go to the market on Friday, sometimes Saturday, and list on Monday. The rest of the week he would spend at home, monitoring and shipping his sales. However, tomorrow was "Sometimes Saturday", and he had suggested they spend the day together as a family exploring the town. She had loved the idea.

"Of course! Why would it not be okay?" Velveteen asked as if it were normally not against her better judgment to let Gideon play with children unevaluated by the Lafayette Academy.

"You should come too," Clover suggested.

Velveteen's face went white. All the bartering, buying, and selling made her uncomfortable – not to mention that one time she had gone with Charlie to a church rummage sale. She shivered. Besides, she would need every extra minute of her days to make the small Toft house habitable. "Thank you so much for the offer, but I have quite a bit of work to do around the house."

"Ah, yes!" Stephen leaned back in his chair. "Quite an interesting place you have there. Mrs Toft was some kind of woman."

"Some kind of woman all right," Granny grumbled, making her entrance into the circle of diners with her shotgun tucked under her left arm. "No good, land-stealing… " There were a few other choice words Velveteen preferred Gideon had not heard.

"I believe you were going to tell us about the house," Charlie added.

"A reason for you all to visit us again." Stephen reached over, extending his hand to Charlie.

"Maybe next time we can return the hospitably. Dinner at the Toft house!"

The mashed potatoes came back up in Velveteen's throat; the ornamented camper vans drove in circles around her brain. She started to sway. But before she lost consciousness again, Danger blurted out, "Blackwells don't associate with Tofts!"

"And we don't associate with pickers!" A dark, burly figure emerged from the shadows cast by the sun's descent upon the market. The faint Scottish accent Charlie had detected in the other Blackwells was stronger and deeper with the giant of a man.

"It's not the time, Shug." Stephen stood up and faced his uncle.

"It's how we make a living. We don't need your kind coming in and cheapening the place, Price. We've worked to make it what it is. I see you on your phone. I know what you're up to! We aren't some barn or back alley pawnshop. Do you hear me, *picker*? Your kind is going to overrun the place; you just watch. *Will you take less*?" he mocked. "No, we won't take less, Price."

"Uncle, that's enough. Let our friends be. We'll talk about it later."

A much calmer sibling ushered Shug Blackwell away from the fire.

"Don't mind him, Charlie. We've made a lot of changes over the past few years. Renovations cost us a piece. He gets hung up on it. He has his own mind about things. Anything new doesn't sit well with him."

Velveteen swallowed another sip of the highly caffeinated soda. "Does that mean people too?"

No one answered.

"Who wants an egg?" Granny Blackwell interrupted the awkward silence, holding the jar of magenta boiled eggs Gideon had seen in the market the day before. "You can't be a Blackwell unless you eat the eggs. Isn't that right, Clover?"

Clover smiled and then mouthed *I'm so sorry* to Velveteen.

Granny unscrewed the lid of the jar and proceeded to pass it among the family members. Danger dug his fork inside, pulled out an egg, and took a bite. "I only like the outside, so I don't eat the yellow part. Go on, get one."

Gideon shook his head. "No thanks."

"Aww, come on. They're not going to hurt you."

"Maybe next time."

"I bet your mom will do it, just like my mom did!"

Danger shoved the jar onto Velveteen's lap, sloshing the concoction of vinegar, beet juice, and spices on her dress. Velveteen coughed at the pungent aroma. "Oh my, uh…" She coughed again. It smelled like their front yard.

Charlie cringed, but seeing his wife's discomfort and knowing she would force the egg down to avoid being rude, he stood up and grabbed the jar. "Who would have thought – purple eggs!" Charlie stuck his fork in the jar, pulled out an egg, and took a bite. His cheeks tightened and he forced himself to swallow.

Velveteen watched, praying her husband wouldn't gag himself to death.

"Well, that's a first."

The Blackwells laughed.

Danger stood up and shouted, "He ate the egg!"

Clover collected Velveteen's plate from her lap. "You owe your husband big for that one," she said under her breath. "They're sour, horrible, taste like death, and she's had them since Easter. She's been trying to sell the things to the tourists."

"We should probably be going; it is getting late." Velveteen attempted to wipe the pink stain off her dress.

Clover gave Velveteen a gentle hug. "Please, don't be a stranger."

Velveteen smiled. "Thank you so much for having us. It truly was a lovely evening." She meant it, sort of. At the core of all the eccentricity, she felt unusually welcomed, but at the same time terrified by Shug Blackwell's attack on her husband and stunned by the ritual eating of pickled eggs.

On the short drive down the hill, Gideon leaned up between his parents. "Dad, what's a picker?"

Charlie made eye contact with his son in the rearview mirror. "I am, Son."

CHAPTER 6

Charlie Price took a sip of his coffee and glanced into the pleading eyes of his wife.

"Don't go, Charlie."

"Last night you were practically begging me to take Gideon to the market."

"Who knows what that man will do to you! What if he tries to skin you alive?"

"Skin me?" Charlie loved it when his wife plunged into the overdramatic. Most often, he eagerly anticipated what she would say next.

"He might! Did you see the size of his arms? And what was that tattoo… a butcher knife? I bet it's what he uses to skin his victims, and I bet he lives in the rooster! Only crazy people live in roosters, Charlie. Do you think he is crazy? Crazy people do crazy things! And what was it he called you?"

"A picker?"

"Yes, picker! He uses a butcher knife to skin the pickers! I don't think you should go. It's not safe."

"Sweetheart, I cannot confirm or deny whether or not Shug Blackwell is crazy. But I can tell you this – he doesn't skin people… at least not when they're alive."

Charlie waited for her next defense as he stared up at the crack in the ceiling from the comfort of their sofa. Even in the tiny house, the couch was as comfortable as it had been in their grand city home. A few patches of glue and a scrape or two remained on the walls from Velveteen's first home renovation project, but overall, she had managed to leave the room looking open, airy, and cozy.

Simple. In the city, even though she was not only educated in the art of design but perfectly capable, she had hired contractors and decorators to paint the walls and arrange the furniture because that's what the acquaintances had told her wives of bankers were supposed to do. In Coraloo, she was attempting to do it herself.

"I like what you've done with the room," he told her honestly, impressed with her accomplishments.

"Don't change the subject!"

"I bet you can find something to go over the couch at the market. Coraloo draws a lot of high-end decorators."

"I know. But *extras* aren't in our budget right now."

Extras. He knew she was using it as an excuse. She hadn't asked him for anything since the move. He hated that there were even things she considered *extras* – possibly personal items she needed but would never ask him for. *Extras* weren't even a thought before *The Rooning.* "Do you need something? What is it? If you need something, we'll get it. I probably have twenty items listed that could sell at any minute. Just tell me what it is. You know I'm no good at guessing."

"I don't need anything, Charlie."

"Nail polish, those round stretchy bands you put in your hair, underwear? Do you need clothes? What is it?"

"Underwear? Really?"

"I don't know what you girls call them… *pan-tees.* We can handle a few small extras right now. It's been a good week. What do you need?"

He loved the thrill of the hunt and even more when the *ping, ping* rang from his phone, alerting him another item had sold online. But he didn't like being so tight, wondering how and if they could pay the next month's rent. Still, he was determined to make this work.

She bit her lower lip and stroked her long hair. "All right; you asked. I need your skin safely on your body." She giggled.

It took Charlie a minute, but he realized she was trying to change the subject. She hadn't meant to plant the daily seed of self-doubt and fear as to whether or not he could provide for his family, but the truth of their current financial situation, the *extras*, had entered his head and there it would stay until he could work his way out of the mental box.

He'd try to play back. "That's a good thing to need; however, you should know one of the vendors had a working guillotine the other day. Would you rather have me skinless or headless?"

"A guillotine! What would one even do with a guillotine?"

"Melon slicer. We could set it on the patio and use it in the summer."

It wasn't the strangest thing Charlie had seen. One time someone tried to sell him a nineteenth-century Moldavian chest once belonging to the real Professor Abraham Van Helsing of *Dracula* fame. As a lover of classic literature, Charlie had almost bought the thing for sheer fun until, on closer inspection of the eclectic contents, he had to inform the vendor he doubted Professor Van Helsing could have used mentholated salve to slay a vampire and whatever was in the other vial was illegal to sell on at least four continents.

"Go with me – go with me to the market. It's not what you think. Listen, I sold a sax last week. We'll move the budget around a bit. We could use a day out, together. I'll take the day off. We can stroll the shops, grab a bite to eat at Granny's. It won't be like the last time."

The last time. The church rummage sale. When they went to pay – Charlie with his arms full of brand-name kitchen appliances and a pair of bookends resembling two Shelties holding rifles – the lady taking the money was none other than Mary Beth Rogers. Velveteen had disguised her mortification behind sunglasses and a delighted smile, then she prayed that Mary Beth had no idea what was being sold at her own fundraiser. Velveteen had thought quickly. *"I hope you can use these to help some poor soul, Mary Beth. Shall I have Charlie leave them here?"* From that point on, Velveteen shied away from *shopping* with Charlie.

"And what will Gideon do while we *stroll*, Charlie?"

"He has plans with the Blackwell boy."

"Which one?" She laughed again at her own jest.

Charlie smiled. "Does it matter? He wants to be with kids his age. You told him he could go, remember?" He knew what to say next. "I bet Melba would go the market."

"Don't you bring her into this, Charlie Price. Besides, Melba is staying with me this morning. We have plans."

"Oh?"

"Yes, she's teaching me to dye my hair."

Charlie puffed out his cheeks to contain his most recent sip of coffee, swallowed, and let out a combination of laugh-filled coughing.

"It's not funny, Charlie. I thought you would be proud of me."

He pulled her to his lap and kissed her. She was beautiful, and even though he could see the stress of *The Rooning* had forced a few gray hairs to emerge from her crown – he would never tell her. She had stayed with him. Most women – at least among their "acquaintances" – would have run straight into the pockets of another wallet. She must still love him, which was a good thing, because he still loved her.

"What does he have against you, this Shug fellow?"

The burden of budgets and bills began to fade as his mind jumped back to the market. "I didn't know the rules. I asked for less. In his shop. It was a French horn – a few dents here and there, but overall in great condition. I could have doubled my purchase price."

"But he wouldn't take it?"

"No." Charlie laughed. "*You don't haggle with the Blackwells,*" he mocked the heavy voice of Shug. "Old Shug has quite a shop. I bet I could flip every item in the place. I'd make twice what he's asking. But, it's all right; I'll leave it all for the tourists. The vendors bring in enough variety to support us for a long time – as long as Shug lets them stay. They have him all worked up for some reason."

"And what if Shug makes them go?"

Charlie didn't blame her for thinking ahead. If he had thought ahead in the first place, they might have survived *The Rooning*.

"Then, I find another way to make money."

She parted her lips to speak, hesitated, and then the words fell out. "Like going back to work in the city?"

The word "work" brought up the insecurities he fought daily to suppress. "Is it what you want? To go back to the city?"

"I… I don't know."

Their new lifestyle was supposed to be settled, no looking back. But she had said "extras" and now he was hearing she wanted to move back to the city.

He put down his coffee, stood up, and rubbed his hand across the back of his neck. "I'll do whatever *you* want, Velveteen."

"Charlie!" Her voice cracked and her eyes pleaded for a forgiveness he could not give her because she had not done anything wrong. He had hurt her feelings. He hadn't meant to… Maybe he had. Talk of money always hurt. "If *this* – all of this – makes you happy, then I'm happy."

He forced a smile. "Good, this makes me happy." He lied. He enjoyed picking, sharing stories with the vendors, and surrounding himself with the ambiance of Coraloo. He had all but stopped searching online auctions and sorting through the postings of newbie listers on eBay – they always listed too low… good for him, bad for them. He liked Coraloo, and he liked the Blackwells for that matter, but he wasn't satisfied. It wasn't enough. He couldn't shake the nagging feeling of uncertainty that came with each pick. Would it sell, or would it sit? They were okay for now, maybe for a few months, but what then?

An hour later, against Velveteen's will, the boys took off for another day at the market. The idea of Charlie crossing paths with the likes of Shug Blackwell made Velveteen more than a little uneasy. Charlie had informed her the man's tattoo was not a butcher knife but rather a very pricey antique Oakeshott type XIV medieval sword – he confessed he had snuck a photo of the man's left arm and researched the artwork. But she wouldn't put it past Shug Blackwell to blacken the eye of her husband.

Charlie's life with the bank had been safe and had brought them consistency, plus a whole lot of *extras*. What he made now from picking paid the bills and allowed her enough for groceries and, sometimes, paint. Whatever "extras" she needed for herself she picked up in the cosmetic aisle of the grocery store. But even then her "extras" didn't always make it home. She'd watch as the cash register tallied the total, worrying she might have to put something back, and if the total was less than what she had in her purse, she would add in the bottle of polish, tube of lip-gloss or one of the higher end bottles of shampoo that had their own shelf at the grocery store and promised to hold her color longer. This week, the hair-coloring kit with the head of a much younger woman on the front had made it home.

Velveteen didn't know what she wanted. She had plans for the Toft house – the interior design student in her had mentally decorated the entire place – but could they really live like this? She felt like a child on a seesaw, waiting for Charlie to take his turn so she could end up on top again. But if she were up top, where would he be – never knowing exactly how much money they would have, no savings, and what about Christmas? Her country Christmas party was most certainly out of the question.

Who would they invite anyway? Doctor Eyeballs and his posse of nurses?

Velveteen studied her reflection – dark shadows under her eyes and evidence of age forcing its crease between her brows. She hoped Charlie hadn't noticed her collection of grays. *The Rooning* had added at least three years. She pulled up her forehead and then pushed back on her cheeks. She couldn't afford the fancy creams she had once pre-ordered from the department store, but she had read that coconut oil was a more natural alternative and cost effective too. She had already purchased a jar of the fleshy goo, but was waiting to open it until after she had dug out the last of her Ode à Plis.

She lifted the box of colorant and carefully removed the contents, laying each one on the counter. She unfolded the instructions and set aside the plastic gloves that were clearly far too big for her petite hands. She could do this. How hard could it be? If Melba DuMont could dye her hair with cherry tree bark and black tea leaves, then Velveteen Price could do it with this over the counter "salon approved" substitute. There had been nearly fifty boxes to choose from on her weekly supermarket excursion. It had taken her a little under an hour to choose the right color – Cocoa Blanket. The swatch on the side appeared to match her locks perfectly and guaranteed to cover the gray.

Velveteen carefully mixed the contents from bottle A into bottle B. She shook it until the white gel morphed into a foggy brown. She then proceeded to carefully massage the mix through her hair, starting with her roots and moving to the ends as the paper had instructed. She squirted the rest of the solution into the palm of her hand and smeared it generously across her scalp to add an extra layer of colorant to the roots. Velveteen lifted the instructions with her goop-smeared, blackened hand, set her timer for thirty minutes, and gasped as her eyes caught sight of the unused gloves. She quickly turned on the faucet with the back of her Cocoa Blanket covered hand. *No! No! No!* This couldn't be right. She knew the taps could be temperamental. She turned the handle as far as it would go. Still nothing. Not even a drop.

Velveteen rushed to the kitchen and maneuvered to turn on the tap with her elbow – nothing. *You've got to be kidding!* She pulled open the refrigerator door and surveyed the possibilities – *aha!* Velveteen reached for the water pitcher with the disposable filter. Almost empty, but better than nothing – and surely the water would be turned on again soon. She removed the pitcher with her forearms, set it on the counter, squirted dish soap on her hands, and scrubbed. Hoping the dye had not set too long on her skin, she dumped the container of filtered water over her soapy appendages and watched as gray soap seeped down the drain. She reached for a hand towel, and to her relief, the palms of her hands were free of color, but when she flipped them over, that's where the real damage had been done. Not only did the dye settle into a heavy black line underneath each fingernail, but also all ten nails were so dark she might as well have hit each one with a hammer.

Okay, nothing a little polish can't cover. She hadn't intended to break out her fall shades just yet, but desperate times called for pretty – and dark – polish. As she tried to remember where she had placed her tray of polishes, a slight beeping of an alarm echoed from the bathroom. Her heart stopped. She fled to the back of the house and stared in the mirror at the matted, wet, obsidian nest piled on top of her hair.

Please let there be water. Please let there be water.

She rotated the knob. *Drip.*

CHAPTER 7

Velveteen reapplied a layer of lip-gloss, straightened the cushions on the couch, hid Charlie's unsold items in the cupboard, and lit her second bergamot and lavender candle. *This will have to do*. She sighed.

There was a knock on the door. She checked her make-up in the mirror and adjusted the towel wrapped around her hair. She smiled and opened the door. Her eyes widened as Clover, Granny, and two girls she had not seen before holding milk jugs of water stepped across the threshold of the Toft house.

"Tofts, ugh!" The old woman flung her head back and then proceeded to thrust it forward with a hard spit on the floor.

"Granny!" Clover gasped.

"It's all right." *It's not*. Velveteen steadied her footing, reminded herself the disinfectant was under the kitchen sink, and ushered them into the kitchen. "Thank you so much for coming. As you can see, I have gotten myself into a situation. Charlie is at the market, and I didn't know who else to call. If you hadn't given me your number last night –"

"We are happy to help. Granny closes up after lunch or when she sells out, and the girls were happy to get out of work today. I had just finished up my canning for the day when you called. Here, I hope you like tomatoes." Clover handed Velveteen a mason jar of ruby red tomatoes. "Do you make salsa? They are great in chili too."

Velveteen stared at the jar. *Salsa? Chili?* The woman in front of her was not only beautiful without a stitch of make-up but also found time to can foods and make homemade salsa while homeschooling five children. Velveteen felt oddly exposed in her under-education of home economics. She hoped Clover didn't notice that she had forgotten to dust. Oh, and the bathroom. *Please, Lord, don't let them see my bathroom!*

Granny interrupted her musings. "I shouldn't be here; none of us should. Blackwells don't associate with Tofts. We're probably all going to catch something. Then we'll get the runnin' offs and die!"

"The *runnin' offs*?" Velveteen asked reticently.

Clover's face went sour and she shook her head.

"Oh! I see." Velveteen smiled sweetly, forcing herself not to think of the old woman sitting on her commode. "Well, I guess it is a good thing I'm not a Toft. No, um, running offs from me!"

"*Humph.* No matter, one lived here and died... thank God, and good riddance."

"Granny!" Clover snapped again.

"Thieves, the whole lot of them!"

"Granny, we're here to help Velveteen, remember?"

"Velveteen. Like the fabric?" Granny chuckled.

Velveteen shifted on her self-pedicured feet. Was Granny making fun of her name? Because, if she was, she definitely had a few things she could say about the names coming out of those camper vans...

"These are my nieces Greer and Gavina," Clover quickly added, changing the subject. The girls smiled.

"They're both single." Granny elbowed Velveteen in the side. "So, if you got anyone you can hitch them up to, that would be all right with me."

"As long as they're not Tofts, correct?" Velveteen laughed.

Granny frowned. "One should not joke about such things."

"Well, I guess we should get to it. It's my –" Velveteen unwrapped the towel from around her head, releasing a sticky mess of black matted hair. She cleared her throat, choking back tears. "My hair."

Granny let out a cackle so loud Velveteen didn't know whether to be offended or to laugh with her. "Oh, what a mess you've got yourself in, city girl! If the Tofts had taken better care of the place, you wouldn't look like you've got yourself dipped in a pile of poo."

Velveteen flopped down on the couch, making sure her hair didn't make contact with the upholstery. What had she done? Why had she called them? *Because I'm alone – alone in Coraloo.*

Clover reached out her hand to Velveteen and helped her stand. "It's not so bad. Let's get you rinsed out."

Velveteen hung her head over the sink as Clover and the girls poured icy cold water through her long locks. Clover reassured her it was going to be all right, but most of what she said was a blur through the gurgling sound of water and Cocoa Blanket chugging down the drain. She kept her eyes closed and ignored the pressure in her cheeks from all of the blood flowing to her face. She fought the tears; she tried hard to cry only in private places so no one would see – it was bad etiquette to draw that kind of selfish attention. But here, with her body slumped over the sink and a woman she had met less than twenty-four hours ago pulling clumpy black globs of color from her hair, she heaved quiet sobs.

Melba would be disappointed.

As if sensing her distress, Clover pressed her fingers into Velveteen's scalp. The tension released from Velveteen's shoulders, and the tightening in her neck vanished.

It took five gallons of water – two runs by Greer and Gavina a half-mile back up to the camper vans – until the water ran clear.

Clover handed her a dry towel. Velveteen draped it over her head in such a way as to hide her face. She privately wiped away the smudged mascara, and then twisted her wet hair into the towel. Clover stared at her sympathetically; Velveteen wished she hadn't.

Velveteen excused herself, dried her hair, and took a minute to run a flat iron through her locks. It wasn't so bad – much darker than her usual milk chocolate, but she could get used to it. She dabbed concealer under her puffy eyes and elongated her already long lashes with fresh mascara – mascara was a must on any occasion.

Much better. She took a slow, deep breath, practiced her smile in the mirror, and returned to the Blackwell ladies.

They were laughing, sitting comfortably around her designed-to-be-vintage kitchen table. They had made themselves at home – fixed their own coffee and poured glasses of water using the water they had brought with them. And was there something baking in the oven… blueberry maybe? She closed her eyes. It was exactly how she had imagined the ramshackle thatch-roofed quarters of Melba DuMont to smell.

Clover blew steam away from her mug of black tea. "Granny is making muffins."

Velveteen looked curiously at the dirtied copper-mixing bowl in the sink. "I didn't know I had the ingredients for muffins."

"You don't have ingredients for anything, missy!" Granny cackled.

"I don't cook much."

"You don't say. Then why so many nice pans?"

"They were gifts." She didn't want to tell the woman they were going away presents from the ladies in the book club, and they were quite expensive, not to mention beautiful. She only kept them to add to the ambiance of her kitchen and never intended to use them. At one point, she considered giving them to Charlie for resale, but she couldn't bear to part with them – not yet. They were new, shiny, and looked so nice arranged in the cupboard.

She changed the subject, noticing Clover had not a single gray strand among her ringlets. "You must have done this before." Velveteen ran her fingers through her raven hair.

"Actually, no."

"Oh." Velveteen fought to keep her jaw in place, poured a cup of coffee, and joined the ladies, wondering how long they planned to stay in her tiny home. It was far bigger than the camper van – their cottage had rooms, a full size stove, and a place to eat that was not surrounded by crumb-hungry dogs, but today, it wasn't big enough.

"All right, so out with it." Granny set her cup down, placed her elbows on the table, rested her chin in her wrinkled hands, and glared at Velveteen.

"I'm sorry?"

"What are you doing here?"

Velveteen wished she could say her fortune had been whisked away by a villain who wore a long black cape – specifically the infamous Count Horace from her Melba DuMont novels – and she had been tragically banished to a life of service, but the Blackwells were no fools. As if the question had been an invitation to tell their life story, she openly spewed every inch of the past year all over the table. She left nothing out – the food trucks, the acquaintances, and even the macarons.

Velveteen had no trouble remembering the moment – four months after the Christmas party, on a Tuesday morning, surrounded by fourteen of the city's most prestigious women. Her living room had smelled of bergamot and lavender, and the macarons from Francine's on 5th perfectly complemented the turquoise and sage hues in the silk drapes. She had once told Charlie only ten percent of the book club was actually about the book; the other ninety percent was about the atmosphere. On that day they were to discuss the passage where Count Horace tosses Melba out in the street and tells her to never return. Melba then walks for four days until she faints in front of the farm of Raul Le Moge. Velveteen recalled trying so hard to connect her life with the heroine – internally telling herself Charlie would fix everything, that they would be okay. That day. *The Rooning.*

"I believe it is important we discuss Melba's immediate reaction to her removal. Our heroine has been physically tossed out into the street and told by her uncle, Count Horace, to never return."

The other women shook their heads and whispered words like "unbelievable" and "how could he?"

Velveteen continued. "If all of us could be as strong as Melba DuMont –"

The doorbell rang. The women seated proudly in her living room didn't flinch.

"Excuse me." She would have called for their housekeeper, Constance, but they had been forced to let her go the week before. Velveteen didn't dare address the absence of their housekeeper to the other ladies.

She sauntered through the vestibule to the front door and casually opened it. On first appearance, the man in his khaki trousers and wrinkled white-collar shirt did not look much different than her regular deliveryman. Had she ordered something and forgotten about it? It used to happen all the time. But not now. Charlie had asked she keep her orders to necessities – and new pumps were not a necessity.

"Good morning, ma'am. If I could simply acquire your signature, I will be on –"

"You can leave it in the office to the left." She wasn't expecting a package. But how lovely for her acquaintances to see a mysterious parcel arriving at the door. She would tip him, laugh at his surprise, softly shut the door, re-enter the gathering, and dive into the surprise package after the ladies had gone. Maybe Charlie had sent it. Maybe it was his way of telling her by some miracle, life was to resume as normal.

But instead of a lovely parcel, he handed her a manila envelope. Her heart lurched in her chest. Charlie had warned her it could happen. He had put off making their *house payment so they would have money for utilities and food. Even if Charlie found work, they were too far behind to catch up.*

"Are you from the bank?" Her voice quivered.

"Ma'am if you will simply sign – "

"Are. You. From. The. Bank?" Her face flushed, her heart sank, and her mind spun as she read the name of the bank holding their mortgage. She handed the large orange envelope back to him. "No thank you. Not today."

But he persisted, looking over her shoulder. She stood up on her tiptoes in an attempt to block his view from the eager, inquisitive faces of the book club. Her guests were not his business.

"You don't have a choice, Mrs Price. If you don't sign, I will be forced to take harsher actions. I don't think you..." He paused, glanced at the ladies once again, and then turned back to Velveteen's burning face. "I don't think you want that, do you Mrs Price?"

She stared at him for a few minutes, stunned and disorientated.

That's when she asked him. That's where it all began – with the question.

"Sir, would you like a treat?" It was all she could think of to curb the curiosity of the ladies behind her – to treat this rogue as if she were thankful for his visit – to cover the fact she was being thrown out into the street by this khaki-wearing Count Horace.

"Um, yes. Yes, please."

She sauntered back to the ornate round cocktail table she and Charlie had purchased in Spain and lifted the sterling silver tray from its home without even a glance to the ladies.

She fully intended to serve him the treat, but in those few steps back, the once wiry young woman her mother had strived to suppress behind Mrs Vanderschmidt's cotillions and coming out parties hatched another plan. The first one was a brilliant aqua. She picked it up and chucked it at his forehead. The man was so stunned he did not realize a green one nailed him on the shoulder. The next one she threw harder and faster, one after another, a rainbow of flying pastries gracing her professionally decorated entry hall.

The man tried to run, as if suddenly forgetting from which direction he came. She tossed another, hitting him on the back of the neck.

He turned and faced her. "Crazy woman! I'll take your house and your stupid macaroons!"

Heat spread through her, flaring into an internal sea of smouldering rage. Stupid maca-roons? She gritted her teeth, arm poised to drive the treat directly into the man's heart. "They're macarons, not macaroons, you imbecile! One 'o', not two." She let go of the macaron and watched it fly directly at the man's chest.

When it was done, the agent had gone, and the envelope lay on the floor. Velveteen dropped the tray with a resounding clang. With the aplomb of a stage actress, she straightened her dress, stood tall and addressed the ladies. "Imagine the gall! We already have home security."

She exhaled, feeling a freedom from a heaviness her heart had carried for months. But the gravity of her confession soon took hold. There was an uncomfortable silence – confirmation enough that she had said too much. Would Charlie be upset that she had told them everything? They had never discussed keeping their past a secret, but there was an unspoken understanding between them that, in order to reach the simplicity they both desired, they would have to put their former lives behind them and never look back.

The women sat stunned around her kitchen table. Clover placed her hand on Velveteen's. Granny, however, leaned back in her chair and crossed her arms. "*The Rooning*, huh?"

"Yes, that's what we call it." Velveteen smiled at the memory.

"And you tossed macarons at the half-wit?"

"Yes." Did they think she was crazy? Did she care?

"Tell me about the macarons."

"Excuse me?"

"The macarons. I want to know about the macarons."

Velveteen looked to Clover for an answer, but she simply shrugged.

"They were from Francine's… on 5th."

"Can you make them?"

"Well… no."

"We'll fix that too. Go on."

Fix that… too? "The ladies in my book club – they adored them."

"What did they cost you?"

"I don't exactly recall."

"You do."

Velveteen choked down the lump in her throat. "You're right, I do. Sixty-six for two dozen."

"Are you joking?" Greer shouted, spraying coffee across the table.

Velveteen shook her head.

"What did they say? About the macarons?" Granny leaned back in her chair again and crossed her arms.

"What did who say?"

"The ladies of course!"

"They didn't say anything. I sat back down and returned to the discussion."

The oven beeped, but Granny did not move; she just stared at her. The oven beeped again. Gavina scooted away from the table.

"Stop," Granny instructed. "She'll get them." She held her gaze on Velveteen, who was presently struck with fear by the old woman. Granny nodded. "Go on."

How unkind! No one had ever spoken to her like this. Velveteen stood up awkwardly, releasing the gaze of her fascinated visitors, and slowly stepped toward the stove. She could feel their eyes, questioning her abilities as a homemaker. Of course she could take a pan out of the oven… couldn't she? The oven beeped again. Velveteen jumped. She searched the cabinet drawers trying to remember where she had placed her linen dishtowels. They were hand embroidered and would have to do, because she had always found potholders too bulky and unattractive.

She located the towels, folded them in half, pulled open the stove door, and removed her ceramic muffin pan. She turned off the stove, ended the timer, and returned the towels to the precise location where she had found them. The sugary scent of sweetened blueberries filled her with an odd sense of accomplishment. She turned to the ladies and smiled as if she had made them herself.

Granny frowned. "With butter."

"Shouldn't they cool?" Velveteen asked.

"I'm the guest."

Velveteen shuffled to find a saucer. During *The Rooning* she asked Charlie to sell her fine china and chose to save the simple white place settings they had received as a wedding present. Her hands shook. Before *The Rooning*, she enthusiastically entertained socialites and politicians. Why was this so difficult? It wasn't that she didn't know how to entertain guests; there was something about the Blackwells that made her uneasy, even uncomfortable – like she couldn't hold to the domestic standards of fermenting boiled eggs and lacing everything in bourbon.

She opened the fridge – no butter. "I'm sorry, but at the moment –"

"Just serve them. The others first."

Without question, she did as the matriarch demanded. Clover smiled as she sat the plated muffin in front of her.

Velveteen exhaled and served Granny last as instructed. But as she leaned over to set the plate in front of her, Granny pretended to duck out of the way, holding her hands up in defense.

Again, there was silence.

Then, Granny burst out in laughter. "Just in case…" she gasped, "you throw it at me." A wave of giggling surged from the other three. Releasing her long-held breath, Velveteen realized she could not keep her face straight and joined in the folly. Then she cried for the second time that day. Large, public tears fell from her eyes. Granny stood up and wrapped a purple scarf around her neck, a gesture of unexpected acceptance. Velveteen tried to say thanks, but could only nod. It smelled like fish and grease and kind of made her feel like she might vomit, but it was one of the most selfless gifts she had ever received.

"*The Rooning*!" Granny shouted with a raised fist. "You need some work all right, but I'll get you straightened out in no time. We'll be over for book club next week. I'll pick something good, nothing sappy and dismal. I don't like the naked books neither, so don't be getting your hopes up." With that, the old woman stood up and hobbled toward the door. The nieces followed after her like obedient puppies.

Clover hung toward the back, fanning her nose. She waited for the others to leave. "Oh, good Lord that thing smells! You don't have to keep it. There's no telling where she got it. If Granny sees something lying around, she takes it, whether it belongs to her or not. And if she thinks you need it, you'll own it. She once gave a set of false teeth to a six-year-old at the market. I tried to remind her that when children lose their teeth they grow back, but she wouldn't hear of it. It's some sort of twisted form of kleptomania. Suits her, don't you think?" Clover's laugh was forced.

Velveteen nodded sweetly. The wretched smell of the scarf mingled with the events of the past few hours, leaving her in a conflicted mess somewhere between feeling better and mortified. That woman was clinically insane. Who was she to say Velveteen needed *work*? More than anything, at this moment Velveteen wanted a bath – a long, hot, bubbly, lavender-scented soak to remove the stench of Granny – but that would have to wait until they had water again.

"She means well. She really does."

"I know." Velveteen didn't know. She had never known her father's mother – or her father for that matter. He was gone before she could walk. And mother's mom had passed during childbirth with her aunt. Mrs Vanderschmidt was the closest thing she had to a *granny*. She couldn't imagine the financially endowed widow talking about the *runnin' offs*.

"Well, I'm looking forward to your book club. Don't be a stranger. You are welcome at our place anytime. Just walk right in. Okay?"

"Okay."

The door shut behind the clan, leaving Velveteen speechless. Hosting a book club in Coraloo had not even crossed her mind – the book club was a part of her life she preferred to leave behind along with the macarons.

CHAPTER 8

*W*ork. Charlie tried to forget Velveteen had mentioned it. *Picking is work*, he reminded himself – again. *Just a different type of work.* Even though they could really use the money, today he didn't feel like "working". If Gideon hadn't been so excited to hang out with Danger, Charlie would have stayed home as Velveteen had requested.

Maybe we should move back to the city? Maybe there's an opening... somewhere. He didn't want to go back, not to the city at least – maybe some other town where the residents weren't privy to his error. He had been successful once; he could do it again. But there had to be another way – a way to support his family but stay clear of the suit and office – free of the chains of expectation, bondage, and failure life in the city had brought them.

Charlie checked the online auction site from his phone for the third time that morning. Nothing new had sold within the last twenty-four hours. He needed to be at the market today.

"Can I go ahead, Dad?"

"Is Captain Turnlip a third-generation space pirate, son of the infamous piratess Madam Celestia?"

"Yes! Thanks, Dad!" Gideon took off with a grin.

Charlie stood in the doorway as anxious tourists brushed past him. He breathed in the scents of Granny's treats and listened to the metallic *click, click* of unlocking shop doors, ready to welcome travelers into their coves. The vendors straightened up their tables, and mild chatter filled the air. The Coraloo Flea Market was awake once more.

"First time?"

Charlie turned around and faced a gentleman staring down at his phone. "Excuse me, are you talking to me?"

"Place is supposed to be a gold mine." The man's gaze held firmly to his handheld device. "'Largest market this side of the city,' it said. My wife thinks she made me come with her for some fancy ribbon. What's so special about ribbon? She ties up the packages and then the person throws it away! Me, I came for that." He pointed to the vast sea of vendors. "You?"

"We live here." Competition soared through Charlie, a burst of energy to find a better deal than the man with the phone. He was tempted to direct the man toward Shug's shop – a lecture on the protocol of the Blackwells would keep the newbie away for a while.

"A local!"

"No, far from it. We moved from…" He didn't want to say it. "We moved here about a month ago."

"Is it true what the paper said, that the Blackwells are a strange bunch?"

"The paper said that?" Charlie had read their description as "eclectic and eccentric" – those words fit them to a tee – but he thought "strange" was unfair.

"I like to read between the lines. Said there was a show of some sort."

Charlie shoved his hands in his pockets and straightened his shoulders. "On the weekends the Blackwell children put on skits for the tourists. Get your coins ready. They'll have the boot out for you." He gazed confidently out into the market – his market, an expert. "It's all in fun. Have you been to see Granny? Her sweets are the best around. When they're gone, they're gone. She closes up shop and heads home." Maybe a local.

"You don't say. I am hungry. What do you recommend?"

What would a local recommend? "The sticky bun, but take an hour or so before you drive home. It's got a kick. And be sure to grab a jar of her apple butter. She grows the apples right out back."

"Is that so? All right. I'll do that then. But don't buy all the good stuff! Save some for the rest of us."

The rest of us.

Until now, Charlie had only seen two other pickers – "antiquers" – and they were from out of state. He didn't class himself as an "antiquer"; if he could turn a profit, he didn't care if his picks were manufactured yesterday. The market was busier than usual. In the distance, one of the Blackwell children yelled, "I have no reason to lie to you, pirate!" Then there was a round of applause.

First show of the day. Gideon's getting his fill of pirates. In the city, he would never have let his son run off alone, but Coraloo was small, safe – welcoming.

In their first week, neighbors on both sides of their little cottage had dropped off an assortment of breads, sweets, and words of wisdom. Father Milligan stopped by and offered to pull the weeds; Velveteen happily accepted and then immediately regretted doing so when the priest showed up the next morning with the church choir. As was the case with the realtor/doctor, it seemed the priest was also the choral director and they had a scheduled practice that day, which they decided to hold in the Prices' garden. Velveteen said it very well could have been a lovely experience had the soprano not been unabashedly tone deaf and fallen victim to an alto's ire. Out of the corner of her eye Velveteen had seen the sly smile on the alto's face as her foot *accidentally* crossed the soprano's path, sending her tumbling into the hydrangeas. It was proposed that Velveteen referee the dispute. Three days later a woman with pale pink hair by the name of Sylvia Toft showed up at the house offering Velveteen a perm in exchange for an honest review. Velveteen gracefully declined the offer.

Charlie grinned at the memory of Velveteen's re-enactment of what she fondly referred to as "the soprano sabotage".

In a matter of minutes, the market was packed with shoppers. Ladies weaved in and out of the crowd with hand-stamped bags from the Blackwell shops. A few men sat, waiting outside the boutiques, talking about their drive into Coraloo, the weather, or how the market would be better suited if it had a bigger parking lot so patrons weren't forced to abandon their vehicles on the streets below and hike up the hill. A chandelier in desperate need of a paint job hurried past Charlie on the right – he doubted the owner would restore it. On his left, a giddy girl, most likely a university student, was paying the vendor's asking price for a typewriter.

She could get it for less.

Then, among the sea of commerce, the silver French horn he had spotted on his second exploratory trip to Coraloo floated by. He watched as the new owner, a gentleman in a slimming pantsuit and brow-line vintage-style glasses, held the horn by its bell. Charlie had learned to study people in his months of picking, especially his type. He definitely was not a musician, nor was he a picker – he wouldn't have bought it from Shug Blackwell. This man had clients; most likely high-end clients who wanted to use the horn as a focal piece in a trendy speakeasy-style nightclub or reservation-only restaurant that served entrées the size of a thimble.

This was Charlie's chance. He wanted that horn and he knew exactly how to get it.

"Sir!" Charlie shouted after the man. "Sir!"

The man whipped around and faced Charlie.

"Excuse me: how much did you pay for the horn?"

The man took a second to study Charlie's shoes and haircut before looking him in the eyes. "Four-hundred fifty."

Charlie coughed. "Four-fifty!" He had paid half the price in the past for similar instruments, but this horn was different. It was Shug's horn. "Wow, steep. You must play."

He doesn't.

"No. I have a client – a collector of sorts."

Of course you do. "Your client is a musician?" The horn would be his before the day was over.

"No. She's a visual artist. Instruments are her muse."

"Sounds interesting." Charlie pretended to examine it. He tilted his head to the right and nodded. "It's a great horn. Thanks." He walked away. The seed had been planted. Charlie walked over to a woman selling used tablecloths – he had no use for table coverings.

There was a tap on his right shoulder. Charlie smiled and whipped around. *He's curious.*

The man adjusted his glasses and shifted his weight from one foot to the other. "Do you think I should have asked if he would take less?"

The idea of yet another victim to Shug's lecture was entertaining; however, in truth, he wouldn't subject anyone, except maybe his deal-forcing former co-worker who was now sitting in his chair at the bank – Carl Rogers – to that kind of torture.

"You got a great deal!" *For a decorator.*

"All right then, thank you."

Charlie gave the man a few minutes to step back; then he went in for the pick. "Wait! Can I see it?"

The man willingly handed the horn to Charlie. Charlie ran his hand around the bell; the name King Schmidt was eloquently engraved into the horn. Brands were good, but this horn wasn't solely about value; it was about his pride. Charlie had only held the horn for a brief moment on his first encounter – not enough time to read the inscription. "I'll give you five."

The man would counter, but this was Charlie's game, and he played it well.

"Six."

Charlie studied the instrument, obviously running his hand over a dent in the mouthpiece. "Five-fifty?"

"Done!" The man's bleached white teeth gleamed in the light of the glittering chandeliers. Both parties had won. Charlie got his horn, and the decorator was departing with an extra hundred.

Charlie pulled out his cash. He counted the bills until he got to five hundred and fifty, leaving him with only ten. He took the horn and watched as the man went back into the market in search of more instruments for his client to deconstruct and display. Charlie's head felt light and his stomach empty. This was all he had left in the money set aside to pick for the day. He doubted the horn was really worth more than seven; the return would not be good. He had made it a practice to at least double his investment.

Music is money, but not this time.

"How did you get it?" Charlie turned around and found himself standing face to face with the red-bearded Shug Blackwell.

"I bought it off a decorator. He's going home happy."

"I said you couldn't have it."

"True, but you didn't say the decorator couldn't have it, and I bought it from him."

"Listen here, Price. This market belongs to my family. You see that woman back there?"

From where he was standing, it didn't look like anyone was back there – no customers and no Granny. The bakery was closed. *She sold out. Good for her.* He was on unstable ground with Shug, so he nodded.

"This is her home; it's our home. We're not some cheap swap shop waiting to make the best deal." His breath smelled sour and bitter. "Look around, Price. These shops have been here longer than you have been alive, and I plan to keep it that way. The likes of you cheapen the place. All these fancy ladies don't need to see you making deals. Next thing you know they'll be asking Granny for a discount on her muffins. I won't have it.

I've got plans and you're not going to mess it up. This isn't the place for you, Price. Leave." The man turned his back to Charlie and walked away.

Go back to your hole of underpriced antiques. I've got what I came for. Charlie was glad Velveteen had stayed behind.

Charlie Price wasn't afraid of Shug Blackwell, but there was no need to stay around if he didn't have money to spend. With the French horn securely in front of him, Charlie set out to find Gideon. He knew what his first port of call would be.

Stephen Blackwell rested his elbows on the bookshop counter and watched Charlie as they talked. "Did Shug have a talk with you?"

"I guess that's what you would call it. How did you know?"

"You've looked over at his shop about a half dozen times since you walked through the door. Don't worry about him. It's not our way to say anything negative about the family, but if you haven't figured it out already, old Shug is a tough one. He's taken care of Granny since he was a boy. He's the oldest of her sons." Stephen laughed. "He thinks it's his life mission to protect us. He loves this place; it's his home, but a lot has changed over the years. We voted to bring in the vendors not long before you showed up. It's the only way we can keep the lights on. Shug voted against it, but we had to try something."

"Why would he vote against it?"

"This place has been home to the Blackwells for years – most of them artists, some of us collectors. I guess he doesn't like change. It's either we change enough to make it all worth it, or we are overtaken by some management company that will replace Granny's with a food court."

"But it's busy! From what I can see, the numbers don't add up. You're a businessman – how can you be in the red? And the article in the paper and the magazine?"

"The article was my idea. I contacted them. After we renovated the place, I thought it would be good if people saw it. Sure increased foot traffic. I thought Shug was going to have my head when the van of photographers showed up."

This made Charlie think about Velveteen's fear of skinning.

"I guess the town is just too small for the market." Charlie couldn't help but let his eyes wander to the Kipling.

"Shug found it for me, at an auction. Half of my inventory came from that auction. I was unpacking the boxes and there it was."

"I've been looking for it most of my adult life."

"Haven't we all? 'We have forty million reasons for failure, but not a single excuse.'"

Charlie had a strange feeling Stephen Blackwell wasn't using his favorite Kipling quote in reference to the book. He glanced out the door toward Shug's once more. "I'm not worried about Shug." He had bigger issues than Shug on his mind – like how he would pay the bills if the horn didn't sell. His stomach knotted with the thought. They'd started over. It had been months since he'd had to hang up on a debt collector. "I should be going. You haven't seen Gideon around by any chance, have you?"

"Check out back. I thought I saw them headed that way."

Charlie left the bookshop and studied the shoppers going in and out of the shops – their hands full of packages, old lamps, discarded shutters, and framed artwork. How could the market be struggling? It didn't make sense, especially if the Blackwells owned the building. A new sense of responsibility filled Charlie – he had to help keep the market going; he might be a picker, but he was also a local. But first he had to sell the French horn… and let Shug Blackwell know he wasn't leaving town without a fight.

CHAPTER 9

1877

Mungo Blackwell removed the beeswax from his tan leather satchel and rubbed it through the thick red hairs of his mustachio pulling them into an upward curve at the ends. He resembled his father, Mumford – tall, nearly six-foot-two with a bushy red beard he would wear for the rest of his life. Mungo ran his finger down the scar on the right side of his face. The wound that started at his hairline and ended at the base of his neck was a reminder of his encounter with a bloat of hippos while crossing the Nile en route to the viceroy of Egypt. Mungo wriggled his toes in his boots – the perfect fit, as it should be, considering he had made them himself.

Thunder drummed in the distance. The ship balanced on the turbulent waters as the mist of the sea sprayed Mungo's olive skin – his father had called it the gift of his mother. Mungo longed to have known her, the quiet voice he had never heard but which carried him across the grainy deserts and through the darkest jungles of Peru, searching.

Mungo had never liked traveling by boat – it took too long to get wherever the wind was taking him – but he wouldn't complain; it was the only way to get to the other side of the world.

Mungo stared into the eyes of the pirate king as the ship rocked back and forth against the storm-torn waters. Salty winds blew through his cotton shirt and threatened to knock him to the ship's deck, but Mungo would not avert his gaze. His father had taught him to always look a pirate in the eye, because it was a known fact a pirate's shiftiness could be determined in a single blink. As this was his second sea voyage – his first in the company of the Royal Navy – he had not yet validated this lesson on the mannerisms of pirates; however, he was not in a position to take chances.

A swaying lantern cast an eerie glow across the ship as Mungo stood at the other end of the captain's blade.

"I don't believe ya!" the pirate bellowed.

Mungo bowed before the captain. "I have no reason to lie to you, pirate. The encounter with the knights is as I say."

"No one crosses paths with the Knights of Odenbon and lives!"

"I bring a gift from his royal highness." Mungo reached into his satchel and produced a stone large enough to replace the pirate's missing eye. "A man would do anything to find his soul, Captain."

The pirate lowered his sword. "Ay," the captain agreed, taking the sparkling blue diamond of Odenbon from the hand of Mungo. "Is this soul a woman that draws you into peril, Blackwell?"

"Could be, Captain. I've never known."

"You are an odd man, shoemaker. I will spare your life so you may find your soul. And as for the stories you tell of the gold…?"

"It is where I claim – north of Barataria."

"And why shouldn't you have the gold for yourself?"

"I have enough, Captain."

At this the Captain raised his one visible eyebrow. "And why shouldn't I take yours as well?"

Mungo ran a finger along his mustachio, pulling the salve through the red hairs to reform the hook at the end. "I'd like to see you try, Captain."

"Ay!" The pirate captain sheathed his sword and slapped Mungo on the shoulder. "Then to Barataria!"

"Captain, we had an agreement."

"Ay?"

"Safe passage, for the gold?"

"You have my word, Blackwell. Safe passage. My crew will cause you no harm. And my boots?"

"I can fix that."

The pirate leaned in and whispered, "You will ensure they are a better pair than Odenbon's?"

"Of course, Captain."

"You are a stoic of gentle demeanor, and a rarity of strength and wit. May all who come under the craftsmanship of Mungo Blackwell be as surprised as I. We go east!"

Mungo closed his eyes and allowed the onset of rain to soak through his clothing. Maybe he would find his contentment in the east.

CHAPTER 10

Velveteen set the porcelain plate of muffins in front of Charlie and Gideon. There was a pause, possibly a moment of shock, as Charlie tried to make sense of the presence of the goodies. Had she had them shipped from Francine's? He hoped not. No, she wouldn't have made such an expensive purchase. Not now. But he had told her they had a little extra. Did she drive to the city just for muffins? Surely not. They hadn't made a trip to the city since the move. Maybe she made them? She hadn't baked him anything since his twenty-seventh birthday – her butter cake tasted delicious, but her dishevelled appearance and flour-dusted hair made him suspect the making of it had not been smooth. That year had changed everything for him. It was the year he received his first promotion and along with it a substantial pay increase. He swore she would never need to bake him another birthday cake ever again, and so she hadn't.

Charlie and Gideon stared at her, waiting for a cue to dive into the unexpected treats. They had eaten an early dinner – early enough that the tavern had not yet run out of deer meat – and so they were both in eager need of an evening snack.

"Go on." She held her hands over her face to hide her smile.

Gideon reached first and took a bite, allowing the crumbs to fall from his chin and onto his plate. "It's *so* good! I didn't know Francine's delivered."

Velveteen blushed. "They don't."

She didn't have them delivered. Relief. Charlie could scratch that off his list of questions. Her response would do; he would not have to inquire any further. He took a bite. They were delicious. The blueberries popped in his mouth, and the buttery sweetness of the muffin tempted him to have another. It was one of the best pastries he had ever eaten. He didn't need to know where she had gotten them, but he was curious. "They are very good."

Velveteen watched as they devoured Granny's treats. She flipped her hair over her shoulder and then quickly placed her gray-stained fingernails behind her back. "Would you like another?"

"Of course! How could I pass up these *delicious* muffins?" He eyed her curiously. There was something different about her – possibly her hair. No matter; she wasn't going to give up the origin of the muffins easily. He could barely stand it. His inductive reasoning had led him to the smell of baked goods wafting through the cottage, but Velveteen didn't bake… or cook for that matter.

"So, Gideon, who was at the market today? Did you learn about the pirates?"

She's changing the subject.

"Yes!"

"He did more than learn about one. He gets to be one." Charlie took another bite.

"The fierce pirate raised his sword and pointed it directly at the chest of Mungo Blackwell!" Gideon shouted, jumping up from his seat and onto his chair. He pointed his fork at his mother and glared at her with one eye squinted closed. "No one has fought the Knights of Odenbon!"

"Odenbon?" Velveteen asked, shocked by her painfully shy son's sudden burst of enthusiasm.

Charlie leaned into her. "They're letting him play a part."

"It's not a big one, but I'm a pirate! I wanted to be the Maharaja of Kuru, but Danger said I'm too young."

"What great stories!" Velveteen laughed.

"They aren't stories. Danger says it's their history. And I read about it in their book."

"Don't let the Blackwells get in your head." She pulled her hair back with both hands and then let it fall again.

What had she said earlier about her hair? "I wouldn't be too quick to pass them off," Charlie added. "They are an eclectic bunch."

"I'm not sure how I feel about him having his head filled with all that nonsense, Charlie."

Gideon yawned and stepped down from his crow's nest with a look of defeat smeared across his face. "May I be excused?"

"Of course, you one-eyed pirate." Charlie loved seeing his son act out the adventures of Mungo Blackwell with the other boys. True or not, he was having fun.

Gideon wrapped his arms around his father's neck. "Night Dad." And then kissed his mother on the cheek. "Night Mom."

"Goodnight. Now go climb in bed, or I'll make you walk the plank!"

Gideon lifted his fist and roared, "Argh!" then ran up the stairs.

"You shouldn't encourage him," Velveteen chastised.

"Why not? It's good for him to be around the other boys. For once he'll have friends at school."

"They don't go to his school, remember? Clover homeschools them."

"Maybe you should give it a try." Charlie was hopeful; Velveteen rolled her eyes. "No homework, no schedules, he would love being home with you." Charlie sensed Velveteen did not like where this conversation was going. "I'm sure Clover would help. Maybe you could do some classes together." Velveteen twirled her mug around in a circle, watching the tea slosh back and forth in her cup. "You could teach art!"

"Do you also want me to move into a camper van?"

"Of course not! I'm not suggesting you become a Blackwell. But remember – this is our fresh start. We can go about life differently here – no parent–teacher conferences or uniforms."

"But he looks so nice in his uniform."

"I thought you were open to trying something new?"

"I've tried enough something new for one day."

He watched curiously as she twisted the tips of her hair between her thumb and forefinger. She had definitely done something to her hair.

"So, you had a successful day at the market?" She was changing the subject again.

He could play that game too. Now was not the time to discuss their finances. "Have you seen my suit?"

"Your suit? Oh Charlie, does that mean you have an interview? Charlie, that's fantastic! Is it in the city? What are they offering to pay? Why didn't you tell me you were applying again?"

There was an awkward silence, a moment where Charlie wished he could tell her he had been offered a six-figure salary with benefits, but that would be a lie. "It's for the market, Velveteen."

"You are interviewing for a job at the market?"

"No." He rubbed the back of his neck. *Job.* He loathed the word. A *job* meant a boss. He didn't want to talk about this. He wanted to go back to the muffins and the pirates, but it was too late.

We've been through this already. Why is she bringing all this up again? He tried to change his thoughts – she hadn't said anything wrong. Why wouldn't she assume he needed a suit for an interview? Where else would he wear one in Coraloo? He hadn't worn one since the day he'd bought the Waterman.

"Oh… So the market, how was it?" She leaned her head against the back of the chair. She was disappointed, probably trying to pull herself down from the instant where she hoped he might have a real job.

"I had an encounter with Shug Blackwell today."

"Of course you did. I see the oaf didn't skin you alive."

"No, but he did say I was cheapening the market. That's why I want the suit. I figure I will bring some class to my new profession. Stephen says the vendors are a recent addition to the market. I guess it was a last-minute attempt to cover the cost of maintaining the building. But I ran through the numbers in my head. It seems to me that since the place belongs to the family, and with what the vendors are paying them, it shouldn't be a problem."

"What happens if they lose the market? What happens to us?" She cleared the table, forgetting to ask if he was finished, and sat back down.

Her mind is somewhere else.

"If Shug Blackwell has anything to do with it, he will chain himself to the door before he lets anyone take it from his mom."

"Granny?"

"The old crank herself."

"But what if something happens? Maybe we should have a backup plan? Have you thought about trying to interview again?"

Why is she bringing this up?

Charlie leaned back in his chair. "I don't want to go back. It's not who I am anymore, Velveteen. It's not me." He couldn't give up this easily. He had already failed in business; he would not fail in this too.

"So this is who you are?"

"Didn't we have this conversation this morning? You said you wanted this too – a new start, a simple life like Melba What's-her-name." His voice was louder than he had intended.

"I want running water, Charlie!"

"We don't have water?"

She raised her eyebrows.

"Oh, right! That's why we had to go out tonight."

"I don't know what I want, Charlie. But I think we need to be prepared. We need to be ready, just in case."

"In case of what?" He knew what she meant – in case *it* happened again, in case they fell face first into another *Rooning*.

"I don't know! In case we have a need... Like water!"

"Like in the city?"

"Charlie! I didn't say that! Where is this coming from?"

She hadn't said it, but he'd wondered about it every day since they moved to Coraloo. He was ready to call this home. But Velveteen always sounded as if they were on furlough, passing through until something better came along. "Were you even happy in the city?"

"Yes." She paused. "No. Not completely. I don't know. It was easier. I didn't have to rely on anyone. I knew what I was doing."

He didn't understand. "What do you really want, Velveteen? Is this not enough?" He hadn't meant to be so firm.

"It's enough, Charlie!"

"Then what is it? Something is bothering you! Tell me what it is so I can fix it!"

"Why does everyone want to fix me? I'm not broken! I just want water!"

"Vee, what is going on?"

Her voice softened. "I don't know, Charlie. I can't explain it. I'm... unsettled, that's all."

There was a quiet, uncomfortable silence between husband and wife. He didn't want to fight; they never fought before *The Rooning*. However, there was an intimacy about their recent heated discussions, an unveiling of the heart, and a deeper look into the woman he loved. His wife needed something he was not able to give her... something she would never tell him. Why?

Her eyes were teary, heavy, and tired. Before *The Rooning*, he would send her to the spa when she appeared on the edge of exhaustion. She would return a glowing ball of social updates, smelling of mint and rosemary. Now, he could barely send her to the grocery for shampoo.

"Vee, I don't want to fight. If you need something, you have to tell me. I'll find a way, but please don't ask me to go back to the city." He reached across the table for her hand, and then he squinted, rubbed his eyes, and looked at her again. "Did you do something to your hair?"

She stared at him as if he had lost his mind.

"You colored it today... you and Melba! It's a tad darker, isn't it?"

"A tad?"

"Is that the color you chose? I mean, darker is great. Do you like it?"

"It wasn't supposed to be darker. I've been trying to tell you – there's no water, Charlie."

Was that really all she wanted? Water? He walked over to the kitchen faucet and turned the handle. A gentle stream of water trickled into the sink. "Hey, look at that! It's working now!" He grinned at his frantic wife.

Velveteen slumped down in her chair and buried her head in her hands.

Charlie rubbed the back of his neck. He'd missed something. "This has nothing to do with the water, does it?" He had read hundreds of books in his lifetime, but not one of them had told him how to decipher the mystery of the female thought process.

"I had no one else to call! And my hair, and my hands, and Granny – she made me serve her, and we have no butter... I need to buy butter. And then! Oh and then..." Her voice shook, as the heat of her anger rose. "She forced me to tell her about *The Rooning*! And they dumped the water..." She motioned uncontrollably with her hands, acting out the process. "And that woman! That woman! She wants to *work on me*! But Clover, she's so lovely, and she brought me a jar of tomatoes. I'm supposed to make salsa, Charlie."

Charlie Price tried to comprehend his wife's explanation of what had happened that day. "I don't understand: why were they pouring water on you?"

Velveteen shook her head, unable to speak.

"Sweetheart, we'll figure it out. Let's make an appointment for you with, what was her name?" He didn't have the money, but he would find a way.

"Sylviaaaa," she wailed. "It's not about my hair, Charlie. Okay, maybe a little about my hair. It's about –" She paused, thinking. "Well, it's really about…"

Just then, there was a ping to Charlie's phone, followed by another, and then another. He cast a look to where he had left his phone sitting on the coffee table and then back to his wife. Three of the many items piled into the cupboard, under their bed, or in the garden shed behind the Toft house had sold. The thrill of the sell sent his mind racing. He fought the temptation to run for his phone. Was it the French horn, or possibly the box of vinyl records he had decided to sell as a set instead of individually? It could wait. She needed him now. He needed her. He opened his mouth to speak, to ask her what her breakdown was really about, but he didn't know how to ask.

Velveteen pushed her chair away from the table and sighed. "Go ahead."

He opened the app on his phone, studied the message, and laughed. He laughed so hard, he had to sit back down. "Well, how about that! Three items in one day! And one of them I've had listed for some time now." Relief.

Velveteen kissed him on the forehead. "I'm proud of you, Charlie Price."

"Are you?"

She nodded. "I am. I have to get my head around it sometimes… literally." She pulled her hair into a ponytail, let it fall over her shoulders, and forced a smile.

"Did they really pour jugs of water over your head?"

She held her hands up to display the number five. "Granny gave me a scarf too, but I don't think it was hers to give."

"She stole it?"

"Quite possibly."

"Vee, I'll do anything to make you happy." He meant it.

When they were dating, they passed by a department store window – at the time a store far more expensive than either of them could afford.

He stopped her in front of the mannequin wearing a pencil skirt and silk blouse. "One day, you will shop here. You will walk in and they will fall over one another to clothe the famous interior designer, Velveteen... Price."

"Price? That sounds nice."

"I love you, and I will do anything to make you happy for the rest of my life."

He asked her to marry him the next day.

She didn't like the way the phrase had rolled off his tongue – *my new profession*. His new profession confined her to the financial mercy of whatever unsold items she had stuffed in the closet earlier in the day. It wasn't so much that she missed the freedom of ordering whatever she wanted online and hopping in a cab for an afternoon of shopping whenever she desired – they hadn't always lived that way – she missed the freedom of picking up a special treat for Gideon at Francine's or surprising Charlie with tickets to a touring Broadway production. She missed the convenience and the ease; she had taken their blessings for granted. She would happily go to work and help pay the bills if she knew what to do, but Charlie, for whatever reason, wanted her to stay home. When she brought up the idea of her getting a job, he shut her down. She did not mind staying home, but it was easier before *The Rooning*. Maybe her mind had been too occupied with other *things* to think about a career. She had never really wanted a career anyway – design school was more of a hobby, one that she was happy to revisit to make their home in Coraloo more livable. Here she was learning to simplify, but even simplicity had its costs. She didn't need much… maybe a little consistency. Yes, that was what she desired most of all – consistency.

"Let me buy you something! What do you need… other than water?"

His question aroused a sense of childlike helplessness. *What do you need?* There was nothing she needed from him in this moment. It felt selfish to take the money he had earned and spend it on herself. It had been easy before *The Rooning*, but not now – not when she could see worry and nights of troubled sleep exposing its true nature through deep creases on his forehead.

She had circled a throw in a catalog last week. It was silly – they didn't need it – but she imagined how lovely it would look draped across the arm of the couch. But she would never mention something so silly to Charlie. There were other things they needed – things she could easily pick up on her next grocery run.

"There must be at least one thing you want. What would Melba ask of her prince if he offered to buy her anything she wanted?"

Velveteen forced a smile – the intensity of their argument held its grip on her. She kissed her husband on the lips, lingering longer than usual. *What would Melba ask for?* "She would ask for nothing, only that he forgive her." She loved Charlie even more now, with all the uncertainty and upheaval they had been through, than she had before *The Rooning*. She hadn't fallen in love with his money – he didn't have any back then – she had fallen in love with his determination. She only wanted him to find something that made him happy.

"And if he refuses?"

"He would never refuse her."

"And why is that?"

"Because he loves her muffins."

"Her muffins?" Charlie raised his eyebrows playfully.

She frowned at his innuendo.

"Oh!" He grinned. "But she doesn't make muffins."

"How do you know?" she said with her hands on her hips. "I made a cake… once!"

"I told you she doesn't make muffins!"

"You tricked me!"

"So where does Melba buy her muffins?"

"Melba wouldn't buy muffins. She'd make them… however, Granny made mine." Velveteen frowned at the memory of the rude woman making demands in her kitchen. She still needed to clean the spit off of the carpet.

"Granny gave you a scarf and made you muffins? She must like you."

"I think she was afraid I would throw them at her! She is definitely the queen of the crazies."

"They're not crazy… *unique*, that's all."

"Did I tell you Granny informed me I'm starting a book club in Coraloo?"

"That's fantastic!"

"Oh, I don't know. I don't feel much like thinking about it. It can't go well. But for now, Charlie Price," she said in her most sultry voice, purposefully suppressing all talk of jobs and consistency, "Let's go pick out that suit."

CHAPTER 11

A wave of financial peace washed over Charlie after a few of the smaller items sold – a rare original U.S. World War 2 tail gunner helmet and a vintage industrial stapler he'd acquired on one of his earlier trips to the market.

It was a tedious, time-consuming process: first in the listing, which required him to photograph each item dozens of times, from every angle, zooming in on dates, serial numbers, and engravings and noting any scratch or dent. Once sold, the item had to be packaged carefully in bubble wrap, placed in a box, and shipped to its destination – to arrive, he hoped, within two weeks. Inevitably, there were occasional delays, which equalled unhappy customers – Charlie's least favorite aspect of the job. Still, when an item sold and he received positive feedback from the buyer, Charlie took a certain satisfaction in his "work", especially when the funds came in and brought him a measure of financial security.

As if the helmet led the charge, his phone alerted him another of his flea market treasures had sold. He checked the details, tucked the phone in the pocket of his slacks, adjusted the cuffs of his button-up shirt, and straightened the bow tie he had chosen as an added touch of sophistication. Charlie Price stepped boldly through the archway of the Coraloo Flea Market – out of the comfort of his blue jeans and strapped into the confines of the gray wool double-breasted pinstriped suit. He'd show Shug Blackwell pickers had class.

Suddenly, he was an outsider looking in – a stranger, an oddity, and no longer a cog in the movement of the market.

The suit had given him the illusion of confidence, like the air of empowerment he had felt in his years at the bank. As he eyed the vendors – some of whom he thought of as friends – Charlie couldn't shake the uncomfortable sensation that his conspicuous appearance would only serve to outclass the sellers, putting him on equal footing with the husbands with heavy wallets who slugged behind their wives carrying a bag in each hand. Charlie didn't like it and considered walking back to the Toft house.

The last time Charlie had worn a suit was thirteen months ago. He had waited for the call, standing with his hands in the pockets of the very same Burberry suit, staring down at the row of food trucks lining the street in front of Heritage Financial. Other than a few jobs during his years at university, Heritage was all he had ever known. Two weeks before, Charlie told Velveteen that Edgar Green had announced his retirement; she went out and bought a dress. Edgar's party commemorating his years of service to the bank would also usher in Charlie's promotion. It had only taken eight years of long hours and late nights to position himself as the next vice president of the one-hundred-year-old establishment.

He recalled how, on that suit-wearing day, hungry patrons waited in long lines for curry-infused burgers, deep-fried churros, and authentic Vietnamese cuisine. The memory played out before him, as clearly as it had happened.

He pulled back the sleeve of his suit coat and checked his watch, crossed his arms, and continued to ponder the exchange of money taking place below him. It could have happened to any one of those poor entrepreneurs.

The phone rang. Charlie sighed. "Hello... yes, sir." He placed the receiver back on its cradle, took another look at his minimalist, but sophisticated – as Velveteen had labeled it – corner office, and proceeded to the conference room.

One empty chair waited for him at the head of the table. Board members, bank president Ralph Walsh, vice president Edgar Green, Carl Rogers – whom Charlie blamed for this disaster – and a handful of other senior employees waited for him with forced smiles.

"Have a seat, Charlie," Ralph directed.

"I prefer to stand."

"Understood. You know why you're here?"

"I have a good idea."

"Son, you approved the loan. We have no other choice."

Charlie passed a glare toward Carl.

"You see, Heritage Financial has been in my family for nearly one hundred years…"

Charlie tuned out the long-winded old man. He had been subjected to this spiel at every corporate event, conference, and on the day he was offered the position of vice president – pending Ralph's retirement. He smiled and nodded, pretending to be engaged, but his mind wandered back to the elusive Kipling.

He could blame the Kipling for this debacle; after all, that's where his mind had been the day Carl Rogers tossed the proposal for the rolling gut trucks of death on his desk. Charlie was good at his job and never doubted his instincts. His instinct told him to pass, but Carl pushed. Mid-conversation, Charlie's finder called and said he had a real lead on the book. The rare leather-bound edition had eluded him at every auction, antique bookshop, and online dealer. That day, his mind consumed by the Kipling, and against his better instincts, he signed for the loan.

"Charlie…" Charlie Price returned his attention to his boss. "It's a bad situation we are in. That truck chain you loaned money to spread a trail of salmonella poisoning over a five-block radius. The poor owner is being sued by two law firms and a neurosurgeon. Those lads at Dudley and Dudley are threatening to come after us next. We're looking at a class action lawsuit. Charlie, we can't afford the press, especially in this economy. The shareholders are looking for someone to blame."

It was his first major blunder in eight years. The standard documents were there, right in front of him with the other necessary paperwork: registration with the local authority, a food service license, and a health and safety policy. But more trucks meant more employees, and required a written hygiene management plan, which the client didn't have. The Dudleys had caught Charlie's oversight. Chances were, the policy wouldn't have stopped the stomach-wrenching deluge. Either way, he'd made a mistake, but he wasn't going down without a fight. He refused to let Ralph Walsh and his cohorts blame him for the overactive bowel movements of some eight hundred people, including the Dudley brothers, who were forced to postpone all cases for two weeks after the younger Dudley failed to make it to the men's room mid-trial.

"Sir, the data more than demonstrates the food truck industry is on the rise," Charlie protested. "Have you looked out the window? There's a fellow out there selling turnip tacos… and the people are loving it!"

"You made a mistake. Your name was on the loan, Son."

"His business plan was solid!"

Ralph leaned back in his chair and placed his hands behind his head. "Dudley and Dudley won't stop until they've drawn blood."

"So you're sacrificing me?"

"No, Son. We're firing you."

"Charlie?" A friendly voice.

Charlie jumped. The past was the past. He could not change what had happened on that day in the city.

"I walked past you three times before I realized who you were. Are you planning to leave us?" Stephen Blackwell asked with apparent concern for Charlie's professional appearance.

"Oh, no – this, it's for fun."

"I've worn my fair share of monkey suits, and I wouldn't exactly call them fun."

"Oh, this will be fun, I promise. You haven't seen Shug around, have you?" Charlie surveyed the market.

"He's around here somewhere, most likely in the shop."

Charlie only half paid attention – his mind caught between the memory of his professional death and making sure Shug Blackwell saw him.

"I don't know what you have up that expensive sleeve of yours, but it can't be good."

Charlie adjusted his cufflinks – the cufflinks Velveteen had bought him when he informed her Edgar Green was retiring. They were books – tiny gold books monogrammed "CEP". He should have pawned them; last week they could have used the money, but there were some things he could not let go.

"Do you want me to tell Shug you're looking for him?"

Charlie laughed. "No, I have a feeling that after our last conversation, he has his eye on me already."

Even though Charlie could not see the shop owner, there was no doubt Shug was watching. While he waited for the inevitable confrontation, Charlie allowed his methods to mesh with his new image. He used bigger words and handled each object as if it were a rare artifact. To his surprise, his ruse was more of a detriment – the regular vendors laughed and not a single new vendor would take his offer.

"Ah, ha!" Danger shot up from underneath a table of automobile parts. "I knew you worked for the FBI!" The boy proceeded to quiz Charlie on his secret identity, code words, and concealed weaponry – all the while Charlie scanned the crowd of eager shoppers for Shug. "Are you on a mission? Does Gideon know who you *really* are? Do you have a codename?"

Charlie laughed. "I'm not a spy, Danger."

"That's what they all say."

He tried to change the subject. "Gideon said something about pirates and pygmies. Are you putting on a show today?"

"It's pygmy day, and it's not a show, it's –"

Charlie laughed. "I know; it's history."

"Mungo Blackwell was a spy too, Mr Price."

"Why am I not surprised? Go on now. I'm sure the other pygmies are waiting for you."

The boy would not ease his interrogation. "How long have you been a spy? Is your wife a spy? You can tell me!"

Charlie gave in. "As long as you promise not to reveal my identity to anyone –"

"I promise!" Danger nodded vigorously, his eyes wide and his mouth gaping.

"I am on a mission. It involves the Chinese government. Top secret." Charlie glanced over his shoulder, pretending he was being watched. "I need your help."

"Sure! Of course."

"I think you can handle it." Charlie pulled his wrist to his chest, tapped the tiny gold book, and then brought it to his ear. He nodded, shot a quick look down at Danger, and then darted his eyes from side to side. "Number one says, you're clear."

"Wow! Can I have one of those communication devices?"

"Sorry, kid, you have to graduate from the academy. Here's what we need from you. Keep a sharp eye on the tourists, got it?"

"Got it. What am I looking for?"

"Chinese vases. It's what the ninja monks use to smuggle in the goods."

"Ninja monks. Yes, sir. I can do it, sir."

"I'm counting on you, Danger." Charlie didn't say another word. Danger took off into the sea of shoppers.

Forty-five minutes later, while in deep debate with a vendor over the cost of a vintage record player, Charlie suddenly found himself handcuffed and facing the head constable of Coraloo.

"Hey! What's going on?"

"Not a word until we figure this out."

"Can you at least un-cuff me? My son's friends are around here." Charlie was relieved Gideon was in school and not with him at the market to witness whatever was going on.

"Fair enough."

The constable unhooked the metal bracelets. Charlie rubbed his wrists.

"Now, I mean it, Mr Price. Not another word. For the sake of your boy, we'll walk out together like nothing's wrong."

Charlie followed the constable out of the market, through the stares of curious customers, down to the center of the town, and into the municipal building. The building stood three stories high, the tallest building in the town of Coraloo, with the law enforcement office and a two-cell jail on the bottom floor, a courtroom and municipal offices on the second, and the mayor's office on the third.

Charlie sat in the hard metal chair of the law enforcement office as the constable filled out his necessary paperwork. "Whatever you're writing on that paper, I didn't do it."

"Uh, huh." The constable kept his eye on the paperwork in front of him.

"I don't work for the Chinese government!"

"A lot about your story doesn't add up, Mr Price."

"Like what?"

"You're telling me the only reason you moved to Coraloo is so you can buy from the vendors and resell it all for more, and you're supporting a wife and child doing this, Mr Price?" The constable shook his head disapprovingly. "That's some story, but I'm not buying it. Right thumb…"

Charlie let his head fall to the desk, and then allowed the constable to roll his right thumb on the pad of ink, and press it onto the paper with his other prints. "This can't be about my personal life. Why am I really here?"

"Espionage."

"Espionage! It was a joke! I was just playing with the boy!" Charlie tried to throw his hands up in the air, forgetting he was cuffed to the desk.

"Granny doesn't think so." The constable put down his ink pen and leaned back in the slat back rolling chair.

"What's Granny got to do with this?"

"Danger insists you moved to Coraloo as an undercover agent with the Federal Bureau of Investigation. The Blackwells don't lie, Mr Price. Granny was fearful of being found out – don't ask." Velveteen's theory about the crazy grandmother seemed more plausible by the moment. "That woman has more secrets than Carter's got liver pills."

"Carter?"

The constable passed over Charlie's confusion about a person named Carter and their liver pills. "So, she called it in, saying a man posing as an FBI agent and quite possibly a black market antiquities dealer, easily identified by a gray wool double-breasted pinstriped suit, was working the market today. We don't like trouble, Mr Price. Why are you really here?"

"I told you."

The constable chuckled. "Nobody's going to believe that, Mr Price. I doubt you even believe it yourself. I'll give you some time to think about it. Let's clean you up first." From a shelf above the filing cabinet, the constable took down a mason jar of clear liquid. "Here. It'll take the ink off. Just don't drink it."

Charlie unscrewed the lid, releasing a pungent aroma like that of turpentine. "Whoa! Is this stuff legal?"

"Nope. Confiscated it years ago. That's our last jug. A couple of the Toft boys found a family recipe and decided to have a go at it. They had a go at it all right! Pretty sure one of the boys bought and paid for a new car before I found what they were up to. All right, Mr Price, in you go."

Charlie stepped into the brick jail cell and sat down on the blue ticking stripe sheet covering the cot. The space hardly evoked a sense of fear and discipline. It was more like a quaint reading nook with a neatly folded white blanket at the foot of the bedding and a stack of old cloth-bound books resting on a wooden nightstand. He probably could have pushed the cell door open and walked right out if he wanted, but he didn't want to.

Charlie laid his head against the wall. *I'm in jail.* He laughed. *I'm in jail.* He reached for one of the books – *Paradise Lost.* He'd read it. He grabbed another – *Frankenstein.* A favorite. *What kind of prison has their cell library stocked with literary classics?* He laughed again. Forty-five minutes ago he had strolled the market dressed like a banker awaiting a verbal confrontation with Shug Blackwell. His wool pinstripes were ironically fitting for his present situation.

Velveteen flung herself against the metal bars. "Oh, Charlie! I only heard moments ago! I'm going to get you out of here! I love you…"

She turned dramatically to face the constable who was sitting at his desk directly across from the cell. Charlie would've hated to be the constable right about now as his wife, appointing herself as his legal representation, frantically tried to convince the constable they were not a family of undercover spies, or black market distributors, or – as the story had grown largely out of proportion – a smuggler of illegal jasmine into China. She flailed her arms in exaggerated movements and plopped her hand on her hip emphatically when she was trying to make a point.

Oh how he loved her.

The door to the office opened again. Charlie pressed his body against the bars and craned his neck to see who else was joining the fray. Seconds later, Stephen Blackwell opened the cell door. Charlie reached out and shook his hand.

"I promised Roy a batch of Granny's bourbon balls if he'd give this whole thing a rest. Just be glad he didn't call in the volunteer officers. You know he thinks something's really wrong when he calls in those two old goons." Stephen patted Charlie on the back. "He's just doing his job."

"I know. Thanks, Stephen."

Charlie took Velveteen by the hand and led her down the streets of Coraloo to the Toft house. By the time they arrived, Gideon had heard all about the event and was so pleased with his father's successful portrayal of the FBI agent who smuggled illegal jasmine via the black market into China, he wanted to convince Danger the whole thing could be acted out next weekend at the market. He'd call it, "A new page in the history of the Coraloo Flea Market". Velveteen forbade it.

CHAPTER 12

"What will the book club be reading this month?" Charlie snagged a cookie from Velveteen's sterling silver serving tray. When he had offered to sell the tray for her, she asked him if she could keep it, saying something about holding onto a piece of life pre-*Rooning*. He had suggested she hang it on the wall as a memory of *The Rooning*, but she said it was too fancy for their country life decor.

"I don't know."

"They'll be here in what, forty-five minutes? It's unlike you to not have figured out what you all will be reading."

"Granny is bringing it."

"But you always pick what the group is reading."

She pulled a lemon cake from the oven, set it on the counter beside her tray of break and bake chocolate chip cookies, and smiled at her accomplishments. "Not in Coraloo. Nobody argues with Granny."

"Maybe that's why I was arrested." In his former life, he would have hired an attorney to sue for defamation of character. In Coraloo, he was pretty sure he was a celebrity among the children. "You're right – nobody argues with Granny."

"You were arrested because you are a spy. Look, Charlie! I made a cake!"

Charlie liked this shift in Velveteen. In the past two weeks she had tried more than a dozen recipes from the *Unofficial Melba DuMont Countryside Cookbook* – most of which found a home in the trashcan, but she had perfected the lemon cake.

The sunlight streamed through the windows of the cottage, mocking the chilly fall afternoon. Their cottage hardly resembled the leftover life of the Toft family. It was light, bright, and airy – the way Velveteen had imagined it could be.

Charlie was impressed with how she had taken their old things and made them look new. She had a gift for it. It was hard to believe she had given it up. A year before *The Rooning*, a move like theirs would have required a contractor, construction crew, and an interior designer for each room. Now it seemed that every day she was tweaking and designing. Charlie looked forward to coming back after a day at the market to be welcomed with, "Charlie, come look what I've done!" It was a joy he had not seen in her in years. Last Friday, he returned to find her pulling up the orange living room carpet with a crowbar she'd uncovered in the garden shed.

"What are you doing?"
"Wood, Charlie! Solid, beautiful wood!"

At times, the Toft cottage felt like home to Charlie; at other times, he had the urge to upgrade to something with more square footage – possibly with his own office where he could sort and price, list and sell, without having to move his wares from the kitchen counters and table whenever they needed to sit down for a meal. The desire was an old one, the feeling of never having enough, always wanting more. He caught himself once or twice perusing online real estate sites, forgetting their goal of living a simpler life. A bigger house meant bigger payments. *Discouraging.*

Currently, his latest picks were shoved under the bed in Gideon's room – out of sight. Velveteen had insisted he move them from the kitchen. She had worked hard preparing the house for the Blackwell ladies. She wanted them to experience the luxurious book club she had hosted in the city – minus the macarons, of course. She had rearranged the pillows on the sofa for a solid hour and stared at the rack they called a wardrobe for another hour or more, deciding what to wear. It had to be perfect. She had to show Granny that Velveteen Price did not need an ounce of work.

"Are you walking Gideon to school?"

Charlie frowned. "Not anymore. He rides his bike with the boys."

"So what are you going to do?"

"I guess I'll just sit at the table and list. I have a couple packages to take to the post office, and then I'll be back." The cheerful disposition on her face switched to a blank stare. Had he forgotten something? They celebrated their anniversary in July, and her birthday in February.

"Don't you have somewhere to go?"

He quickly glanced at the calendar on his phone. Empty – free of lunch appointments, meetings, or required professional development trainings. "No."

"Charlie, you can't be down here for my book club!"

"I'm sorry, what did you say?" His mind was stuck on the emptiness of his calendar. It was what he had wanted – his days free to be with the family and not filled with the slush pile of paperwork and conference calls.

"My book club, Charlie!"

"Right, so where do you want me to go?"

"Away! Please..."

"How about Gideon's room?"

Velveteen had yet to get her hand on the room. The cowboys on the walls reminded Charlie of the scenes acted out by the boys at the market. Being confined to the rodeo would force him to get some much needed listing done of the picks he had stashed away: old tool chests, some containing tools; a vintage overhead projector; a box of spoons; a set of coasters; and three boxes of items to be sorted. It was always fun to go back through his picks – but clearly not today. Velveteen's plans somehow made him feel agitated, uncomfortable, and aware of his boredom.

"You've never been home during book club. I wasn't expecting it. You'll make me nervous."

"Nervous? I'll shut the door. You won't even know I'm up there."

"I can't explain it, Charlie." Velveteen walked in circles, mumbling to herself. "I guess I'll say I am painting in there; we'll keep the door closed. They won't have to see his room. But what if they venture upstairs, they'll wonder… Charlie, are you sure there is nowhere to go?"

"It's a Thursday; the market is closed."

"What about Stephen? Can't you go do whatever it is he does on the weekdays?"

"I don't understand why this is a big deal."

"I don't know why it's a big deal, it just is! I was not planning on you being here!"

He sighed. "I don't have anywhere to go, Velveteen. Do you want me to sit in the street?"

"Of course not." She blushed.

The mantel clock rang the half-hour – Velveteen had thirty minutes to freshen up her make-up and make sure the house was perfect for the ladies. She had planned through every detail, except Charlie. Gideon clomped down the stairs and into the kitchen. He grabbed a cookie, and with his backpack slung across his shoulder threw open the door.

"Hey!" Charlie called. "Not even a goodbye?"

"Sorry." Gideon wiped a crumb from his lip with his forearm "Bye!"

"Hold up! What are you doing after school?"

"Practice. Mungo's getting married!" Gideon started out the door again.

"Wait!" Velveteen called to her son.

He rolled his eyes and stepped back inside.

"How does the house look?"

He shrugged. "Good."

"Do you think they will like it?"

"It's just a house."

"It's not *just* a house; it's our house. The Blackwells aren't used to being in a house. They live in camper vans." She paused, noticing Gideon's contorted stare. "Why are you looking at me like that?"

"The Blackwells have a house."

"Gideon, we ate on the lawn in front of their camper van. I think I would know if they have a house."

"That's not what Danger said – gotta go!" He quickly kissed his mom on the cheek, gave Charlie a sideways hug, and ran out of the cottage.

"What do you think that was about?"

Charlie scratched the back of his head, realizing he hadn't spent enough time talking to his wife. "They have a house in the suburbs."

"What!"

"They rent it to tourists."

"Oh, so it's like an investment."

"Well, it was their house, until Stephen got word the market was in trouble. He was an attorney – took some time off to help out the family. Took over his father's shop a few years ago and decided he liked his new life better."

"Are you telling me they have a house, and they *choose* to live in a camper van?"

"Something like that."

Her face was white, her hands shaking. What else did she not know about the Blackwells? Were they royalty in disguise, hiding from the paparazzi and the duties of palace life? Or were they like her, a bouncing ball ping-ponging from simple to socialites and back to simple again? *Simplicity.*

She surveyed the room with a newfound sense of despair. "It's not enough! Charlie, you have to go to the store... fresh fruits... cheese, whatever you can find."

"Stop! It's perfect. You're perfect. They are coming to see *you*, not the house."

"Why would they come to see *me*, Charlie? I'm just the host. The food, the atmosphere – it's all-important. What if they're uncomfortable or they're hungry and my cookies don't taste good, then they don't eat them, and then they faint from starvation!"

He put his hand over his mouth to hold in his chuckle.

"Don't make fun, Charlie Price."

"Sweetheart, we're not in the city anymore. You don't have to impress anyone."

"I know..."

He had forgotten, despite her insistence hosting a social event such as a book club did not cause her extreme anxiety, that she was always a complete wreck the morning of. She would allow herself to get so swept up in every detail, from writing lists of "questions for discussion" to deliberating on which pastry would be best for each woman's particular dietary requirements, that she would elevate a simple social gathering to a black-tie affair. Before *The Rooning*, he would go to work, leaving her mid-tizzy, and return that afternoon to a wife beaming with confidence over her beautiful success. She did have a flair for entertaining, he had to admit, having attended more than one of his wife's events – though never a book group gathering. The laughs and easy conversation said it all: he knew that not a single attendee would deny they felt like the most important person in the room. Any CEO would have given their left arm to have her knack for entertaining; a successful soiree à la Velveteen was the equivalent of a completed deal or an "attaboy" from the higher ups. However, when she had canceled all further meetings of her book club following *The Rooning*, she hadn't seemed upset, but relieved.

> *"What did you tell them?" Charlie disguised his relief behind genuine curiosity.*
>
> *"I simply explained that Barnaby was ill."*
>
> *"Who's Barnaby?"*
>
> *"Our Maltese."*
>
> *"We don't have a Maltese."*
>
> *"It doesn't matter, Charlie. The ladies don't know that. They believe Barnaby is facing in-home care. Of course I would have to postpone our gathering until he is well. Poor thing…"*

The sight of her frantic attention to the frivolous had brought up memories of the pretentious back and forth they had played with their acquaintances. But this was different – she was different. Hosting the book club wasn't even her idea; it was Granny's, and no one argues with Granny. Without Velveteen even realizing it, she had entered the arena, fighting to find her normal in Coraloo.

The book club will come to a close, and tonight she'll tell me how wonderful it was. "I'm going upstairs. You won't even know I'm here." His mind now bounced between his empty schedule and Velveteen's book club. *This will be good for her. She'll love it.* "You've got this."

There was a knock on the door.

She had carefully written out the invitations on her monogrammed stationery and tied each one with hand-dyed ribbon Charlie had procured from the market. The ribbon had been an extra, a surprise she was confused to receive. Did they have money for extras? She never knew. She had felt selfish even thinking it and quickly brushed the thought away, grateful for the gift.

"I know just how I plan to use it!" she had squealed.
Already? That was fast.
"It's perfect, Charlie."
"I thought you would like it."

And now they were here. This may have been Granny's idea, but it was a Velveteen Price exclusive.

Velveteen glanced in the mirror to brush down any stray hairs and purse her lips together. *You can do this. You can do this.* She had chosen a fitted pair of blue jeans and lightweight sweater. Remembering Clover's casual style on their visit to the camper vans, Velveteen took off her heels and dropped them into the umbrella stand by the front door. She felt naked and uncomfortably exposed, so she pulled her size six pumps back out and slipped them on. *Much better.*

Velveteen opened the door to find the same Blackwell ladies she had seen a month ago at the camper vans cleaned up and dressed nicer than any of her acquaintances from the city had ever dressed for her book club. Clover's ripped jeans and baggy shirt were replaced by a smart sheath and a pair of floral heels – Velveteen had a similar pair in black.

Granny had wrapped a thick braid around her usual bun and sat a pillbox hat on top.

Very Jackie-O.

Granny's purse hung across the crook in her arm. In her other arm she held six copies of *The Heiress of DuMont.*

Velveteen bit her lip. Of all the billions of books in the world, Granny had chosen her favorite.

"Lord, don't let us catch whatever that Toft left in this hole of house. Amen!" Granny snarled before she crossed the threshold. She stepped inside and examined the house from right to left. "You should have painted those walls by now, Velveteen."

For a moment, Velveteen forgot what was going on. How was she to reply to this woman? She swallowed the lump in her throat and regained her bearings. "Please, have a seat." Velveteen set the event in motion by offering cups of tea served in her wedding china and complimenting the ladies on their floral frocks and sparkling jewelry. Soon she was in her element, gliding across the room doing what she did best: entertaining. The cottage was welcoming, warm, and smelled of bergamot and lavender – it was the way she had envisioned it when Charlie floated the idea of Coraloo, minus the bumblebee in the kitchen.

Granny shoved a piece of cake in her mouth. "More lemon zest, Velveteen," Granny practically shouted. "It needs more zest!"

Clover tugged gently at the sleeve of Velveteen's sweater. "Don't let her fool you. It's not because she's hard of hearing that she speaks louder than everyone else in the room. She has to be the center of attention, and your lemon cake is divine."

Velveteen sat down in the armchair across from Granny, staring at the emerald-eyed woman on the cover of the book. She had the very same book resting on her bedside table – except her copy was bookmarked, had underlined passages, and was well worn around the edges. Its sequels – two, three, and four were lined up neatly behind it.

She looked up at the ladies. What had she expected? Had she really thought they would arrive in their everyday clothing with Granny in her apron and Clover in her tattered jeans? The ladies sitting around her coffee table in their finery could give her acquaintances in the city a run for their money.

Velveteen straightened in her chair – a tinge of normalcy, hints of their former life inching their way through her soul. She liked it.

She felt her anxieties disappear as the ladies pointed out the detail of a hand-painted family portrait commissioned shortly after Gideon was born and complimented her on how the Toft cottage was much improved from their first visit.

Their first visit. Velveteen caressed the tips of her hair in remembrance. She would need to touch up the color in another week or two. For the first time since *The Rooning*, she had a semblance of control. In this moment, she was not dependent on Charlie. She was on her own. Nothing could change her Melba moment.

"Ladies –" Velveteen started, holding Melba firmly.

"We're going to read this one!" Granny took command of the room.

Velveteen froze, her body unwillingly falling deeper into hiding among the plush fibers of the armchair. She had always been the one to lead the discussion. She had planned to give her well-memorized speech on the importance of being prepared and ready to participate. It was why, after the former group's discussions repeatedly steered in the direction of monogrammed accessories and charity balls, she had declared the book club invitation only.

"It looks like a good one!"

A good one? Velveteen thought, not paying attention to how much sugar she was adding to her tea. *It's a great one. It's my favorite!*

"It made me think of you, Velveteen."

"Granny!" Clover interjected.

"Well, it did! Rich girl has to move to the country. It's what it says on the back of the book."

At this point another cousin leaned over and forcefully whispered something in Granny's ear.

Velveteen's hands shook.

"What do you mean *offensive*?" Granny said to the cousin. "This Melba sounds like our Velveteen."

Velveteen set her cup on its matching saucer. She straightened her back and glanced at the tray of break-and-bake cookies. "Granny, would you like a cookie?"

"Did you make them yourself?"

Velveteen smiled, picked up the silver tray of *Rooning* fame, and walked it over to Granny, an unsavoury cocktail of anger mixed with a sudden nausea churning inside her. How dare this woman mock their situation? Velveteen stopped by her side and debated her next move.

Granny reached for a cookie and took a bite. "Needs salt. How about I cook next time?"

Velveteen clinched her teeth and tightened her grip on the serving tray. Images of flying chocolate chips filled her head, and then another thought – if she chucked a cookie at the old bag, would it kill her? Would she fall over backwards in her chair with her stocking feet dangling in the air exposing her undergarments? Velveteen grinned. These ladies did not know the Melba that she knew. They did not know the Melba that took matters into her own hands.

Granny looked into the rigid eyes of Velveteen. "For certain, I don't want anymore. Sit back down."

"Granny!" Clover jumped up from her seat on the sofa to take the tray from Velveteen's hands. "Velveteen, she's not well; please look past this."

"What do you mean *I'm not well*?"

"It's okay, Clover." Velveteen's stomach tightened and her breath shortened. *Not well.* "Melba is my favorite. I think, I think…" She could no more than speak than she vomited straight into the lap of Granny Blackwell.

Clover ran to the kitchen.

Velveteen couldn't move. "I'm so sorry…" *I'm not sorry.*

Granny stood up – the mess of regurgitated attempts of multiple pastry samplings sliding in clumps to the floor – and waddled off, seemingly unconcerned, to peer the wall of photos. "Told you they needed more salt. We'll meet in the market next week."

Velveteen hardly noticed Clover wiping her face with a warm washrag. "I'm so sorry. I think I just got so caught up in everything. Really, I'm fine. The book club must go on. I made a cake, Clover. I made you all a cake."

"We'll do it another day." Clover put the strands of hair attempting to stick in Velveteen's mouth behind her ears.

"You own a house, a real house, but you live in a camper van. Why do you live in a camper van?" Velveteen fell back into the chair where Granny had been sitting. The smell from the vomit overpowered the bergamot. The heat of sickness returned to her throat. "How do you all fit in there?"

Clover laughed and continued to wipe Velveteen's face. "Where's Charlie?"

Velveteen pointed to the ceiling. One of the cousins went up and came back down with a concerned Charlie Price, while another diligently tried cleaning the floor. A vomit-covered Granny perused the room examining the belongings of the Price family as another cousin followed behind her attempting to scrape the rest of Velveteen's distress off her dress.

Charlie placed a hand on the forehead of his wife. "Are you okay?"

"I don't think so. I need to go lie down."

"I think that would be a good idea."

"Charlie, I… what was it Gideon called it – *puked*. I puked on Granny Blackwell."

"I can see that. To avoid puking on anyone else, you'd better go upstairs."

Granny took a picture of Charlie and Velveteen off the wall, blew on it, wiped away her breath with the back of her sleeve, and hung it back. "I think you could have found a better place, Mr Price. You know old Toft lived here."

He still had not heard the full history of their little house. "Yes, Granny."

Her voice softened. "You have a real gem – you know that, don't you? She just hasn't found her shoes yet."

"Her shoes?"

"But don't worry; she'll find them. She's looking for them."

Charlie couldn't help but wonder if the old lady was well and truly out of her mind. All Charlie could think about was their closet in the city – the closet where Velveteen had lined her shoes up by heel height and color. She had sold several pairs online and donated another load to a rummage sale where he ironically had seen them the following week while picking.

"I think she's wearing her shoes, Granny. Can I get you anything?"

Granny examined him from his blue jeans to his *Rust Feeds My Wanderlust* t-shirt. She ignored his question. "I don't think you're wearing the right shoes either, Mr Price. I like the ones you wore with that fancy suit much better."

"You thought I was a spy."

She leaned in to him. "I still do, Mr Price… If that's your real name. My Shug has his eye on you." It was suddenly clear. Granny hadn't had Charlie arrested. It was Shug. "She didn't wear her scarf today. Tell her to wear it next time. Oh, and don't let her make a fuss out of nothing. I'll host the book club at the market."

What was going on with Granny's strange obsession with footwear and accessories? Of what concern were Velveteen's wardrobe choices to her? He wanted to tell Granny that Velveteen would rather go barefoot than step foot into the Coraloo flea market. Instead he said, "I'll remind her about the scarf."

CHAPTER 13

1887

Mungo Blackwell circumnavigated the world twice until his journey found him at the foot, actually the feet, of the Maharaja of Kuru. The maharaja had sent for the infamous cobbler after learning there was no finer shoemaker in the world. Mungo talked with the portly man at some length before determining the maharaja's slippers were to be hand-beaded with gemstones found in Colombia and sewn with silken threads from China. Mungo even added minuscule bells to the tips of the upturned toes so the maharaja's feet would jingle when he strolled through the halls of his palace.

The maharaja was so taken by the handmade foot coverings he invited Mungo to stay for a feast in his honor and, as a gift for his services, presented Mungo with crates of cardamom, black pepper, cumin, coriander, and cinnamon. Mungo had no desire for exotic spices; he did, however, long for conversation. While he had met many souls on his travels, Mungo Blackwell was lonely, so he gratefully accepted the maharaja's invitation.

The aromas of the feast – fenugreek, mint, and masala – filled the air. Arranged before Mungo was a vast array of lamb, chicken, vegetables, and sweets prepared by the maharaja himself. It was said the maharaja's culinary skill was so praised in the kingdom, the former maharaja had stepped down and named Maahir maharaja of all Kuru.

But it was not the sumptuous feast that caught the eye of Mungo; he was captivated by something – someone – else. Sarra was the most beautiful creature he had ever laid eyes upon, and he would make her a pair of the finest shoes, if she would allow him, just to be in her presence. In all of his travels in all of the lands of the world, there was none as beautiful as the future Maharani of Kuru.

The curse had kept Mungo wandering ceaselessly, but the nineteen-year-old daughter of the maharaja gripped his heart and paused his quest. Captivated with the stories of his travels to faraway places and his brave, adventurous, gentle spirit, she had fallen in love with the cobbler – a man who had seen farther than the gardens of her father's kingdom.

Mungo thought it would be easy to wed the daughter. His father had told him the story a hundred times of how he had wed Mungo's mother because of a pair of shoes. Mungo would make a thousand pairs of shoes for the maharaja, if that was what it took to marry his daughter. And for one thousand pairs of shoes, the Maharaja of Kuru agreed.

For three years Mungo served as Maahir's personal cobbler. Every morning he woke, watched the princess walk through the garden, and, his heart aflutter, he set out to create that day's pair of shoes. He had leathers imported from the States, fabrics imported from Europe, dyes from the east, and jewels from the west.

But the maharaja did not intend to let his daughter go so easily. She was his only heir, and should he die, his kingdom would pass to his lazy brother, Sust, and Sust's beast of a wife, Beakal. Maahir would rather drown in a bowl of curry than see Sust at the head of the table. So, unbeknownst to Mungo, the maharaja devised a plan.

On the one-thousandth day, Mungo presented Maahir with a pair of white slippers. As Mungo had quickly learned with the presentation of each new pair, he inhaled the incense burning beside the throne, held his breath, and gently removed the pair from the previous day. Before exhaling and taking a new breath, he slid the new pair onto the feet of the Maharaja of Kuru. Once the stench of his unearthly foot fungus was covered, Mungo bowed, exhaled, and stepped back. The princess and Mungo stood in desperate anticipation of her father passing his blessing; instead, Maahir clutched his chest and pretended to fall to the floor dead.

Sarra, now the Maharani of Kuru – forced by law of the land to reign and one day marry her cousin, Prince Parth (who was presently twelve and resembled a plump squirrel) – grieved for her father as his epitaph was read: it noted worthy accomplishments, his collection of shoes, his milk dumplings in sweetened pistachio milk, and how much the kingdom loved him. It was in this moment, to the shock of them all, the maharaja, realizing his selfishness and dishonesty, stepped out from behind a silk curtain and gave his blessing to his daughter.

Mungo and Sarra married right then and there at the funeral of the Maharaja of Kuru.

Chapter 14

Charlie Price checked his watch for the time and the stairs for movement. An assortment of family photos – snapshots of Gideon's firsts, a picture of the three of them in front of the Eiffel Tower on vacation in France, and their wedding photo – hung staggered on the wall in an assortment of gilded frames. Charlie studied the man in the photograph. That man had a vision, a plan for the next twenty years of their life. The blond twenty-something in the tuxedo was proud, slightly arrogant, and ready to conquer the world. Charlie sighed. He didn't know that man anymore – he didn't want to know him.

He walked to the kitchen and surveyed the room, trying to recall why he had gone in there in the first place, and then retuned to the bottom of the stairwell. Velveteen said she was well enough to go and insisted that if her episode had been contagious, she was no longer able to infect anyone now a week had passed.

"It's time to go!" he called up to her. She did not reply. He slumped down on the sofa and ran his fingers through his hair. He stood up again and walked to the stairs. "Vee! We're not going to have enough time!" Finally, he gave up and sat down on the exposed wood step. He yawned. His eyelids drooped and his mind wandered. Over the past few weeks, good picks had become harder to find. Shug had been right. More pickers were frequenting the market – pickers with bigger budgets willing to take bigger risks. Charlie's most recent find – the 1960s Rolodex and box of refills – should have been a win but sat unsold in the corner of the kitchen beside his other auction finds. The *ping* to his phone had become an addiction. He found himself checking his ringer on a daily basis to make sure it was on and scrolled through his listed items regularly to see if he had accidentally marked an item as sold.

Charlie convinced himself they would be fine. If the French horn sold, it would sustain them for at least another month or two – another pick like that and they would make it comfortably through Christmas. Gideon had already been dropping hints about the limited edition *Star Pirate* to be released on December 1, and Charlie had never gone a Christmas without buying Velveteen a gift. The item, his next big sell – it was out there waiting for him. He knew it.

Finally, Velveteen emerged from the upstairs with thick, round, black-rimmed sunglasses covering her hazel eyes. She wore fashionably fitted blue jeans and a thin ivory sweater that hung delicately off her shoulder. She stepped lightly down the stairs in high-heeled shoes that matched the tattered and piling purple scarf she had labored to drape stylishly around her neck. Charlie had dutifully remembered to tell her to wear it. Velveteen had scowled at him and said she would think about it.

"Don't say a word, Charlie Price. Let's get this over with." In her hand she carried her worn, dog-eared copy of *The Heiress of DuMont*.

He had so many comments he could make at this moment: *It's kind of warm for a scarf, don't you think?* Or, *Is that scarf from the Melba DuMont collection?* But he held his tongue. He did not want to jeopardize this moment – the moment when she would step foot inside the Coraloo Flea Market for the first time. He had planned to leave early, so they could have some time alone, just the two off them strolling the market like one of the many couples he watched every weekend shopping the Coraloo.

"Are you sure it's closed today, Charlie?"

"Absolutely. With the exception of a few Blackwells and your book club –"

"It's Granny's book club."

"Right, *Granny's* book club. We'll be the only ones there – no Mary Beth Rogers, no decorators –"

"No professors?"

"No professors."

It was a joke between the two, in memory of Velveteen's least favorite professor at the university, meant to mean someone judgmental and without the capability to see someone's worth.

"Okay, Charlie. Let's go."

The town was quiet today, the tavern closed until noon, and the residents a short drive away – most employed by a producer of high-end handbags, the supermarket, or one of the other areas of commerce that had passed over Coraloo to settle thirty minutes away in the next town over. It had crossed Charlie's mind to jump in the car and experience what life could be like on the other side of the hill, but he did not see what good it would do, nor did he have the nerve to find out. He half feared one of the businesses would hire him on the spot. The consistency would be welcomed, but what then? He'd work his way to the top; maybe they would make him V.P. Is that what Velveteen wanted – to have her husband enslaved by a system of commerce and marketing ploys? Was that what he wanted? *No.* That life no longer had anything to offer him as far as he was concerned. They had gotten away and were trying to do their life over – another way.

In three months they had nearly done it – downsized their lifestyle, dramatically decreased their spending, but – there was the *but*, the *but* that turned him on edge and needled at his boredom. They weren't done yet – they weren't there yet. Something was missing.

Velveteen Price stopped in front of the stone archway and read, NO DOGS OR TOFTS – GRANNY BITES!

After the book club, Velveteen had joked that she was contemplating telling Granny she was actually a Toft. Now, standing by the sign, she chuckled. "If Shug skins you alive, and Granny eats me for dinner, what will we tell Gideon?"

Charlie laughed and hugged Velveteen to his side. "Are you ready?"

"Ready as I'll ever be," she said, taking a step forward.

"Wait!" He halted her and placed his hand in front of her face. "Close your eyes."

"You want me to close my eyes?"

"Yes, just do it."

She pulled her sunglasses down on her nose.

"For me."

"Fine." She huffed.

He didn't know if she really closed her eyes, but he wanted her first look at the Coraloo to be as magical as the first time he had set foot into the building – the day he decided to pack his family up and move them away from invitation-only events and the monotony of nine-to-five accountability.

"Can I open them now?"

"Yes, open them."

Rows of strung fairy lights twinkled brilliantly against the raftered ceiling, the three gigantic crystal chandeliers were ablaze, and something – something sweet and rich – was producing an aroma that infused the air with such sweetness Charlie couldn't help but be drawn in. The cool fall air snuck through the cracks in the walls and chilled his cheeks. He watched her, hoping to witness her awe of the hidden wonder, the hidden surprise of the majestic Coraloo.

Velveteen removed the sunglasses she had used to hide her tired eyes and slid them into her purse. He had hoped for a reaction: a squeal, a *wow* – anything. He had her in his place, his sanctuary, his hope. He needed to know for sure she was okay. They hadn't spoken much over the past week – only trivial conversations about Charlie's latest pick or Granny's upcoming book club. She didn't look well, or maybe it was that she didn't look happy. He used to be able to decipher one from the other.

She stepped toward one of the shops. Closed.

"This is Stephen's."

Velveteen placed her hand upon the cold glass window and peered inside. "The bookstore... his father's."

"Yes! And over there... " he pointed to the flower shop, "fresh flowers brought in from all over the world."

She nodded.

"And over there, beside the antiques... not the one with the dishes... the other one... that's Shug's."

"Shug, the skinner?"

"Yes!" He laughed.

"Where did you say the vendors are, Charlie?"

He had told her before, but she hadn't taken it in then. But now she was showing interest, right? He would happily tell her again. "The market is only open on the weekend. That's when the vendors arrive." He stepped away from her until he was standing in an open space under the center chandelier. "And this... this is where the children put on their plays about the family."

"It's a conundrum, the whole thing, isn't it?" Her voice was soft, calm, captivated, as Charlie had hoped she would be. "So strange, breathtaking. But the pirates and the pygmies... the Blackwells... It's like a whole other world and we're simply passing through."

"A bit... but Gideon is having fun with it."

"And that shop, the one with the colors?"

"It's where I bought the hand-dyed ribbon – Stephen's aunt, I believe."

Velveteen ran her hand along the fabricated fronts, stopping occasionally to silently study the contents of each shop. She stopped and inhaled. "It's bergamot and lavender."

"Aunt Moira's. She has everything in there from cooking herbs to candles. She makes it all herself."

"Aunt Moira. You talk about them like they're your own family, Charlie. She was at the book club –" The words trailed off. "I didn't know she made candles. I didn't realize they did any of this."

"Talented. Every one of them."

Velveteen didn't answer.

Charlie placed his hand on the small of Velveteen's back and pulled her toward him. "What's wrong?"

"I thought I could do it, but I can't. I don't know how, Charlie. I can't make ribbons or jams. I can't even can tomatoes. I could never homeschool Gideon, and I can't pretend to like this scarf. I tried. I really tried, Charlie. I don't know who I'm supposed to be or what I'm doing. I can't even host my own book club!" She flung her arms out in despair, sending her book flying across the stained concrete floor. "And I can't do simplicity." At that moment there was a light crack; Velveteen fell to her right, frowning down at the broken heel of her purple pump. There was a pause, a silence between them. "I think I need to go back, Charlie."

Charlie did not know what to say to his crumbling wife. He had to hand it to her; she had given it a good go – completely transformed their home, learned to bake a lemon cake, and even tried to host the book club – but she was right, she didn't belong in Coraloo. Maybe he didn't belong here either.

"What are you doing here, Price?"

Charlie slowly turned around.

Shug towered above Charlie with his arms folded across his broad chest and a scowl protruding from his beard. "Shouldn't you be in jail?"

Charlie was in no mood to deal with Shug today. "Seems like there was a bit of a mix-up."

"Seems like it."

"I'm flattered you think I'm an emissary for the Chinese government. Was that what it was? Oh, wait. I believe I was a spy. You –"

"You need to go, Price."

"We were on our way out."

"No, I mean you need to go and never come back."

"I have as much right to be here as anybody. I'm a part of the market, Shug – what I do keeps the rhythm. The vendors rent space from you, I buy from the vendors, somebody out there buys the item from me, and I come back. I'm happy, the vendors are happy, and the market continues."

"You're not one of us, Price."

"What's the difference between you and me? Huh? You go to auctions and estate sales – swipe what the family of the dead don't want, and then you sell it and call it an antique. We aren't different, Shug."

"Nothing is ever good enough for you. You always want less, you take what's not yours, and then you sell it for more. You're taking advantage of people, Price. You're cheapening the market. What we do is art; what you do is pretend to be something you're not."

Charlie gritted his teeth and glared up at Shug. "You don't know me."

"I know all about you, Charlie Price. I've known about you since the day you moved in. What was it the paper said – 'Can one man really kill a bank?'"

Charlie felt the color draining from his face. Shug had done his homework. There was nowhere to hide, not even in Coraloo.

"We don't need your kind here, Price. Leave." Shug turned his back and walked away.

Charlie clinched his fists. *Your kind?* Who did Shug think he was? King of the market? He turned to face Velveteen, to explain, to let her know for the one hundredth time that everything was going to be okay, but she was gone.

Velveteen squinted in the light of the market. She felt dizzy, out of sorts, and a tad nauseous. She feared if she didn't get a sip of water or lie down, she might recreate the sickness incident at the book club in the middle of the market. "Charlie?" He didn't respond, caught up in heated conversation with a man nearly twice his size. "Excuse me, Charlie?" Again no reply.

She could not stand there any longer and listen to the mouths of two egos fighting over the shopping rights of a flea market. It would be horrible to abandon him to the fate of Shug, not that she thought she would be of any physical assistance should the beast-man decide to whip out his blade and do his deadly deed. But what good could she be dehydrated and doubled over? Charlie would have to fend for himself. She'd cry for help if she heard him scream. She grabbed her purple footwear and walked barefoot through the market.

Charlie was right; she did love the market. Despite her reservations, she knew she would. It looked exactly as he had described it. It was the real reason she had at least six months of excuses lined up to keep her away – those she told Charlie and those she told herself. She didn't want to get too attached. She didn't want to get too comfortable, because what if *it* happened again and they were forced to leave such a wonderful place behind. But it didn't matter; she didn't belong here, surrounded by the Blackwells' handiwork, nor did she belong with the acquaintances, with all their small talk and fancy crudités. She didn't belong anywhere.

Velveteen closed her eyes and listened to the stillness around her. She wriggled her painted toes on the cool concrete and slowly breathed in the aroma of warm, sweet dough drifting from the kitchen. The scents reminded her of home – not the Toft house or their former townhouse in the city, but recollections of memories collected in both. She tried to remember the days before *The Rooning*, to revive her happiest memory... Charlie... Gideon. She imagined herself sitting on their sofa wrapped in a blanket, watching Charlie carefully turn the pages of one of his recently acquired novels, and Gideon, eyes wide, earnestly studying the images and short bits of dialogue, flipping the page to read the next adventure of his space pirates. She fought back tears; all she wanted was a place to call home.

Velveteen wandered aimlessly to the back of the market where she stopped in front of a lengthy antique case full of pastries. Above it a sign, intricately painted in gold with dainty purple flowers weaving in and out of each letter, read *Granny's*. When Charlie told her Granny sold food at the market, she had expected an indoor equivalent of a ramshackle food truck, not a pastry shop as quaint and orderly as Francine's on 5th. She had read the articles Charlie placed in front of her and heard the stories filtering back from the decorators her acquaintances in the city procured, but all her mind could envision was a mobile diner, rusted around the edges, and a foul stench of reused grease pouring out the pay window. The Blackwells were full of surprises.

"Hello!" Surely there was someone around who could find her a glass of water. She was exhausted and oddly thirsty. Charlie said she should take it easy – she had not stopped working on the house since they moved in. Every day it seemed she found something new to sand, tighten, or repaint. She laughed at herself and her own persistence. Their first weeks in the Toft house were a blurred memory – had she really pulled all the wallpaper off the walls, ripped up the carpet, painted the kitchen, and cleared out the garden shed?

Velveteen stood on tiptoe, leaned over the counter, and called again, "Hello!"

No answer.

She set her pumps on one of the long hardwood tables and laid her head down on her crossed arms. If she could rest her eyes for a brief minute, she might feel better – not well enough to handle an hour of Granny attempting to explicate in her own words the world of Melba but well enough to walk home.

"Those aren't the right shoes for you."

Velveteen groaned at the familiar voice. A hand plonked a glass of water down by her arm. She considered pretending to sleep in hopes Granny Blackwell would go away.

"Come on Miss Melba. I need your help in the kitchen."

CHAPTER 15

Velveteen lifted an eye toward the family matriarch. Had the woman said she didn't like her shoes? And did she call her *Melba*? The last time Velveteen had seen Granny, the woman's Sunday best was covered in partially digested cookie dough. Velveteen glanced out into the empty market, hoping Clover would show up early, hoping Charlie would rescue her – he always rescued her – but not today. She would have to save herself, just as she'd done before he stumbled into her life. Back when it was her and her mother. Back when her expectation was that she would be independent and have a career – before her mother's boss, Mrs Vanderschmidt, swooped in and taught her the art of pretending among the elite. Before she'd realized what she really wanted, what Charlie gave her – to be a wife and a mother.

She'd gone through too much to let this person she barely knew get the best of her. She thought about leaving it all – Granny and the book club. But that's not who she was. Velveteen Price did not give up. And maybe, if she helped Granny with whatever she needed help with, she would finally leave her alone about her shoes and whatever else the bat chose to nag about.

Velveteen gathered her shoes and, questioning whether or not it was sanitary, walked barefoot behind the counter and into the kitchen. It was pristine with its gas stove – far nicer than the one she had in the city – a great industrial stainless steel refrigerator, so shiny she could see her warped reflection, and the floors, spotless.

Granny tossed a crisp white apron at her face. "That's for thinking about throwing a cookie at me! Don't deny it, Miss Melba. I know what you were thinking! And this –"

Before Velveteen could blink, her face was covered in white flour.

"… is for getting your insides all over my Easter dress!"

Velveteen glared at her, refusing to blink, fighting back tears of frustration. She wouldn't give Granny the satisfaction of seeing her cry again. Why did this old woman hate her so much? Did it have something to do with her son Shug and his obvious dislike of Charlie? Had she said something to the Blackwell matriarch that had offended her?

"Here," Granny said, shoving an empty stainless steel mixing bowl at her. "Recipe's on the counter. When you get to the folding, be sure to scrape the sides, gently – too much and they'll crack. Nobody likes a cracked macaron."

Surely this woman would not dare ask her to make the one thing that haunted her dreams – that element of her former life that, once a delicacy, was reduced in a moment of rage to a miniature tactical weapon. She had sworn to herself she would never set eye upon their defiance again! Was this old woman that hateful, that bitter, that vexed by the mere presence of Velveteen she would ask her to do such a thing? Velveteen had bared her soul, shared with her the darkest moment of her life. Why did the beast taunt her so?

"Macarons, Miss Melba. I'm going to teach you, city girl, how to make a proper macaron. That way you don't have to spend all of your husband's hard-earned money on overpriced meringues from hoity toity no-flavor bakeries."

An angry, raging fire burned throughout Velveteen. What did Granny know about how she spent her money? She'd bought the macarons from Francine's because she could. They had the money then. It hardly made a dent in their bank account. She couldn't buy them now if she wanted to. They would be a ridiculous purchase and she would never spend her husband's "hard-earned money" on anything they didn't need. They had agreed upon their life then, just as they had before they moved to Coraloo. She would stay home with Gideon, manage the house. It was what they *both* wanted. She wasn't ashamed of it.

That was it – Velveteen had had enough. Granny had already stolen her book club, and now she was asking her to make… She tossed the apron on the floor, slammed the bowl on the counter, and turned to leave. But then she had a thought. *That's what Granny wants. The mule wants me to walk away. I won't give her the satisfaction.* Velveteen jerked the apron off the ground and tied it around her waist. *How hard can it be? If the gun-toting granny can do it, then so can I.*

She studied the list of ingredients: almond flour, cream of tartar, powdered sugar… She carefully measured them out. *Sift together dry ingredients twice and set aside. Whisk egg whites until foamy, add cream of tarter… medium speed.*

She would need a mixer; Granny's large freestanding one stood on the counter. She hadn't a clue how to use it. Granny had her back turned, rolling out pastry dough for the next day's treats. Velveteen read over the directions once again – she definitely needed a mixer. Quietly, she searched the cabinets of spices, bowls, bakeware, and finally, small appliances until she found the hand mixer – still in the box.

Relieved, she clicked the whisks in place, and then cracked the three eggs into a separate bowl. The yellow yolks stared at her bug-eyed. Those weren't supposed to be in there. She attempted to carefully remove the centers with a spoon, but the blobs held fast. This wouldn't work. She pulled up her sweater sleeve and reached into the bowl; the yolk split, spreading its ooze throughout the whites.

"Ugh!"

"Separate them before you put them in the bowl," Granny giggled. "Use the shells."

Does my tormenter have eyes in the back of her head? Velveteen dumped the contents of her first attempt in the trashcan, wiped out the bowl, and tried again. *Use the shells.* She gently tapped the egg on the side of the bowl, and witnessed the clear fluid seeping through the cracks. "Ha!"

She eased the crack open a little more to allow more of the white to fall out. When the yolk began to pop through, she shifted the egg. "Can you do that, Melba DuMont? Can you do that!" she said louder than she had intended.

Velveteen glanced over her shoulder. The cantankerous market icon was busy stirring a concoction of blueberries and lime juice on the gas range and appeared to have not heard her.

She separated the second and then third egg, added the cream of tartar, and carefully switched on the mixer. Gradually the blend began to foam, then took on a silky, glossy sheen. Per the recipe, she added the sugar one tablespoon at a time, increased the speed to medium high, and beat the mixture until hard peaks formed. Written in a beautifully scrolling handwriting in the margin were the words, *Don't over beat!* "Now she tells me," she mumbled. Then, *add lime zest and coloring.*

Sift the dry ingredients into the wet. "More sifting? All right." Gently fold the mixture. Run the spatula clockwise from the bottom, being sure to delicately scrape the sides, cutting the batter in half.

As the mixture came together, Velveteen's anxiety subsided, replaced by giddiness. She suddenly saw herself removing the tray from the oven, the tops and bottoms of her *homemade* macarons perfectly smooth and round with a slight sheen. The edges would be gently crinkled, exactly like the ones she bought from Francine's.

She wondered if the concoction in front of her tasted as good as it smelled. With a sideways glance toward Granny – *was she actually measuring her pastry with a ruler?* – Velveteen dipped her finger gingerly into the gooey concoction. Then she did it again, this time savoring the hint of citrus. She licked her lips.

"Don't eat it all." *It's true – she does have eyes in the back of her head; or maybe the place is full of security cameras watching my every move!* "On second thought, you could use some extra meat on those bones. You gotta give your man something to hold on to."

Velveteen whipped back around, her index finger still in her mouth. She had half a mind to do an encore performance of *The Rooning*, this time with the uncooked batter. For a moment she could almost taste the satisfaction it would bring her to scoop out a handful of the white goop and fling it at Granny's head, watching it slide down the layers of her wrinkled neck.

She returned to her happy place. *Line pans with parchment paper... Pipe into one and a half inch concentric circles...* "Pipe?" She had watched a baking show or two enough to know what this meant, but she had never done it. Why had she never done it? In fact, at this moment she wasn't sure how she had found herself to be so inept in the kitchen in the first place. Maybe it was because her mother had never cooked, and once she married Charlie, she never needed to. She scoured the well-stocked kitchen once again until she found what looked like the cake decorating tools she had seen on television.

She could do this. In one hand she clutched the plastic bag; in the other she held a silver nozzle. Before her stood the perfectly blended batter; she gazed from one to the other. Suddenly she felt a rush of anxiety, like she was a tenth grader faced with a quadratic equation: how was she going to get all that goo in the cone-shaped bag?

"Put the nozzle in the bag," Granny barked.

Oh, this woman! Velveteen dropped the nozzle into the bag. "I would have figured it out." And then proceeded to scoop the blend into the pastry bag.

She squeezed the bag and allowed the green batter to flow into a splotch on the pan. *Not exactly a circle.* She tried again, and again, until she had twenty-seven roundish blobs on her pan. Her daydream began to fade as she realized her expectations of perfectly chic Francine's-esque macarons were not in her future. She lifted the pan and tapped it twice on the counter as instructed, then thirty minutes of resting and then eighteen more to bake.

Velveteen waited – excited, anxious, and nervous all at the same time, watching through the stove glass for the formation of the crinkled edge, distinguishing the iconic dessert. She stepped away to wipe down her work area, but then rushed back over, stooping in front of the stove once again to check in on her creations. It wasn't looking good – the ruffled feet were bursting out of the bottom, the tops were textured and bumpy, and a rigid crack was developing down the center of each one. The timer buzzed. Velveteen jumped.

She frowned at the trays of a failed attempt in front of her. *Why did I think I could do this?*

Granny stood on tiptoes looking over Velveteen's shoulder. "Oven was too hot. And you over beat them."

"I followed your instructions!"

"Not my job to tell you when it's getting too hot. And not my instructions. Sometimes you gotta figure it out for yourself. Then next time –"

"There won't be a next time."

"Then *next* time, you'll know what to do differently. There's always a next time, Miss Melba. I've been alive long enough to know. Here." She handed Velveteen a bowl of blueberry lime curd. "Finish them."

Velveteen carefully piped the blueberry-lime filling on top of a pastry and then placed another on top. Her thoughts drifted from the kitchen to her life – to Gideon, busy at school, and Charlie, trying his best to make things work for them – and soon she became lost in a rhythm of squeezing and stacking as the pastries filled the trays in rows of tasty green-purple filled circles.

The room was quiet, still, refreshing. Despite the wonkiness of her creations, she was proud of what she had done. Granny was right – there would be a next time. She would do it again, and next time, even if there were a hundred next times, she'd get it right.

"Granny Blackwell –" Velveteen set down the piping tool and wiped her hands on the apron. "I'm sorry I… I was sick… I didn't mean…"

"No harm. I smelled like sour sausages for a day, but I can't blame that on you." She turned and faced Velveteen, a mixing bowl in the crook of her arm and a spatula in the other. "I have more grandbabies than you have high heels, Miss Melba. I can handle it." Velveteen considered correcting her, thinking maybe the elderly Blackwell had truly confused her with the heroine of their novel.

The muffled voices of Granny's Coraloo book club approached. "I'll set these on a tray, Granny."

"No tray for you, Miss Melba. You're taking them home. This," she said, pulling from the oven the most beautiful latticed apple pie Velveteen had ever seen – not even Francine's could make one so lovely – "is for our book club."

Velveteen followed Granny out of the kitchen to where three of the Blackwell ladies waited with their individual copies of *The Heiress of DuMont* resting in front of them. Velveteen's book was lying somewhere in front of the ribbon shop.

"Sit," Granny instructed. Velveteen sat. "How's that husband of yours? He seems changed these days."

After an hour and a half in the kitchen, with few words exchanged between them, Velveteen was uncomfortable, but not surprised. She'd almost forgotten about Charlie, left to fend for himself with Granny's formidable son. Well, she hadn't heard any screams of agony, so she could only hope that he'd emerged from his "talk" with Shug in one piece.

Granny was openly discussing her personal life. "Changed?"

Granny lifted an eyebrow, wiped her greasy hands on her apron, scraped the sweat off her forehead with the back of her arm, and sat down beside Velveteen. "Men are a squirrely bunch – you've got to watch them closely. They won't tell you what's on their mind. You have to figure it out yourself. He doesn't like his shoes; he's not comfortable in them. Can't get them to fit right."

In the past, Velveteen considered having extra shelving added to their walk-in closet to accommodate her collection of shoes. Some might class her among those said to have a fetish, but she didn't talk about them nearly as much as Granny. This woman was obsessed with shoes.

"Charlie told you he didn't like his shoes?"

"Of course he didn't tell me! What kind of man tells a woman about his shoes! Just pay attention, trust me. I'll get you both sized up before I'm done with you." There it was. Velveteen suspected the woman had some kind of motive. Granny Blackwell was playing tricks with their minds, twisting their intentions, dropping subliminal hints about shoes, and making her bake macarons, all for some sort of mental reprogramming. Next thing, Granny would be taking them shopping for a camper van. Velveteen gasped. *Granny wants to turn us into Blackwells.*

"Velveteen!"

"Yes?" Startled, Velveteen stood up and awkwardly accepted the welcoming hug of Clover.

"How are you feeling?"

"Better, I think."

A few of the other ladies came to greet her as well, withholding any conversation regarding the incident in the living room. Had Velveteen thrown up on one of the acquaintances, she would have been hot gossip for at least a month, and that was saying a lot since fresh gossip usually died within a week – unless something more intriguing came along – like Charlie Price's termination from Heritage Financial. She had been at the salon when it happened, a hive of gossip if ever there was one. She'd already heard the news so wasn't surprised to get Charlie's call.

"Can you meet me at the park?"

Velveteen Price walked through the park fully aware of the stares. Still she held her head high. Her freshly highlighted locks glistened in the sunlight, the yellow chiffon, smocked waist sundress complementing her petite frame. The Heiress of Dumont peeked out of the Italian leather handbag in the bend of her arm that perfectly matched her nude pumps. She smiled when she saw Charlie and then let him tell her his terrible news.

"I already heard. I'm so sorry, Charlie." She hugged him, holding him to let him know she was not going anywhere.

"How –"

"Jennifer was at the salon today."

"Jennifer? How did Jennifer know?"

"Jennifer's nanny and Mary Beth Roger's nanny bumped into one another at school. And you know how much Jennifer can't stand me since Mary Beth and I became best friends at last year's Christmas party – although obviously she still pretends to like me. Well, Jennifer's nanny was going on about how I won't let Jennifer in the book club, and Mary Beth's nanny said there might not be a book club soon… and then the whole thing came out. So of course Jennifer's nanny told Jennifer, who loathes me – it's not my fault she refused to read the book. I asked her politely, truly politely, not to return if she felt so strongly about straining her eyes. Anyway, Jennifer walked into the salon and started running her mouth about Heritage and the

whole salmonella incident. That's when Carol... you know Carol... turned my dryer off, so I could hear the whole thing. Then, you called. Sweetheart, I am so sorry. We will get through this." She touched his cheek with the palm of her hand and then kissed him, lingering with him to let him know she was his.

"Did you hit her?"

"Of course not, Charlie Price!"

"But you wanted to, didn't you?"

"Hit? No. Accidentally pour my tea down her imported silk blouse? Yes. I showed restraint and politely asked if she had read anything good lately." Velveteen grinned. "Enough about me, what happened, Charlie?"

He told her the rest.

Velveteen sometimes imagined the acquaintances were continuing to talk about the "fall of the Price family", as though it was the next volume in a saucy series. Surely the elite had not bought her story about their impromptu move to Coraloo. But she'd been part of high society long enough to know all it would take was a slip-up at the cosmetic surgeon or for one of their nannies to land on a hidden gem of a scandal, and the Price family saga would vanish.

"Velveteen? Are you okay?"

"What?" Velveteen snapped from her reverie.

"I lost you for a second. Is everything okay?"

Is everything okay? Clover had no reason to be nice to her, no motive, no social ladder to climb. Why couldn't Velveteen believe someone wanted to be more than an acquaintance? She started to answer, yes – a reflex, an insistence that she was perfectly fine and no further questioning was needed. But in truth, she wasn't quite sure. So she simply smiled.

Clover squeezed her shoulder kindly and then walked away.

Velveteen sat at the table drawing imaginary circles with her finger as Granny rattled on about Melba's misfortune. She picked at the crust of her pie – hungry enough to stuff every one of her boxed blueberry-lime macarons down her throat, but at the same time nauseous from the syrupy sweet aftertaste the pie left in her mouth.

"The old count up and kicked her into the street!" Granny shouted, slamming her fist down emphatically.

The older ladies nodded and shouted words like *scoundrel* and *cad*. It was not at all how Velveteen had run her book club. She had carefully studied the text, researched the author's notes and lectures on the novel, and carefully prepared questions that aligned with the external and internal conflicts. The acquaintances never cursed or threatened to bring physical harm to the villainous Count Horace – unlike Aunt Sorcha, who implied she was talented in the use of a fileting knife.

"But," Granny continued, "she didn't even fight back!"

Velveteen remembered discussing this scene back in the city. Her discussion had centered around the demureness of Melba, her strength as she pulled her fallen body from the muck left by the spring rain, and how she had gathered her bags and did not consider for a moment to look back on her former life. Melba pressed on, forcing her feet to tread the path of hardship, her strength emerging, denying Count Horace the tears of her humiliation and embracing the challenge of the simple life before her. *Simple.* But while Melba's cowardice had not come up in book club, Velveteen had thought exactly what Granny Blackwell had just said: *She didn't even fight back.*

Velveteen stared at a chink in the aged brick wall as Granny tried to convince the women that any kitchen tool can be used as a weapon, and had Melba DuMont been more concerned about herself and less concerned about the loose thread on her ball gown, she might have been able to knock Count Horace in his nether parts with a cast iron skillet.

She smiled and returned her focus to Granny Blackwell.

"I guess we'll find out what missy frou-frou does next. Read the next two chapters and we'll talk about it next week."

Velveteen was accustomed to reading a book a month and meeting to discuss the novel in its entirety. Granny's method was "meet and eat". The longer they could make it last, the better.

"Granny Blackwell?" Velveteen gathered her half-eaten pie and fork and followed Granny into the kitchen.

"Yes."

"I'm not her. I'm not Melba."

"Oh?"

"I fought back." Velveteen lifted the box of macarons.

"But you're losing the fight. You don't know who you are, do you? Are you Velveteen Price or are you Melba DuMont? You can't play dress-up forever."

She parted her lips to speak, to defend her identity, but Granny was right. Velveteen stared at the box. "What do I do?"

Granny Blackwell shook her head and crossed her arms under her voluptuous bosom. "You eat them," she slurred.

"Right…"

Granny stood up and then suddenly fell heavily against the sink. Velveteen rushed to her, catching her before her head hit the edge of the wooden countertop.

"Help!" Velveteen called. The weight of the woman pulled down on her. "Help!"

Granny Blackwell's arms hung heavy, limp at her sides, and her left eye drooped.

"Granny!" one of the cousins shouted and assisted Velveteen in lowering Granny to the floor. "Get her some water."

Velveteen stepped back.

"Granny!" Clover shouted into the wrinkled face of the woman. "Can you hear me?"

Granny opened her eyes. She tried to speak, but the words were incoherent.

"We need to get her to Dr Toft!"

"No," Granny slurred. "Not a Toft… the other one."

"We're not arguing about this now, Granny! Fie, run and get Shug!"

Granny mumbled something. The cousins, aunts, and granddaughters all leaned in close to her.

"Are you sure?" Clover asked.

Granny nodded and pointed at Velveteen.

"Will she be all right?" An odd sensation of worry for the woman came over Velveteen. She needed Charlie. He would know what to do. He always knew what to do.

A siren wailed in the distance. In minutes the back door to the kitchen swung open and two men with a gurney, followed by a frantic Shug, rushed in to attend to Granny. Velveteen watched in horror as they checked Granny's blood pressure and lifted her onto the rolling bed.

"The spells are coming more frequent. It's her sugar. We've tried everything to have her watch what she eats. It's no use," Clover explained. "She's stubborn. Said she's done everything she needed to do in life – death can have her now."

"Wow, that sounds exceptionally morbid."

"Blackwells look at life a little differently than most people."

Granny called from behind them, her voice raspy and garbled. "Did you tell her?"

"Not yet, Granny."

"Tell me what?" Velveteen asked.

"She said the color is bad on you. She wants you to take it off."

"Take what off?"

"The scarf." Clover laughed. Velveteen slowly unbound the bundle of purple yarn and cradled it close to her chest. "She gave me a brooch last year that she took from cousin Elspeth and then demanded it back so she could give it to Elspeth as a birthday present."

"A bit of amnesia?"

"No, a bit of stubborn old woman."

Velveteen sensed a bond forming between her and Clover – a real, unaffected bond, unlike her forced affiliations of the past. Forced was easy. She was wise in the ways of forced; *real* was uncharted territory.

"And there was one more thing. There is no telling what she means by it, so make of it what you will. She wants to know when you're going to tell him."

Velveteen's cheeks flushed. Her voice cracked when she spoke. "Tell him what?" In the distance she could see Charlie rushing toward the scene – so handsome, so hers, so... unscathed. His eyes locked with hers.

"It's okay. We know – it's a family gift, or curse, depending on how you look at it. We have a way of figuring things out... Granny has a way of figuring things out. But if she's right, and she usually is, you need to tell him, Velveteen. It's not fair for him to not know."

"I can't. Not yet."

CHAPTER 16

Charlie Price rubbed his finger over the raised threads of the circular badge. As a third-generation Boy Scout, he recognized the tiny embroidered eagle at its center from his grandfather's collection. He peered over his shoulder to the heart of the market where Gideon – who had expressed no interest in sleeping outdoors or learning to carve a bear out of a block of wood – and the Blackwell boys were currently pretending to smear beeswax on the face of Stephen's niece. Before Coraloo he and Charlie would take regular Saturday morning walks through the city to the Outer Limits of Earth comic book shop. They'd pretend to be space pirates, keeping a careful lookout for alien cab drivers and laser-toting deliverymen. Charlie missed their time together, but it was good to see Gideon so happy. He never would have imagined his shy son would be practicing amateur theatrics with a troupe of rough and tumble Blackwell children, in only a matter of weeks.

Charlie typed *Boy Scout felt patch* into the app on his phone. He scrolled through the vast array of patches, narrowed his search to the UK, and made an offer on the red and blue 1940s Seaman's badge.

"Will you take three for it?"

The man with a toothpick hanging out of the side of his mouth nodded. Charlie took out three bills and handed it to the man.

"You're joking, right? Threehundred."

"Threehundred! For a patch? No thanks."

"I've got more. I'll take six-fifty for the whole lot."

Awaiting the sale of the French horn, but having a succession of higher value items to sell, Charlie had brought all the money he had – hoping for the big find, the one that would take him to a new level of picking. He had formed the habit of reinvesting the profit, and setting the rest aside for incidentals. If he bought something for four and sold it for twelve, he kept four and reinvested the remaining eight. Today, he'd brought it all.

In the beginning, the thrill of the sale gave him a rush of adrenaline that carried him to the next pick. It didn't matter how big or how small the item; sometimes it was the shock that he had actually done it, that something he had bought – a toaster, a vintage board game, an antique dress form or whatever it might be – could double in value. The Waterman was the start of it all, but in the past few weeks he'd wanted to go bigger, sell bigger, get more return on his investment. The French horn had set him back – more than forty views, but no bids. He hadn't told Velveteen they were getting tight, but had asked her to make her homemade pizzas for Stephen, Clover, and the Blackwell children who were coming over for dinner. It was inexpensive and his favorite of the foods she had learned to make since they had come to Coraloo. But her idea of entertaining guests was not pizza; she said she would cook up a surprise and had for the first time let him know she might need a bit of extra grocery money. They were tight, but he'd figure it out. She was changing; so was he.

Two weeks ago, when she'd said she needed to go back to the city to transfer medical records, he tried to convince her that it could be done by a phone call or over the Internet. When she refused with a dramatic over-explanation of identity theft, he'd offered to go with her, secretly hoping she would decline his offer. He'd go anywhere with her, but he'd rather not go there. She said she would sort it out.

"Can I see what you have?" Charlie was curious. It was a lot to pay, but the 1940s Boy Scout Seaman's patch was worth at least three hundred on its own. If the vendor had one more in the lot, he could easily quadruple his money. This find would be bigger than the French horn.

Charlie sorted through the man's collection of vintage British Boy Scout memorabilia. There must have been thirty patches in the pile, along with a Baden Powell cigarette card that was surely worth something. "Was your father a scout?"

"Grandfather."

"Mine too. What a coincidence. This was his?"

The man nodded, continuing to chew on the tiny piece of wood. A quick memory of his own grandfather's collection of family memorabilia and its value made Charlie second-guess his initial intent to purchase the collection. He'd never sell family heirlooms – in fact, the idea disgusted him, but with her blessing he had sold nearly everything Velveteen had in her jewelry box. Had he even thought to check its sentimental value? Surely she would have told him if a necklace had been a family antique.

On the other hand, maybe the guy needed the money. If Charlie made the purchase, he would be helping him out. It was the way of the market – the business of exchange was good for everyone. Charlie didn't negotiate, feeling altruistic. "All right, six-fifty it is."

The man handed over the tattered green army box of scouting memorabilia. Charlie handed over the cash. He was about to leave the market when a black case caught his eye. A violin. *Walk away, Charlie.* The fifty left in his pocket nudged him closer. Just a peek. It couldn't hurt. Could be a piece of junk, or the case alone – he'd had luck with cases before. With the box secure under his shoulder, Charlie wiped a layer of dust off the hard black instrument case. He flipped the latches and lifted the lid. He recognized it immediately – a student violin and an easy flip, if he could get the right price. He had flipped plenty of violins like this one.

"How much?" He shouldn't have asked. The French horn remained in the corner of the kitchen – an eyesore for Velveteen and a reminder of impending failure for Charlie.

"Fifteen." The woman rose from her folding chair to face Charlie. He had bought from her before. "And don't you go asking for less."

Charlie laughed. She recognized him. "I don't know. I think I've done well today."

"You could double your money." Her statement caught him off guard. It hadn't occurred to him the vendors – a coalition of junk collectors, families, and retirees – were aware of his intentions. "I know what you do. We all do."

"Then why not do it yourself? You could double your money overnight!"

"Nah. Don't want to. Don't have the time. I'm not ready to quit my day job."

Charlie Price mentally organized the market sellers in categories: the most obvious were the Blackwells – the artisans with their homemade wares and carefully selected antiques, sought after by the decorators and the tourists. Then there were the vendors – the mélange of hopeful entrepreneurs trying to make a sale off auction leftovers, obsolete collections, or personal downsizing. And the pickers – the resellers who'd buy from either of the other two if they thought they could resell for profit. It was the way he had come to know the world of Coraloo. It was his profession, his place in the market – his place in the world. It never occurred to him the vendors produced income outside the market.

"Your day job?"

"Freelance consulting mostly. Small business, turnarounds."

Charlie stared at the woman, his sense of judgment terribly askew. He had envisioned this woman as someone who drove around picking up rummage sale leftovers and cleaning out the attics of deceased family members.

"And you?"

"Me?"

"What do you do?"

"I do this," Charlie replied, tightening his grip on the box.

"You mean you buy our stuff and sell it – that's what you do? And you can live on it?"

Charlie's defense mechanism kicked in. "I haven't always done this. I was in banking. Loans and small business acquisition. My wife and I wanted a simpler life. We wanted to raise our son away from the city."

"Really? You just up and left it all behind. I envy you Mr – "

"Price. Charlie Price."

"Mr Price. Good for you. I think we could all use a large dose of the simple life. I can't say I'm that brave. All right then, ten. I'll give it to you for ten."

"Excuse me?"

"The violin. I'm taking off five for the inspiration."

"I'm not following you."

"You inspire me, Charlie Price. Now, do you have lessons on how to convince the spouse? I can just see myself walking up to my husband and saying, 'Eddie, we're quitting our jobs and moving to Coraloo!' He's going to ask, 'How will we survive?' And I'm going to say, 'Don't you worry about that; we'll live like Mr Price.'"

Charlie suddenly felt uneasy. He hadn't told her about the food truck, *The Rooning*, the Toft house, or his monthly fear of unpaid bills. She didn't know that their quest for simplicity had been forced upon them. They didn't choose it – that was the truth. He hadn't voluntarily left his high-dollar career like Stephen had. Charlie Price had been fired.

Charlie laughed as if the sound of his voice would drown out the word echoing in his brain. *Fired*. "Let me know if you talk him into it."

"Will do, Mr Price." Charlie handed over a ten and took the violin. He had hoped to hold on to a bit of extra, but music is money. The dimming of the lights and the *click, click* of the locks let him know the Blackwells were closing up shop. Vendors tossed mismatched sheets over their unpurchased items, and last-minute shoppers hurried toward the stone archway.

"Charlie!"

Charlie turned at the voice of Stephen Blackwell.

"We're looking forward to dinner tonight. Are you sure you can handle the lot of us? It's all right if you want an adults only night."

"I'm sure. Velveteen said the *whole family*."

"We can't wait! Do you have a minute? I've got something to show you."

Charlie checked his watch. He had time.

The inside of the bookshop was dimly lit and the shuffle and chatter of Coraloo had diminished to the voices of straggling tourists taking last-minute photographs and Innis Wilkinson sweeping up the concrete floors for tomorrow's patrons. Years ago the Blackwells had hired her to clean the place, but found one woman couldn't do it on her own, so they hired her husband, whom Charlie only knew as Mr Wilkinson, to help. Innis didn't speak, which Charlie could only assume was by choice, and she wore a pair of scissors around her neck. They were not the tiny decorative ones on an oxidized chain like those Sorcha Blackwell sold in her ribbon shop. These scissors appeared to be heavy metal fabric sheers. Charlie had asked Stephen about her once, but Stephen had not a clue.

Mr Wilkinson was nearly as puzzling. He walked with a limp and wore his long hair in two braids down the back. What Stephen did know for a fact was that Mr Wilkinson had no reason to have a limp. When he wasn't working in the market, he had no trouble walking in and out of the tavern at unreasonable hours of the evening. So the purpose of the limp was as mysterious as the sheers.

"It's in the back! I'll bring it out!" Stephen called from the depths of the shop.

In the stillness of the late afternoon, Charlie waited. Under the Blackwell-crafted Edison bulb light fixture, the Kipling glowed – a reminder of life before *The Rooning*. Charlie leaned in, examining what he could through the glass. The book had haunted him; it was all he could think about in his spare time. He had hired Marvin three years ago to hunt down the elusive edition. Had Marvin located it any sooner, the Kipling would have been Charlie's instead of stuck behind a glass case in an old shoe factory. Maybe life would have been different if he had acquired the Kipling. Maybe he would have been more focused, maybe he would have noticed the missing hygiene management plan, maybe he would have paid closer attention and seen the reality staring him in the face – the food truck owner didn't know what he was getting into and clearly was not equipped to run a business, let alone distribute food.

Charlie slammed his fist down on the table. He wanted the book more than he wanted anything. *One day*, he told himself. "One day." Charlie examined the case. A tiny gold lever held the glass closed. He wanted to touch it, to hold what could have been his. Charlie lifted the lever, the familiar scent of old leather drawing him in with an almost irresistible pull. He reached for the book.

"I thought you might want to see this!" Stephen called.

The case snapped shut. Charlie stepped away from it, feeling guilty and exposed.

"I'm sorry. I shouldn't have –"

Stephen unwrapped a cloth-bound book. "I came across it at an auction. Look at the title page."

Stephen clearly hadn't heard him. The Kipling case had shut but the latch still hung open. He should tell Stephen.

"Incredible, isn't it?"

"Incredible," Charlie mumbled. He couldn't focus on the book Stephen was holding before him. *What had he planned to do with the Kipling? Hold it? Open it? Take it?* "The Kipling, I…"

Stephen slapped him on the back. "I knew a fellow Kipling connoisseur would appreciate the inscription."

"Inscription?" Charlie focused in on the scratchy lines and gasped. "Is that Kipling's handwriting?"

"Well, if it's not authentic, then it's a heck of a forgery. Notice here," he said, "he refers to her as a *Janeite*. But he didn't write 'The Janeites' until 1926. This is dated 1924. Look how he marked through the typesetting of his name to sign it. Unbelievable, isn't it?"

Normally this find would have sent Charlie reeling, but as much as he tried to focus on the book, his mind was elsewhere.

"You all right?"

"Sorry, just a lot on my mind."

"Like…?"

Charlie shoved his hands in his pockets. "Just life." He breathed in the scent of aged paper and old wood. "When you were a boy, did you ever imagine life would be so hard? I mean, no one ever really tells you that it's going to be this way. Responsibility was taking the trash out, and disappointment was losing the game. I kind of feel like we've been cheated."

"You're telling me," Stephen said. "There should be some kind of handbook, *A Man's Guide to Adulting*."

Charlie forced a laugh. He could sure use a book like that now. He scuffed his foot on the concrete. "But it's turning out well for you. You gave it all up – career, lifestyle, and who knows what else – to run a bookshop in a flea market while your family lives out back in a camper van. Why take the risk?"

Stephen crossed his arms and leaned back against the counter. "We Blackwells have always valued two things above all: faith and family. I guess I forgot about both for a while. My children were growing and so was my list of clients. I saw other families more than I saw my own. Clover and I were like strangers in our own home – we didn't feel like the same people anymore. The business world has a way of blurring a man's focus, if you know what I mean. My marriage, my children – for them I was willing to take the risk."

"But how could you possibly have known you'd be happy? That everything was going to work out?"

"I didn't. That's the faith part."

Charlie shifted on his feet.

"You can't hold on to the past, Charlie. You've got to forgive yourself."

Charlie crossed his arms and sighed. "So you know my story then. Let me guess, Shug told you?"

"He may have mentioned it a time or two. We all make mistakes. Yours happened to make headlines. I've gone up against the Dudleys a time or two. They had it coming." Stephen laughed. Charlie didn't. "Friend, you need to believe in something much bigger than yourself. You have to let go."

"I'm not sure I believe in much of anything anymore."

"My faith, what I believe in, is a love that changes people. It changed me, brought me back home. I believe it could change you – if you let it. Where do you find faith, Charlie? Who do you have faith in?"

Charlie collected his purchases and passed another glance at the encased Kipling. "I've wondered that myself."

CHAPTER 17

1889

Mungo Blackwell recognized them instantly; he had heard rumors, but never had he seen them until this moment – a tribe of people who painted their bodies a cloudy white before they feasted on their captives. With long spears pointed directly at Mungo and his bride, the savages, no more than four feet tall, resembled feral children dressed in elaborate costuming. He had been in worse situations, but never with another. He had something new to fight for, someone to protect. He would not allow the cannibal pygmies of the South Seas to turn her into breakfast.

Mungo surveyed the surroundings, careful not to make eye contact – everyone knows to make eye contact with a pygmy is sudden death. There was nowhere to run out of range of their spears. He had hoped to show his bride, Sarra, the more lovely parts of the islands of the South Seas, but their guide had led them astray. Mungo would deal with him another day.

The circle of fifty pygmies inched closer – chanting "He-hoi, he-hoi, he-hoi!" – until Mungo could smell the death upon their breath.

"Mungo, I'm frightened," his wife whispered.

"I will protect you, my love," he whispered back.

"Hoi!" The pygmies halted. The circle parted. An older member of the tribe stepped forward. Mungo slowly lifted his head to face his captor. The pygmy glared at Mungo and flashed a glance toward his bride. Suddenly, two of the pygmies had his Sarra in their clutches. Mungo was ready. Before they could touch a hair on his beard, he pulled a silver dagger from his satchel and with one spin cut the tips off of every spear. With arms flailing, legs kicking, and deafening war cries clicking from their tongues, the pygmies of the South Seas attacked. Mungo tried to fight them off. But the wiry half-sized natives tackled him to the ground, leaving a streak of blood across his chest. He knocked the mini-warriors off his wounded body, sending them flying in all directions.

"Where is my bride?" Mungo growled.

"My bride," the native grunted, motioning to Sarra, whose hands were bound above her head and tied to a long wooden pole. Mungo glared at the older native, narrowed his eyes, and shook his head.

Suddenly, a great howl echoed throughout the village. The tribe fell to their knees, trembling, as a fearsome woman wearing Sarra's slippers, her upper lip sprouting a bushel of wiry hairs, entered the scene. Knowing not what to make of the strange woman, but seeing her need, Mungo slowly reached in his pocket and handed the woman his can of beeswax.

Mungo waited as the woman fidgeted with the tin can. She thrust it back at Mungo, nudging for him to open it. Mungo twisted the lid, dipped his finger in the buttery goo, and proceeded to twist his mustachio into a hook. There was silence. The woman waved her hand in the air, motioning for the older native to join her – an elder of the tribe, Mungo presumed. The elder proceeded to dip his hand into the goo, removing a glob the size of a walnut. Mungo nodded toward the woman. The woman lifted her chin as the elder smeared the contents of his finger upon her face, securing the unruly hairs to her upper lip. Again there was silence.

The woman turned to face the natives. The warriors cheered. The elder grinned, exposing two rows of rotting teeth. As if the cosmetic miracle had put a series of festive events in motion, two trays of exotic fruits and a bowl of a very foul smelling meat were presented to Mungo, but he refused to eat a bite until they released his bride. The elder was offended and angered, and demanded in his native tongue that Mungo offer a trade for Sarra. But since the natives had confiscated his satchel and knife, all Mungo had left were the shoes on his feet.

The trade was accepted. The Blackwell shoes had changed the course of Mungo Blackwell's life once again. Mungo quickly cut his wife down from her hold and pulled her to his side. He kissed her unashamedly, to the disgust of the natives. But the natives were not done with the travelers quite yet. The woman and the elder insisted Mungo marry them in a ceremony involving a tree trunk and a moldy piece of bread. That night while the tribe slept, with his bride on his arm, Mungo walked out of the village barefoot and ready to go wherever the curse of his grandfather would take them.

CHAPTER 18

Velveteen added up all the possible seating options in the living room and kitchen. It would have to do. In the city, their dining room table seated twelve. She had set their small kitchen table with four plates from her collection of china and carefully folded four cloth napkins, which she placed at the center of each plate. A crystal glass stood to the right corner of each setting and stainless steel flatware – she had allowed Charlie to sell their silver-plated set after *The Rooning* – flanked each plate, with a knife and spoon on the right and salad and dinner fork on the left. She no longer needed Emily Post to tell her how to set a table. Velveteen had set so many tables she could do it blindfolded.

She mentally did her best to squeeze in the six children around the coffee table; however, Fife was nearly as tall as Stephen, had graduated, was taking online business courses, and at sixteen had a full beard. She could squeeze Fife in with the adults, but that would leave Fie with Danger, the twins, and Gideon. Fie, only a year younger than her brother, would definitely feel out of place. She would leave Fife and apologize for their lack of space.

Her grandmother's copy of Debrett's 480-page handbook on style, form, and manners lay on the counter open to a page on "the eating of ethnic foods".

She checked the clock on the stove. Charlie was late. An unopened package for Gideon waited on the table by the door. He had anticipated its arrival before the move to Coraloo. They were both impressed and, truth be told, relieved when Gideon presented them with the money he had earned from selling old toys and asked Charlie to place the order. But Gideon hadn't mentioned the purchase since before the pre-order. Maybe he was no longer interested in the world of *Space Pirates*. He was changing; they were all changing in Coraloo.

The life was what she wanted for Gideon, to replace his fantasy world of space pirates with real friends. She had to admit, even if the Blackwells weren't her top choice in companions, he was happy – and she no longer had to nod and pretend to understand what he was talking about when he set out to explain how ray guns were powered by star energy.

"Vee! We're here!"

We're?

Velveteen tried to talk herself out of her frustration with Charlie. He was supposed to be home – alone – to help with last-minute details.

"No worries, sweetheart," he said sweetly, as if anticipating her irritation. "It's just Stephen."

"Mrs Price, thank you for having us. Clover is walking down with the rest of our clan. Can I help you with anything?"

The shop owner's genteel personality and manners were enough to make Emily Post swoon and John Debrett applaud.

"No thank you. I believe I have it all together." Velveteen pulled back the oven door, releasing the aroma of the Moroccan chicken recipe she had found in a cookbook. For years her cookbooks served to handsomely decorate the end cap of their kitchen island in the city, but in the past month, she'd found the beautifully covered books to be quite helpful in preparing meals.

Charlie had suggested pizza, but she wanted to prove she could do more – even if she had to ask Charlie for extra grocery money, uncomfortable as the request made her.

Velveteen had imagined herself standing alongside Melba when she added the dried apricots and chili flakes to her cart at the supermarket in the next town over. She had to ask the grocer multiple times to assist her in locating such items as cumin seed and chickpeas. In the city, she only shopped for the basics – going to the grocery store was more of a social event where the local gossip was passed over the thumping of melons and the smelling for ripe fruit. Velveteen had never known the difference between a good thump or a bad thump. It was all pretend, a game of charades over who had the healthiest cart of groceries and who would dare purchase the over-processed treats for their wee ones. Most of the ladies had their housekeepers do the real shopping. Since Velveteen had a secret affinity for sweets, she had been known to place a few choice leafy greens at the top of her cart to cover any contraband chocolate that might have found its way into her weekly shop.

She checked her time on the clock once again. The chicken was done. The potatoes were in the warmer, and the Brussels sprouts – she checked the pan… perfectly caramelized – she had read about that online. Charlie and Stephen sat in the seats she had set for the children. She tried to remind herself men don't care about things like straightened toss pillows. There was a knock at the door.

The next hours hinted at moments from their past – entertaining guests, warm scents filling the rooms, and an array of conversation jumping in organized clusters from one family to the next. But unlike the pretentious dinners she had hosted for the acquaintances, this was not pretend. For once she had prepared the meal from scratch, and she soaked up the compliments, which were directly aimed at her ability, not passing phrasing actually meant for a hired chef or socially revered catering company. And the guests were so pleasant that at one point she forget her role as hostess, lost in honest laughter and friendship.

Danger was the only one who wouldn't eat the Brussels sprouts – he claimed he was allergic, but Clover said he wasn't and made him choke down at least one. There was a moment of drama and over-exaggerated gagging, then a confession. Not only was Danger not allergic, but he liked them.

Fife didn't mind sitting on the couch with his younger siblings, but once he had finished his meal, he asked to be excused to return to their camper van. Fie took her book to the Prices' garden, and Danger, Gideon, and the twins ran off to rehearse.

"You should have seen it, Vee! Not only signed, but inscribed!"

"Where on earth did you find it Stephen?" Velveteen asked, calm and proud of the dinner event she had successfully pulled off.

"I actually came across it at an auction we frequent in the city. Strangest thing, come to think of it: I could have sworn I saw you the other day."

"Could have been. She made a trip a few weeks ago." Charlie had not wanted her to go. He had insisted they could get their medical records transferred without leaving home.

"Velveteen, it says right here we can make the switch online."

"I'd rather do it in person, Charlie. Who knows what could happen if our records fall into the wrong hands! I can handle this."

"What could possibly happen?"

"Well, identity theft."

"Identity theft?"

"What if some who-knows-who gets Gideon's information? Then we'll have some yahoo running around claiming he's Gideon Price. Then the who-knows-who robs a bank – or worse, kidnaps the president! Then forever everyone will think our Gideon is a bank-robbing kidnapper! He'll never go to college, Charlie! His life will be forever changed because of the Internet!"

Charlie listened and tried not to laugh. She had to be hiding something. "If you want to take a trip to the city, just tell me."

162

"It's not anything to discuss, Charlie. A quick trip there and back. We agreed that I'd handle the affairs of the home."

"We could all go, as a family." Family. The word hung in his mind. They hadn't acted much like a family lately. Velveteen was quieter than usual and Gideon was off playing pirates.

"You don't want to go back."

The conversation started down a path Charlie was not ready to travel. Going to the city wasn't a hop in a cab. He hadn't been back since The Rooning. For Charlie it was a taboo place… like returning to the scene of a murder.

"Must have been someone else. Was it Monday I made the trip, Clover?" Stephen asked.

Charlie passed a glance to his wife.

Velveteen's face tightened. She forced a laugh. "Still wrapping a few things up… I feel like I will never be fully moved in."

"Monday?" Charlie pulled out his phone, checking his calendar. "That's grocery day, right?"

Velveteen changed the subject. "Dessert! Who would like dessert?"

"Let me help." Charlie stood, dirty plate in hand.

"No… No, thanks, Charlie. I can handle it. It's just a simple bread pudding." She didn't want him to be worried about her whereabouts, but now was definitely not the time to have the conversation. It could wait.

Clover gathered the empty plates and sat them on the kitchen counter. "I haven't had bread pudding since I was a girl!"

"It's simple, really." Simple was an overstatement. The recipe had used such delicate words as "brisk" and "whisk" – in truth, there was really no simple about it. Velveteen thought she might die waiting to see if the pudding would firm up. And then there was the sauce.

Velveteen carefully poured the pungent liqueur topping over each ramekin. Serving the dessert, she was Melba entertaining her unbeknownst prince. But it was obvious that Charlie was unnerved by the revelation of her quick trip to the city. Velveteen avoided eye contact with her husband and pushed aside the dread of having to tell him why she was really in the city the day she had tried to dodge Stephen Blackwell.

"Granny said you had been spending some time with her in the kitchen." Stephen said, licking his lips and then spooning in another bite.

"Granny Blackwell does seem to add a kick of bourbon to everything, doesn't she?" Charlie shook his head, acknowledging the sweet potency of the bourbon sauce. "I thought Gideon had been drinking the first time I brought him to the market."

"Ha ha, very funny. Yes, I have been spending *some* time with Granny before the book club. She knows a lot… about food and things."

"She ought to," Stephen said. "Her father was chef de cuisine at a hotel in France. She was practically raised in that hotel. It's where she met Granddad. There was quite a romance between those two."

Velveteen couldn't imagine Granny living any life other than that of a Blackwell, especially not as the daughter of a renowned chef.

Suddenly, the children came running into the house. "Can we show you?" Gideon asked, out of breath and covered in sweat.

"Show us what?" Velveteen wiped her hands on the embroidered towel and took a seat beside her husband.

"The scene! We have a new one!" Danger interjected, addressing his father.

"Let's see it!" Stephen said, as he leaned back in his chair.

"A scene? Like the ones they do at the market?" After three weeks of consecutive market visits for Granny's book club, Velveteen had come to know the lingo and ways of Coraloo.

"Mom, you have to be quiet," Gideon admonished.

"Oh, so sorry."

The parents giggled at the sincerity of the children and watched in silence as they took their positions on the makeshift stage of their living room.

"Mungo! They're back!" Fie gasped, draping the back of her hand across her forehead and pretending to swoon.

"Stay away from the windows! I'll hang the Toft up if they step a foot closer to our land!" Danger shouted.

Fie clutched her stomach. "Mungo, the baby!"

"I'll deliver it when I return."

"Your house is mine, Blackwell!" Gideon shouted, jumping up on the coffee table and pointing a stick at Danger. "This is Toft land!" Finella stood behind him, arms crossed and eyes glaring – this wasn't their first performance.

"No, you lopsided mongrel! I bought this land and built the house with my bare hands."

Velveteen was fascinated and so intrigued she completely overlooked the fact that Gideon had his foot in a plate of leftover Moroccan chicken she had forgotten in her tidying up.

"Mungo!" Fie called, now lying flat on her back with her knees propped up. "The baby!"

"Then we will fight for it!" Gideon shouted, jumping off the table, smearing sauce on the floor. He thrust his imaginary sword at Danger.

"This sword," Danger said, holding the imaginary sword in his left hand and twisting the tip of his imaginary mustachio with the other, "was given to me by the pirate king of the mid-Atlantic. Never a man lived that faced its blade."

"Mungooooooo!" Fie yelled.

Velveteen watched, bouncing her leg with her chin cupped in her hands.

"Never has the pirate blade faced me," Gideon snarled.

There was a back and forth of movements – up on the table, walking across the sofa – with Fie, like a wild woman, screaming

165

with birthing pains and occasionally stopping her wailing to release a series of controlled short breaths before she screamed again. Suddenly, Gideon thrust his arm toward Danger. Danger stumbled back, then he spun around backward, and with a furious wail, he swung his imaginary sword at the neck of Gideon Price. Velveteen gasped as Gideon stumbled backwards clutching his neck. Then, he fell over.

Gideon sat up and addressed the parents. "We haven't figured out how to show my head rolling to the foot of Mungo, but we just now started practicing."

"Mungoooo, oh, oh, oh, oooooooo!" Fie yelled in character.

Danger rushed to her side with one arm tucked behind his back. "No son of mine will be born to face the tyranny of dishonest men!" With that, he stuck his hand by Fie's feet, where she proceeded to hand him a rolled up bath towel. "My son!" Danger shouted, holding the towel baby in the air.

"We haven't figured out how to make the birthing scene look real either. I'll ask Granny – she'll have an idea," Fie added.

The adults stood and applauded, except for Velveteen, who in her wildest dreams never imagined she'd find herself watching her son pretending to be beheaded and a seven-year-old giving birth to a wash towel on her living room floor.

Later that evening after the Blackwells had gone. Velveteen cleaned up the remains of her successful evening.

"Why didn't you tell me you were going into the city again?"

Velveteen turned to see Charlie staring at her blankly. "I didn't figure you would need to know about such things –"

"Did you have enough money?"

"For what?"

"I don't know, gas, and whatever you were doing."

"Your tank was full. It's not a big deal, Charlie."

"I would have gone with you."

166

"You say that, but you don't want to go back."

"We have everything we need right here." His gaze was deep, and he wasn't doing a very good job of covering up the underlying message of his statement.

That world, with its buildings, its sounds, its residents, was all a painful reminder of the months of silence and darkness after *The Rooning*, where everything he had predicted would happen happened. They'd lost everything. She had fought to hold herself together, afraid that Charlie was so vulnerable he would lose his will to live if he thought for one second she was going to leave him. She made sure to tell him where she was going, and how long she was going to be gone. And if she needed to cry she hid in the closet so he wouldn't see her. Her husband had been sucked so deep in depression that when he came home and started selling off everything, she would have sold the shoes off her feet to make him happy.

"I had fun tonight." She changed the subject.

"Are you happy?" He changed it back.

She pulled her hair away from her face and then let it fall down her back. It seemed as if they'd had this conversation before. "Yes. No. I don't know. What was the question?" She laughed.

He wrapped his arm around her waist. "Do *I* make you happy?"

"Of course."

"I would have gone with you." He kissed her on the forehead. "You just had to ask."

She just had to ask. But she wouldn't. "Charlie, I…" She wanted to tell him, but not like this. Granny was right. He deserved to know the truth. But how would he take it? She had noticed glimpses of *The Rooning*'s darkness beginning to surface. But she could not keep this from him any longer. "Charlie, there is something I need to tell you…"

The gentle *ping* from Charlie's phone interrupted her. Velveteen opened her mouth to speak.

"Ignore it." Charlie leaned his forehead against hers. His hands shook behind her back. "What do you need to tell me?"

The phone pinged again.

"You should see what sold." She pulled away from her husband.

He grabbed her hand and pulled her back. "What's going on, Vee? Why are you going to the city?"

She kissed him. And then kissed him again. She would tell him, later. "It was no big deal. Go see what sold. I know it's killing you, Charlie Price."

"It can wait." His voice was cold.

She should have told him about the second trip. She knew that now. "I had something to take care of."

"Why didn't you tell me?"

"I needed to go alone, that's all." It was the truth.

"Why?"

Tell him. This wasn't how it was supposed to happen. He wasn't ready to hear what she had to say. Not now, maybe never. They had been through so much already. "Because… I didn't want you to worry." That was true.

"Worry? About money? Are you trying to find a job?"

"What? No." She laughed. "Wait. Do you want me to find a job? Is that what you want? I will, I mean, I can."

"No! Of course not. I know you can. But I never want you to feel like you have to work. I *want* to provide for you and Gideon. It's not that I think you can't take care of yourself – or all of us for that matter. You're smart, talented, and everyone loves you! If you want to work, if that's what you really want, I'm behind you all the way."

She wasn't fishing for compliments. They had been over this twice before – once shortly after they married and once after *The Rooning*. "Charlie, that's not –"

The phone beeped twice. The buyer had left a message. Charlie shot a quick glance toward his phone sitting on the edge of the kitchen counter.

"Go on!"

Charlie looked into the eyes of his wife, searching her. He smiled. "Okay."

Velveteen turned to face the pile of dishes in the sink. She needed to think, to figure out how to tell him the whole truth.

Suddenly, Charlie picked her up, startling her from the conversation playing over in her mind, and twirled her around underneath the glowing bumblebee. "I'm sorry I've been so on edge, but not anymore. We're going to be okay. We sold the French horn!"

CHAPTER 19

Charlie carefully lined a cardboard box with packing foam and placed the French horn inside, a wave of relief washing over him. He had held onto the horn far longer than his nerves had anticipated, but he could relax for now. The sale of the instrument would catch them up financially, replenishing the funds he had spent on the scouting memorabilia and the violin, and providing an extra cushion for the coming weeks, if not months.

He was excited; Velveteen was distant. After he told her, he expected her to be as excited as he was, but she simply said, "That's great, Charlie," wiped her hands on a dishtowel, and went to bed. Did she know exactly how tight they had been? He could feel it without even checking their account – could she? Was that the real reason she had gone to the city – to find a job – or was it something else?

Financially, *The Rooning* had left them with less than they had when they were newlyweds living in a one-bedroom apartment, with barely enough to buy food and pay the utilities. But despite that, in the days following *The Rooning*, Charlie had felt a closeness with Velveteen more intense, more genuine, than anything they had experienced in their relationship – as though by taking away the wealth something new was revealed. Without him working late at the office, they had more time and talked every night after Gideon went off to sleep – most often he talked and she listened, occasionally interjecting a thought or word of encouragement. She made sure in his darkness he could still see the stars.

"Do you want to go look at the stars, Charlie?"

There were times when his shame got the better of him, and he was numb and cold toward her – he knew it was unfair. She didn't deserve it. It wasn't her fault. That night had been one of his selfish nights.

"We can't see the stars, Vee. There's too much light pollution."

Her smile faded, but she was determined. She took him by the hand and pulled him into the grand master bedroom. On each of the hand-cut crystals of the chandelier hanging over their four-poster bed, she had stuck a silver star. She lay down and instructed him to lie beside her.

"Let's dream a new dream, Charlie. We did it once, we can do it again."

In his hopelessness and distance, she had brought him back, reminded him what mattered. But he couldn't shake the feeling that something had gone wrong. Their recent closeness now seemed overshadowed by her reticence. Her trips to the city bothered him, shadowing his dreams and preoccupying his thoughts. He wanted to celebrate with her, tell her the sale of the horn would cover their rent for the next two months as well as give them a little extra for Christmas if they chose to save it, but she seemed distant. Had he pushed her too far? Maybe *she* needed to see the stars.

Charlie withheld a few dollars from the sale. The market would be open in an hour, and he always got there right when, if not before, it opened. It would be a good distraction; after all, it was his sanctuary. He sometimes envisioned the day he would walk through the stone archway, see his rare Kipling sitting among a stack of old books, and buy it for next to nothing. But on that imaginary day, he might notice another book, more rare than the Kipling. It would be so valuable he would sell it for enough to cover their rent for a year. He'd go back to city triumphant and –

He flopped down on the sofa and smacked the large box with his hand. What would it take for him to go back? To show his face again? Would it ever be enough?

The phone rang. Velveteen answered in the kitchen. He leaned in to listen. "I'm sorry but I won't be able to make it this week." She whispered something he could not hear, then a laugh. "Yes, I'll see you then."

Velveteen stepped into the living room. Faint dark circles shadowed her eyes.

"Who was on the phone?" Silence. "Vee, who was on the phone?"

Her face flushed, she looked over his shoulder, as if not hearing him.

"Vee, is everything all right?"

"Yes." Her smile was forced.

"There's something you're not telling me." He was on his feet. "Please, tell me what's going on. Whatever it is, we'll work through it. It's what we do." The phone rang again. "Are you going to answer it?"

"I'm sure it's Clover. We're supposed to have tea. I need to get cleaned up. I'll call her back."

Another ring. Something was wrong, very wrong. Charlie didn't know what it was, but Velveteen was not acting like herself. All she had to do was pick it up and say *hello*. Another ring.

"You should answer it."

She reached down and lifted the phone to her ear. "Velveteen Price." There was a pause, then a look of horror passed across Velveteen's face. Her eyes filled with tears and her hands shook. "We're on our way."

"Where are we going?" Charlie asked.

"The hospital. It's Gideon."

Charlie bounced his knees, rubbed his sweating palms on his trousers, and stood up. He walked from one end of the room to the other and then sat back down, proceeding to continue with the bouncing. Velveteen's eye make-up was smudged and her left hand continued to shake.

Danger, Fie, and Finella took turns pointing out the discrepancies in the reproduction Van Gogh that decorated the otherwise colorless waiting area. Tiny paths where tears had passed streaked Fie's dusty cheeks. Stephen sat with his arm around his wife.

Charlie pulled Velveteen in closer, the awkwardness of the mystery phone call set aside. Their son was in surgery. For the first time since they had been in Coraloo, Charlie wished, if it made sense to wish for such things, that this had happened in the city. The doctor who moonlighted as a realtor was not his first pick, and if the surgery hadn't needed to be done so quickly, he would have considered rushing Gideon to the city hospital.

Charlie kissed the top of his wife's head – her hair smelled of strawberries. The last time they had been at the Coraloo County Hospital was because she had fainted at the sight of the wallpaper; Gideon had been okay then. Friendly as he seemed, Dr Eyeballs was not the welcome party they had anticipated on their first day in Coraloo. Charlie allowed his thoughts to wander to those early days, when Velveteen had given the tiny Toft cottage a complete overhaul – with what little they had set aside in their budget, the possessions remaining of their former life, and with the limited colors they were willing to mix at the local hardware store. Charlie laughed out loud and then covered his mouth.

"Do you remember the wallpaper?" he whispered in her ear.

At this, Velveteen let out a chuckle. "And the paint – Gideon called it 'puke yellow.'"

Charlie laughed again, drawing the eye of others awaiting news of their loved ones. "It's still puke yellow."

"I kind of like it now."

"You do?"

"Yes, I do."

"Mr Price, Mrs Price." Doctor Eyeballs appeared in front of the couple, his hands tucked in the pockets of his white lab coat, his eyeballs magnified through the thick glass of his spectacles. "He did great – you can go back and see him now."

Charlie reached for Velveteen's hand. Together they entered Gideon's room. His face was bandaged and an I.V. with clear fluid ran into his arm. A slow beep resonated from the box beside the bed. The doctor had said the fracture to his face was not life threatening; however, because tissue surrounding the eye had become trapped, prompt surgical treatment was necessary to prevent long-term complications such as loss of vision or a permanent change in his appearance.

"It's okay; you can talk to him," the doctor encouraged.

"Gideon," Velveteen said through blubbering sobs, "we're right here. Mom and Dad are right here."

"Hey sport." Charlie's voice was broken and forced. "They're taking good care of you. Mom said your new *Star Pirates* came in. I had her put it in her purse. You'll be reading it in no time."

"Can I speak to you both?" Doctor Eyeballs motioned for the couple to join him away from Gideon. "We can't be certain, but there did not appear to be any nerve damage. We will have a better idea in the morning when we remove the bandages."

"Thank you, Doctor Eye… ur… Toft." At this moment, Charlie saw beyond the magnified eyes and straight to the man who had cared for his son.

Stephen peeked his head in the door. "Would it be okay if the children came in for a minute? They want to make sure he's still alive."

"Of course," Velveteen insisted. "They're his friends."

Charlie didn't know who this woman was standing beside him. She liked the puke yellow and now she was willing the Blackwell children – whose antics could quite possibly have blinded their son – to enter the room.

"Is he breathing?" Finella waved her hand above Gideon's face.

"Look at the wires! He's like a cyborg!" Fie exclaimed.

Clover placed a correcting hand on the shoulder of each of her children. "Not too loud. He's resting."

"Aww," Danger moaned. "Who's gonna play the thief? Gideon was the best thief we've ever had. Way better than Fife!"

"Who cares?" Finella said excitedly. "He's got to be the pirate king!"

Fie frowned. "But I'm the pirate king."

"Not anymore! Gideon will have to wear a patch anyway. Only the pirate king wears a patch, so Gideon is the pirate king!"

Fie stomped her foot on the ground and crossed her arms. But the decision was made.

Clover looked down at her redheaded children. "I think it's time for one of you to start talking. Who is going to explain to Mr and Mrs Price what happened at the market? We're going to find out one way or another." At once, all three heads went down, the children suddenly lost for words. "Danger?"

"Well, Mr Wilkinson was changing a lightbulb in the chandelier –" Danger started.

"We were supposed to be practicing our scene. Saturdays are the busiest. We had to get it right," Fie said, as if everyone in the room should have known.

"Mr Wilkinson got the wrong kind of bulb. So there we were, with his really tall ladder –"

"And I said," Fie interrupted, "I bet Mungo could swing from the chandelier."

Velveteen gasped. "Gideon fell from the chandelier?"

"On no, Mrs Price. He didn't make it that far," Danger explained. "He got halfway up the ladder when we heard Mrs Wilkinson rolling her cart. That's when it happened. I yelled up for Gideon to come back down. He couldn't hear me very well, so he turned around. That's when he slid. His face hit the floor so hard I heard it –"

"That's enough, Danger." Stephen placed his hand in front of Danger's mouth.

Danger pulled away. "Mr and Mrs Price, it was my fault."

Finella pushed him out of the way. "No it wasn't. I was the one who dared him to do it."

Fie pushed back at her sister. "I bet him a Mungo he wouldn't do it. I'm the one to blame."

Velveteen covered her tired eyes with her hand. "You bet a what?"

"*Bet you a Mungo…* It's something the kids say, like a dare you can't turn away from," Stephen explained. "We said it when we were children too."

A moan came from the direction of Gideon. Clover ushered Danger and the twins out of the room. A team of nurses stepped up to check Gideon's fluid levels and blood pressure.

"Do you think he would have done it?" Velveteen took her son's free hand in her own and kissed its palm.

Charlie chuckled. "Swung from the chandelier?" He shook his head. "Six months ago, I would have said, *absolutely not.* Now, who knows? Sounds like he was on his way up."

"I can't believe he actually thought he could swing on the chandelier. Charlie, he could have been –" her voice cracked.

"But he wasn't. He's here. We're here – as a family. You look like you could use a break. Why don't you grab a tea with Clover. I'll stay."

"A tea?"

"With Clover. Before we got the news you said you were going to have tea."

Velveteen took hold of Gideon's hand and avoided Charlie's gaze. "Not now. I can't leave him, Charlie."

Now that Gideon was stabilized and he knew he would be okay, Charlie's thoughts returned to the events of a few hours ago: the mysterious phone call, his wife's caginess, the increasing distance, like a gulf, growing between them… He stepped closer and put an arm on Velveteen's shoulder. "Of course," he said. He couldn't leave either. They'd both stay, together.

CHAPTER 20

Velveteen Price inched back the curtain. A bleached blond thirty-something woman with a kinky perm stood on the other side of the Toft front door examining her fire engine red fingernails: Sylvia Toft. The doorbell rang again. Velveteen pinched her cheeks, ran her fingers through her hair, smiled, and opened the door.

"I heard about your son. It is a tragedy the way the Blackwells keep the place – making money off the misfortunes of others. Soon they'll have this whole town turned upside down and running rampant with tourists. How is he? Was it his neck he broke?" The local hair artist rambled on while holding out a mason jar full of what looked like chopped meats, beans, corn, peas, and bits of something Velveteen didn't recognize.

"Thank you for asking about him. It's his eye. He needed surgery, but Dr Toft says he should be up and about in a few days. It was so kind of you to stop by and check on him. Thank you, again." Velveteen tried to close the door, but Sylvia stuck her foot inside.

"Do you like burgoo? I was going to make a lasagne, but I didn't have time to run to the market for cheese. You can return the jar when you're finished. No hurry. I have a whole cupboard stocked with the stew. We made it last Sunday at the family reunion. Everyone brings a can of whatever and we dump it right in – beans, peas, squirrel. How rude of me! I should have invited you so you could see how the *real* residents of Coraloo live. Do you know where I live? There's a sign outside. It's also my shop. I do wish you'd come by. I believe you are the only woman below the hill who has yet to cross my doorstep. And my sister says she has yet to see you in the boutique. Where do you shop?" Velveteen tried to speak, but could not start a sentence. "You must have your hair done in the city. I can't compete with that. I do my own, of course. Pink one week, blond another."

Velveteen glanced back. Charlie leaned against the kitchen doorframe with his hand over his mouth. She narrowed her eyes, furrowed her brow playfully, and tried to silently communicate. *Not. Funny.*

"I have a friend that lives in the city... What's her name? Elizabeth! That's it! Do you know an Elizabeth? It could be the same one. Wouldn't that be something! Silly me. I'm not sure who she sees for her hair, but I believe I could have done better. I don't have much formal training, mind you. But my mother, Nora Toft... Have you met my mother? She says it's a gift."

"It really was kind of you to bring us this soup –"

"Burgoo. It's a stew. Lord knows what's in it!"

"Right, burgoo. I will return the jar –" Velveteen tried again.

"You look exhausted. Your eyes are a bit baggy today. Do they feel baggy?"

Velveteen listened. She was exhausted, mentally and physically.

"I've got my kit right here." Sylvia Toft bent down and picked up a black rectangular suitcase by the handle that looked like something Charlie would have brought home from the market. In gold stamped letters it read: Coraloo High School Cosmetology. "Let me give you a treatment and some color. I have just the shade for those lips – do you normally wear red? You really should or maybe coral. I can lift the eyebrows and add some contouring on the cheekbones. It'll be on me."

Charlie's mouth hung open as Velveteen stepped back, allowing the frizzy-haired woman to buzz through the front door, across the living room, and into the kitchen. Velveteen could not believe what she was doing either.

Velveteen sat in the chair as Sylvia had instructed. She allowed her eyes to close as the woman explained each layer of application – oils, exfoliates, toners, lotions – as she wiped, smeared, and patted Velveteen's face.

"I don't know what you see in those Blackwells. They cause trouble. Think they own the town. They can stay up on the hill for all I care, but we own the valley. Stephen brought the lot of them back, you know. He's a looker. I was sweet on him in high school; shame he's a Blackwell. Not sure what he sees in that woman. I say, if you're gonna leave, stay gone. We were doing just fine before they came back with all their artsy-fartsyness. The whole lot of them used to live on the hill right below the market. You know what houses I'm talking about, don't you? Of course you do, they're gorgeous! But Lord knows I'd never let you live in a Blackwell house! I still say they're all cursed – not the houses, the clan. Everybody knows it. Can't sit still long enough to save their lives. They've been coming and going for years, until one day, I thought sure of it, they were nearly all gone. They left Coraloo, so we took it back. Well, finders keepers is what I say. My cousin bought one of those houses, against my advice mind you. We disinfected it pretty good, but I swear there's no way we got all the Blackwell out of it. Most of the rest of the houses were rented out." Sylvia blabbed on. Velveteen fought to stay awake – she was beginning to find it difficult to hang on to the convoluted chatter of the self-proclaimed make-up artist. "We'll be best friends, Velvy."

Velvy? "Best friends?" Velveteen mumbled.

"I'll leave you here to ferment –"

"Ferment?"

"It's shop talk, honey. I've got to get back to Mom's. She'll be upset if I don't let her dogs out. I'll set the timer on the stove. When it beeps your face will be as soft as a baby's butt. I'll stop over in a day or two to check on you. Oh, won't we be the talk of the town!"

180

Velveteen woke to the monotonous bleep of the kitchen timer. She yawned, wondering if she really had allowed some random woman to slap her down with highly fragranced facial products or if she had dreamed it all. She patted her cheeks, raised her eyebrows, and opened her mouth wide, moving her jaw from one side to the other in order to release the tightness in her face. She groaned. She'd allowed it.

"Charlie!"

No answer.

"Charlie?"

Charlie stared out over the sea of glassware, table settings, used toys, and outdated electronics. *All the same.* Today the aisles of anxious vendors did not look like an easy dollar – more like hawkers willing to shovel their wares into his already packed garden shed. Velveteen had kindly asked him to remove his purchases from the kitchen the night before the Blackwells came over for dinner, and had not given him the go ahead to bring the items back in the house.

Charlie was still buzzing from the successful sell of the French horn and was waiting for the other items to sell. Over the past week he had relished having extra money, enjoyed the freedom of having two months' worth of bills covered, and now, his only concern was for Christmas gifts – even though it was two months away. He had his eye on a collector's edition of *Star Pirate* he hoped to buy for Gideon. But his chances of finding another big win among the vendors seemed slim to none; he would have to find another way. Charlie had considered taking a risk on an online auction site – mostly returns, overstocks, and damaged packaging from large distribution houses and department stores. The items they mentioned were large and would turn faster, with much larger profits. But they would need a bigger house with more storage if he went this route.

It was something to consider, possibly a house in the suburbs with a garage.

Gideon would hate the suburbs. He'd hate anywhere if it wasn't Coraloo.

Since Gideon's accident, the Toft house had been relatively uneventful, with the exception of a few neighborly visitors bringing sweets for Gideon and offering to help Velveteen around the house. How the neighbors received word of the incident was at first a mystery, until Sylvia Toft stopped by to destress Velveteen with a free cosmetics consultation. Not only was Charlie shocked Velveteen had agreed, but he was even more surprised that the conversation between the ladies proved to be extraordinarily informative. As Velveteen tried not to nod off, he listened. Most of the town, including Sylvia Toft, eldest daughter of the infamous realtor Dr Toft, were direct descendants of Jonathan Toft, otherwise known by the Blackwells as "The Thief". Dr Toft had filled the family in on Gideon's unfortunate accident with the Blackwell boys. Mystery solved.

Charlie moved with ease among the vast tables of vendors, oblivious to the market's real draw on the perimeter. As usual, the quaint shops were a mini-city of their own accord, serving a different clientele than the vendors in the interior. Occasionally, Charlie would see a family venture over to the tables, rifle through the wares, and watch the children's faces light up with excitement over a Matchbox car, stuffed bear, or an outdated Barbie doll – new in the box, but no longer a collectible of any value. Velveteen kindly forbade Charlie to bring home anything stuffed, especially if it was once living. "Bugs, Charlie! Who knows what creepy-crawlies live on those things!" she had pleaded.

He reluctantly agreed. However, if he could find a mounted elk, and could get it for the right price, he had seen them resell as high as three thousand – that might change her mind.

There was a roar of laughter – the pirate must have asked for the shoes. Charlie craned his neck, hoping to catch a glimpse of Gideon. Dr Toft said Gideon would have to leave his eye covered for at least a month. Gideon was stir-crazy by his second day home from school; Velveteen was too. After much pleading and vowing he would never attempt to hang from a chandelier – whether acting or not – Gideon persuaded Charlie to allow him to accompany him to the market. Velveteen happily saw them off.

Through the crowd, Charlie could see the dim glow of Shug's shop. A steady stream of customers moved in and out. Charlie turned his back and returned to the disorganized clutter of the vendors. He picked up a red metal toolbox, opened it up, and turned it over. He had sold vintage toolboxes before. They were typically an easy sell.

"How much?" Charlie asked. The fifty-something behind the table ignored him. "Sir, how much?" The man didn't turn.

"How much for the set?" a woman standing beside Charlie asked.

The fifty-something turned and smiled. "For the set?" He emphasized the word *set*.

He wants her to think she's getting a deal.

"Oh, I could take fifteen."

The woman examined the cobalt blue jars and walked away.

"How much for the tool chest?" Charlie asked, trying to make eye contact with the vendor.

"It's not for sale," the man said, looking away. "I put it out by accident."

"Are you sure? I'd like to make an offer." Charlie had purchased many items that were not meant to be sold. He had read that everything has a price; you just have to be willing to figure out what the seller wants.

"No thanks."

"Will you take ten?" Charlie pushed.

"Not for sale." The man took the box from Charlie's hold.

"Okay, no worries." Taken aback, Charlie turned away. It wasn't worth an argument.

He walked on. Many of the vendors he had come to know by first name, as well as what they sold and how far to push them – with the exception of a few newbies like the fifty-something.

"Hey Curt! Do you have anything new?" Charlie sorted through the merchandise of a vendor specializing in old tools and records.

"Not today, Charlie. I heard about Gideon. How's he doing?"

"He's fine. Already back playing with the Blackwell kids."

"Do you get along with them? I mean, the Blackwells?"

"I think so. I haven't met them all. We spend some time with Stephen and his brood."

"No problems or anything?"

"I've had a run in or two with Shug." Charlie spotted a hammer. The handle appeared to be solid wood, but unlike hammers he had passed over before, this particular one had three claws on the back. Charlie stepped away from the table, turned around, and went to his phone. He could easily get five hundred for the hammer. "What will you take for this?" Charlie asked, turning toward the vender with the hammer in hand.

"Price, you won't get anything for that old thing."

"I don't know." Charlie did know. "It's old, and look at the claw on the back. What will you take for it?"

The man scratched what few strands of black hair time had left him. "I can't sell it to you, Charlie."

"Can't sell it? Curt, you'd sell your belt for the right price. Come on, how much for the hammer?"

"I can't do it, Charlie. Sorry."

"You're joking with me!"

The man puffed out his cheeks and then blew out a hard breath of air. He shook his head.

"Why not?"

"I'm not going to lie to you, Charlie. We've been doing good business these past months. But you see, it's Shug. He told us if we sold to you, we'd lose our vendor's license. With Christmas coming, and the market busier than it's ever been, I could use the extra money. The next closest market is three hours south. The hour drive here is hard enough on me."

Heat filled Charlie's face. "I'll buy everything you've got. Name your price."

The man nodded toward Shug's shop. "I can't do it, Charlie. I really am sorry."

"Who else did he tell? Did he tell that new guy down there too?" Charlie asked, pointing to the fifty-something.

"We had a letter about it on our tables when we came in to set up. Sorry, Charlie."

"So, what you're telling me is none of you are supposed to sell to me. Is that what you're saying?" Charlie turned toward the shop of the antique dealer.

"Don't do anything crazy! He's a big fellow."

Don't let him skin you! Charlie could hear Velveteen's plea in his ear, but in his anger he pushed it aside. He stormed toward the shop, ignoring every voice, sound, and smell around him. His eyes focused on the black wooden sign above the shop's entrance that read in heavy block letters: *Shug's*. Charlie pushed past a woman carrying a ceramic dog. He wanted to tell her not to buy it – she'd pay half online.

Shug stood occupied behind the once pub bar turned checkout counter. He looked up. They locked eyes. Charlie's face burned with months of pent up frustration, humiliation, and even a bit of jealousy. Shug's business was doing fine – the Blackwell didn't have a *Rooning* to overcome, a former life to hide from, and a wife and son to make happy. Charlie didn't wait for the words to escape Shug's lips. He stormed around the high-top counter, clenched his fist, pulled back his arm, and punched Shug Blackwell directly in the jaw.

Shug didn't move, but he didn't take his eyes off of the smaller man before him either. His breathing was heavy and his lips pursed. Charlie's hand hurt – but he wasn't backing down. Shug reached down and grabbed Charlie by the collar of his button-up shirt, dragged him past the antiques out into the openness of the market, and shoved him to the ground.

"Get out of my market, Price!"

"You had no right!" Charlie shouted as he stumbled to his feet.

"It's my market. I make the rules."

"So what's next? Are you going to start telling all these people that you decide who buys and who doesn't? Are you going to start asking for identification at the door? How about a DNA test, Shug?" Charlie turned to a man carrying a bouquet of flowers. "Sir, are these flowers for your wife?" The unsuspecting gentleman nodded. "Do you have the proper identification to buy flowers at the Coraloo Flea Market?" The terrified man shook his head.

Stephen stepped into the crowd of spectators and put a warning hand on Charlie. "That's enough, Charlie."

"I have a right to be here, Stephen! Are you on his side? Do you think I should go?"

"Right now, I do. Come on, let's go outside and cool off."

What am I doing? Charlie followed Stephen away from the group, but Shug was two steps behind them.

"Didn't I say you would cheapen my market? Well done, Charlie Price, well done. You've given our dear patrons their best show yet. Get out of here, Price. I don't want to ever see your face in here again."

Charlie turned around to face the giant of a man. With both hands, Shug shoved Charlie back to the ground.

"Shug, go back to your shop!" Granny's voice hushed the whisperers. "Charlie, you need to go home for a bit."

"He's not welcome, Mom," Shug said, wiping the bit of blood Charlie had drawn from the corner of his mouth.

Charlie fumbled to his feet again – his back ached, and it felt like he had sprained his wrist on the way down… the second time.

"Dad, I think we should go." Gideon Price emerged from the crowd. "Let's go home."

Gideon's eyes pleaded to go, to get away, to avoid further embarrassment.

What have I done?

His son wanted to go home. *Home.* Charlie wasn't sure where home was anymore – the city, Coraloo, some unknown place in their future.

"Charlie," Granny said, placing her hand on his back. "Everyone's welcome at the mar –" She didn't finish her sentence. Her eyes rolled backwards, and she began to sway.

"Mom!" Shug shouted as he ran to her side. The woman buckled at the knees and would have hit the ground had Charlie not been there in time to catch her.

CHAPTER 21

Velveteen straightened Charlie's necktie. She had insisted he wear his suit, despite his insistence it was what had landed him in jail.

"Granny did say I looked best in these shoes." Charlie sat down on the bed to tie the laces of his dress shoes.

Velveteen stood before the full-length mirror hanging on the back of their closet door, admiring her own shoes. She had rescued the black velvet high heels with the bow on the back and the black taffeta dress she had chosen to wear from her own "to be sold" pile... just in case. She had never imagined *just in case* would be a funeral.

The dress fit more snugly than she remembered. Of course, it had been more than a year since she had last worn it. She wrapped the purple scarf over her shoulders and bit her lip. After hand-washing the crocheted accessory three times, the stench had finally dissipated. Even though Granny had told her to take it off, she wanted to wear it tonight.

"I'm not sure it's appropriate for a funeral, Charlie. What do you think?"

"I think she would be disappointed if you didn't wear it."

With Gideon trudging behind, attempting to loosen his tie, the Prices stepped into the quiet stillness of the Coraloo Flea Market. Without the vendors, the boundless open space of the market appeared grander than usual, however lonely. Their footsteps echoed in cadence. The dimmed decorative lighting outside the shops cast diminutive shadows across the empty market. Tonight a silent chill hung in the air as if death itself was watching the newcomers walk uncertainly to the funeral of Granny Blackwell.

Charlie paused in the spot where the woman had fallen. "I'm not sure I should be here. I have no desire to upset Shug tonight."

"Of course you should be here, Charlie. Stephen insisted that you come. And I forbid you to take any blame for this. She was not well; Clover told me all about it. She had fought the effects of her diabetes for years."

"Where is everyone?" Gideon spoke louder than necessary, entertained by the echo of his voice bouncing off the walls. "Did we miss it?"

"I'm certain Clover said the funeral was at six."

Charlie glanced at his watch. "And we're sure it's at the market?"

"That's what she said. I'll feel horrible if we missed it, just horrible."

"Shouldn't it be at a church or something?" Gideon asked, fidgeting with his eye patch.

"Let's check out back." Charlie cased the market for signs of movement. "I think I hear music."

"Maybe, but I'm sure she said the market, Charlie."

Velveteen followed Gideon and Charlie through the vacated market toward the back entrance. Then, she stopped. Hundreds of illuminated candles lined the shelving and counter of *Granny's*. Pictures of Granny, drawn by all of the Blackwell children, peppered the floor, along with a scattering of pink chrysanthemums. On the cash register lay Granny's copy of *The Heiress of Dumont*. Velveteen's throat tightened and salty tears fell down her cheeks. She stepped into the empty shop, running her hand along the edge of the display case, absorbing the heady mix of sweetness and sorrow. There were moments when she had hated that woman, but Granny saw through her layers. She'd seen something in Velveteen that Velveteen hadn't been able to see in herself: her battle to be accepted, to figure out who she was supposed to be and what she was supposed to do. Granny had said she would fix her, that she wasn't *wearing the right shoes*. But how was Velveteen supposed to know which ones were the right shoes? Who would tell her now? She stifled a laugh. It was just like the old woman to leave her to figure it out for herself.

Velveteen slipped off her heels and allowed the cool concrete to soothe her slightly swollen feet. She wriggled and stretched her toes and then slipped the heels back on. Tight, uncomfortable. Maybe she shouldn't wear shoes at all.

"Are you okay?" Charlie asked. He'd doubled back and had been watching her, allowing her to process in her own way.

She shook her head.

Granny had wanted her to tell Charlie. But now was not the time; he had too much on his mind, and so did she. Velveteen kissed the palm of her hand and laid it on top of the book. "I'll tell him, Granny," Velveteen whispered. "I'll tell him. I promise."

Charlie pushed open the door at the back of the market and peered outside. The music stopped as the Blackwells, sitting in their lawn chairs around open fire-pits, caught sight of the family of three.

"What are you so dressed up for?" Danger asked, bounding toward Gideon and breaking the silence.

The Blackwells were dressed comfortably in blue jeans and t-shirts – a drastic casual contrast to the Prices' finery. Granted, the Blackwells were strange, but she at least expected the men to wear a button-up shirt or jacket and the women a dress of some sort. This was beyond everything Velveteen had ever read or studied in her etiquette books. In fact, the scene laid out in front of them looked much the same as it had the day they first visited the camper vans.

"I think we missed it," Charlie whispered.

Velveteen leaned into him. "She said six."

Stephen jumped to their aid. "I guess we should have explained."

"No need," Velveteen replied. "I am so sorry we missed the funeral. We truly meant no disrespect. I must have misunderstood."

"I'm sure you didn't."

"But the funeral –"

"We've already had the funeral!" Danger announced. "Come on Gideon; you're missing all the good food."

"So we did miss it," Velveteen sighed. She was uncharacteristically out of sorts lately, but she was one hundred percent certain Clover had told her Granny's vigil would be at six… *behind the market*. What was wrong with her? How had she forgotten where it would be?

"Come, get a bite of food. We'll explain." Stephen ushered the couple to a series of folding tables lined up with crock pots and aluminum foil baking dishes filled with enough starch and carbohydrates to make Velveteen's former personal trainer pass out in his protein shake. But the macaroni and cheese with added bits of bacon smelled too good to resist.

"Oh, Velveteen!" Clover gasped, once again wearing her stylishly ripped jeans, but this time with a sweater Velveteen was sure she had seen while browsing online. "You look stunning!"

Velveteen blushed. "I believe we overdressed for the… vigil."

Clover hooked her arm in Velveteen's. "Granny would have loved every inch of you. Especially those shoes! They suit you, but feel free to take them off," she said, glancing down at her own pedicured toes.

Velveteen looked at her shoes and considered for the second time that day walking barefoot. As far as she knew, by the standards of etiquette, she was appropriately dressed for a funeral: she had chosen a subtle color – traditional black; the dress was conservative – Audrey neckline; had opted out of a hat. She'd save the gauche, outlandish, and big-enough-to-obstruct-those-sitting-behind-her head piece for the frills of a Derby party, should she ever be invited to one again. The acquaintances would have been pleased. When her mother passed, she'd bought a smart black sheath for the visitation and a belted trench with matching umbrella for the outdoor service, because, as her book said, "One must always be prepared for inclement weather."

And one should be prepared for a Blackwell vigil. She decided to take the shoes off. "Thank you. I guess I misunderstood. I'm so sorry we missed the funeral." Velveteen pulled the scarf around her shoulders a bit tighter – the evening was darkening and the night air blew through her quaffed hair, but mainly she hoped to disguise her dress.

"You didn't miss it," Gavina Blackwell chimed in. "You weren't invited."

Velveteen stopped mid-bite, plastic fork suspended in the air above her Styrofoam plate. Charlie cast hurried glances around the camp. He certainly didn't want his presence to cause a scene.

Stephen rested a hand on Charlie's shoulder. "It's all right; he's not here."

"I can't tell you how sorry I am. I didn't mean to…" Charlie sighed. "The market and Granny… How is Shug handling it?"

"He's been staying in the city a lot lately."

"In the city?"

"He's already mourned once. I figure he's dealing with the finality of it by locating new inventory. A couple of big auctions coming up. He wants what's best for the market. Family is important to him."

"What Gavina meant to say," Clover said, bringing the conversation back to Velveteen's clear mortification, "is that Granny had her funeral years ago."

Charlie swallowed the wrong way, coughed, and sent his mouthful soaring straight into the fire, causing it to flicker and fight against the breeze. "Excuse me? Did you say *years ago*?"

"Well," Stephen said, throwing his hands up in the air, "there you have it."

"But Clover called – she said there was to be a vigil." Velveteen, like Charlie, was visibly confused.

"I'm so sorry, Velveteen. I should have explained. This – ," she motioned with her arms, "this is the vigil."

"So, it's not a *funeral*?"

Part of Velveteen was morbidly curious about the whereabouts of the deceased Granny, but most of her was afraid to ask.

"We already had Granny's funeral," Stephen explained. A series of strung lights flicked on around the awning of a nearby camper van. "I would say it was at least sixteen years ago. Clover and I hadn't been married very long."

Velveteen was totally confused, and suddenly extremely thirsty. "I don't understand."

"Most of the older Blackwells have already had their funerals."

Charlie set down his plate. "Are you telling me you've already had your funeral?"

Stephen shook his head. "No, I guess I haven't had the time."

"You better get on it," an uncle chimed in.

"So let me get this straight, you're going to have your funeral *before* you die?" Charlie asked in disbelief.

This was the most insane notion Velveteen had ever heard of in her life, but then she was eating a potluck dinner behind a flea market in honor of a deceased family member of people she had known less than a year. Melba would be all about this moment. Velveteen's former self would never have believed it possible.

"It's a family tradition, so to speak. It started with Mu –"

"Mungo Blackwell?" Velveteen interrupted.

"Yes."

"Why?" was all that she could ask. "Funerals are for… well, they're for dead people."

"Who's to say we aren't dead until we learn what we are living for?" Stephen placed his hands behind his head and leaned back casually in the folding camping chair. "We all need to know what's missing in our lives. At a funeral people say everything a person has accomplished in their life, but what if they missed something? What if there was one thing you never realized you needed to do? What if you had a chance to go back and do it?"

Velveteen reminded herself to shut her mouth so the hunk of bread she had placed in it would not fall out. She stared down at her plate, forcing herself to chew. Just when she could see the normal in the family, the Blackwells reverted back to the crazy. She swallowed the chunk and, as she seemed to be doing with surprising frequency, said what was on her mind.

"I can't imagine Granny had much missing from her life. She certainly seemed to have it all together."

"High heels." Clover gulped down a drink of soda. "She wanted to wear high heels."

"What?" Charlie and Velveteen said in unison.

The circle of family erupted in laughter.

"It was hard enough to find someone to give her eulogy; both the preacher and the priest had already had run-ins with her. Stephen agreed, but before he could finish she jumped up in front of everyone and declared she'd never worn high heels before. No one else even had the chance to speak." Clover covered her mouth to hold in her own giggles. "She made us girls take her to the city to pick out a pair that day. She said if she was going to wear them, they had to be high and patent leather. We must have hit every shoe store we could find. Cost was of no concern to her. We returned with a pair of size seven-and-a-half black patent leather pumps, and let me tell you, that woman wore those shoes every day for four straight months." Clover stood up and pretended to pull up an imaginary skirt. "She would hike her dress up like this and show the tourists." The family continued to laugh. "She'd say, 'Don't I look a piece of a woman, now!'"

"Oh, oh, oh, and she'd say," a cousin mocked playfully, "*never a man crossed my path that he didn't look at my shoes!*"

"No man ever paid attention to her shoes; they were too busy looking at her buns!" Stephen chuckled. There was a moment of silence, then the family laughed some more. "Her sticky buns, you crazy lot! Get your mind out of the gutter!"

"I liked her buns," Gideon said, leaning over his dad's shoulder. There was another awkward pause, before the laughter resumed and the family was at it again; this time Velveteen and Charlie joined in the merriment. Gideon stood, fists on hips. "What did I say? The first time I saw her I ordered a sticky bun!"

What few memories Velveteen had of the woman flooded her mind, bringing with it a desire to know family – aunts, uncles, and cousins she had never met.

"She would have enjoyed this," Stephen added. "Wouldn't she?"

"That's why we do it the way we do," Gavina added. "But Lord, I've never seen a woman hold herself so high – and I doubt, even with the extra inches, she hit five foot. About month six her arthritis set in, and she had to stop wearing them."

"That must have been so sad for her." Against her better judgment, Velveteen found herself embracing the opportunity this completely unexpected, and downright bizarre, vigil afforded – joining in with remembering and memorializing Granny in a manner contrary to everything she had ever read about funeral formalities. "The one thing in her life she wanted, and her health forced her to quit."

"Oh no!" A woman neither of the Prices recognized, but was clearly a Blackwell by virtue of the bushy red hair pulled into a ponytail on top of her head, jumped into the conversation. "She hated those things! She only wore them to spite us all. We told her they would hurt, but she would never give us the satisfaction of admitting it, so she pranced around in agony for months." Another spattering of laughter carried across the campsite.

"We buried her in them," Stephen said softly. "It was Shug's idea."

"And she is cursing him all the way into the afterlife!" Clover giggled. The Blackwell family exploded once again.

The melodic hum of a bagpipe interrupted the cheer as an uncle played in front of the rooster van. In unison, pulling from the Scottish inflections of their ancestors, the Blackwells began to sing:

> *On to the hills,*
> *Thy soul longs to see*
> *The evermore where death takes me.*
> *Of paths yet trod,*
> *Thy heart will cry.*
> *But alas my dear,*
> *I'll see you on the other side.*

Charlie had heard "Hills of Evermore" once before – at his grandfather's funeral, so many years ago. Listening to the song now, against the melancholy drone of the bagpipes, he was transported back to his childhood. He closed his eyes and allowed the music to enter his soul, stirring something deep within him and temporarily displacing the insecurity and doubt that he'd been carrying with him since *The Rooning*. As the last note echoed across the hill, Charlie clung to the memory of his past hopes and dreams.

He didn't want to leave. He could learn a lesson or two from Granny and from the Blackwells, who did not mourn the loss of their loved one – their matriarch – but celebrated her with story and song, remembering who she was in life and not what could have been had death not taken her. Charlie glanced over at his wife, barefoot and smiling – comfortable and secure. In the distance he could see Gideon – confident and happy – acting out the latest scene in the Blackwell family history. What more could he ask for in this life than this?

CHAPTER 22

Charlie fidgeted with the figures on his spreadsheet, the neatness of its rows and columns belying the clutter that each number represented – an item bought or sold, a worry lost or gained. And at the bottom, the total value of his efforts tallied up in black and white. Not as much as he had hoped; it would never be as much as he hoped.

Velveteen flipped to the next page of her book. Earlier that morning she had offered to print shipping labels, tape boxes, and walk with Charlie to the post office where the postmaster, Norvel Poteet – a Toft by marriage – greeted them both by first name. Velveteen placed a sticky note in the page's center and wrote the words *Melba* and *afraid*; she then glanced down at the notes she had jotted down on the pad of paper.

Charlie opened a new tab on his laptop and logged in to the online auction site as he had done multiple times a day for the past two weeks. The new owner of the French horn had not yet left him a review – the only sure-fire way to know a package had been received. For a few days following the transfer of funds, Charlie considered holding on to the money until he had confirmation the buyer was pleased. But it was one of his biggest sells and he had already allocated the money. With a few recent smaller sells, Charlie had calculated it would also cover Christmas.

However, when Charlie had checked his e-mail the night before, he saw that the Australian buyer had contacted him to let him know the horn had yet to arrive. Online shipping updates said the man should have received it by now. After spending half of the evening on the phone, the missing parcel was discovered in a warehouse on the other side of the country. It would take at least another week for the horn to make its way across the ocean. They had already spent half of the money and could not afford for the horn to be returned.

"Charlie, I have a fantastic idea!" Velveteen slammed her book shut. "We need to have our Christmas party. We'll do it here, in Coraloo! Of course, I'll have to go into the city –"

"The city? Didn't you just make another trip?" A sense of dread descended on Charlie. He'd temporarily buried his concerns about her mysterious trips to the city, but now his worries resurfaced.

"I've been catching up… with a friend."

"You had *friends* in the city?" He never recalled her having any real friends. Before the move she'd told the acquaintances he had taken a position as an antiques dealer in Coraloo. They had heard of Coraloo – though not a single one had stepped a foot in the building; they hired people to do that for them. It did not bother Charlie, but *antiques dealer* sounded too stuffy, too much like life before *The Rooning*. He would hardly call picking through junk shops and rummage sales antiques dealing. He preferred picker, modern day treasure hunter or, even better, finder of wonders. Gideon liked that one.

"I thought I would order invitations from Le Papier. On second thought… I have an idea, Charlie! How about I buy everything from the market? It would save money and our guests would think it absolutely delightful! I think I can do everything else myself. I've gotten quite good at Granny's macarons and the bread pudding was a hit. You said so yourself. Can't you see it – a party in the country? I promise not to spend too much. It will be simple, quaint…"

Quaint.

He had used that word – *quaint* – to persuade her to move to Coraloo. She continued on while his mind recalled their initial plan: simplicity. Had they achieved it here? Their house was smaller, they lived on a much tighter budget, and Velveteen had a glow about her he had not seen in years. They weren't over scheduled, Gideon was doing well in school and had friends… but Charlie was still far from finding the simplicity he desired. The stresses of providing, deciding what to pay first, and dreaming of extras had not left his wonderings.

"Oh, Charlie! It would be so good for us, don't you think? And I don't believe they would mind the drive. They can stay in the bed and breakfast around the corner."

"Why would they want to do that when they can walk? It's not far."

"Not far! Charlie, I hardly think they will want to walk from the city!"

He shut his laptop. His jaw stiffened. "Who are you inviting, Vee?"

She sensed his confusion. "Well, I was thinking the people we always invite to our Christmas party. Who else would want to come?"

"Vee, we haven't talked to any of them in nearly a year."

"All the reason why we should invite them!"

"Why?"

"Why what?"

"Why are you doing this?"

"Charlie, I don't understand. We always used to have a Christmas party. Since you sold the French horn –"

"It's not about the money." It was partly about the money. "I don't understand. Why those people? I don't know those people anymore – do you? In fact, I don't think I ever really knew them even when they were at my house, eating my food. And that Rutherford –"

"Rutherford?" Velveteen opened her book and pretended to read.

"I don't care who his great-grandfather was. There's not enough crab puffs in the country to feed that one. I swear he stuffed some in his wife's purse."

Velveteen giggled and then bit her lip.

"Oh and the Brunswicks. Oh, the Brunswicks! I would absolutely love for him to tell me again how much bigger their house is than ours. He'll have a heyday with this place."

"So we won't invite the Rutherfords or the Brunswicks."

"Or the Rogers. *What are you doing these days, my man?*" Charlie mocked his former banking colleague. "Oh you know, hanging out at the flea market…"

Velveteen held her book in front of her face to hide the huge grin.

"And Carl will say, *And how's that working out for you, my man?* And I'll say… Well, I don't know what I'll say; another reason not to invite them."

"So, I can have the party?"

"Can I invite a few guests?" If they were having a party, he wanted it to be comfortable.

Velveteen jumped up, hugged him around the neck, and kissed him delicately on the lips. "Invite whoever you want. I don't care as long as we have the party. Thank you, Charlie Price! Thank you!"

He hugged her back – his bride, his wife, and his love. Moments of closeness seemed far removed from their daily life. He didn't want to let her go.

"I'll start planning right away!"

"Take it easy on me, okay?" He would have to work harder, maybe lower the price on the Boy Scout memorabilia. It would be a challenge, but he could do it… for her… for them.

The mantel clock chimed a quarter to ten. Velveteen released her grip around his neck. "Now out with you! Are you going to the market?" She paused. "You're sure Shug's still out of town?"

"Yes, don't worry. I promise not to be hung and quartered, at least not by Shug."

"He's been gone nearly a month. Who's running the shop?"

"One of the cousins."

"Don't you find that odd?"

"All I know," he said, setting down his laptop and picking his coat off the coat rack, "is I'm going to the market."

"And when he comes back?"

"I have a plan."

"Are you going to tell me about this plan?"

"Maybe," he said, shutting the door behind him.

Velveteen quickly set a tray of pink macarons – made exactly the way Granny had taught her – on the table, fluffed the cushions on the couch, and then wriggled her bare feet on the wood floors. Even in the cold of November, she liked the way the floors felt under her feet. Opening the door, she welcomed the Blackwell ladies into her home.

Each lady sat in the same seat they had sat in for the past month. They intentionally left the armchair free – it had been Granny's seat; no one dared to sit in it. Originally, Velveteen thought it was out of respect, but later Clover explained that the younger cousins were afraid Granny would haunt them. She had been tough in life; they were sure she'd be a terror in death. It was Clover's suggestion the book club move back to Velveteen's. *Granny's* remained closed; not one of the Blackwell ladies felt comfortable taking her place in the kitchen, even though a few of the aunts were more than capable. Running the concession would mean giving up their own storefronts – their art and their joy.

Velveteen held up a book showing the portrait of a lady in a lavish green ball gown standing in front of a barn. The ladies cheered.

"It's gorgeous!" one of them exclaimed.

Velveteen handed a copy of *The Princess of DuMont: Straw to Silk* to each of the women. This was her second favorite in the series – the first remained her personal handbook for how to handle every social obstacle life tossed her way. She watched as the ladies caressed the matte finish cover, turning the book over to read the back, and thumbing through the pages to get a peek at the new life of Melba DuMont.

"Since we are beginning a new novel, I decided we should start by looking back on the attributes of our heroine." Velveteen glanced at her notes. "Anyone want to start?" She had a few things of her own to say, but etiquette required she allow the guests to speak first. Selflessness was an attribute she was hoping to improve upon.

"Strong," Clover stated. "She lost every part of the life she had always known, picked herself up off the road, and in order to survive took employment as a shepherdess. She had never worked a day in her life, but was willing to do whatever it took to survive."

Velveteen shifted uncomfortably. "I agree, Clover. Anyone else?"

"She must not be stupid either," one of the aunts added. "The woman had to figure it all out. She was patching her dress up with chicken feed sacks and making Ryegrass soup!"

The ladies laughed.

"My favorite part was when she tried to color her hair with cherry bark!" Gavina said. The ladies laughed again. Velveteen forced a smile. She was oddly uncomfortable. "Or when Count Horace –"

There was a knock at the door. Velveteen froze. The macarons were on the table, Melba was the topic of conversation, the ladies were looking at her. *It* was happening again. Charlie had not mentioned they were behind on the rent, but it was possible. It had happened once, why not again? Another knock. Velveteen stood and walked slowly to the door – her hand shook and her heart pounded. If Granny were here, she most definitely would have thrown up on her again.

Velveteen closed her eyes and reached for the handle. *Please, no envelope. Please, no envelope.* There would be no hiding behind deception – no lies this time. These ladies had heard her story, she had told them everything. She could not go through it again – the selling, the moving, the starting over.

Another knock.

She turned the handle.

"I thought you'd never answer the door, but I had a feeling you were in here. Best friends can sense those things." Sylvia Toft stood at her front door with coal black hair, painted on eyebrows, and a shade of lip color that bounced between an icy blue and a shimmering green. Her cosmetic case sat on the ground beside her feet. "I figured you could use another pick-me-up." She winked at Velveteen. "Can I come in?"

"Well, actually –" Before Velveteen could explain, Sylvia Toft pushed past her and into the presence of the Blackwell women.

"Oh – Blackwells! I didn't know you were…" Sylvia stuttered, obviously unnerved by their presence. "Velvy, can I have a word with you? Maybe in the other room?"

"We should go." Clover stood up. The other women followed her lead.

"No!" Velveteen yelped, much louder than she had intended. "No, sit, please. I'm not sure I know… I mean, um, why don't you all discuss the Le Moge family. We'll visit with them later in book two."

Sylvia marched into the kitchen. Velveteen followed, relieved she was not being served a foreclosure notice, but wondering if this situation was not somehow far worse.

"Do you know who is in *your* living room, Velvy?" Sylvia asked with arms flailing wildly.

"Yes, I do." Velveteen did not care much for being called *Velvy*; it somehow reminded her of an automobile part. "It's my –"

"You are associating with the enemy. I told you what happened."

Velveteen didn't exactly recall the entire conversation. She was certain whatever was in the cream Sylvia had smeared on her face – which made her feel as if she had been in the sun too long – had some sort of soporific effect. When she woke, it was as if she'd been drugged. Not only that, she'd had to use half her jar of coconut oil to remove the layering of Sylvia's artistic gifting in cosmetology.

"They're my book club, Sylvia."

"Blackwells don't read, Velvy. They are deceiving you. I'll help you get them out." The woman started back toward the living room, but Velveteen was able to grab her arm before she crossed the threshold.

"No, no, no! They're my friends, and they can read."

Sylvia's smile drew into a taut line. "I'm sorry. I didn't know. There has always been talk in town that your husband frequented the market, but I thought you were above such things. I'll go."

Although opposite in almost every way, somehow this woman with her over-dyed hair and heavy cosmetics reminded Velveteen of the acquaintances – quick to judge and hung up on a family name. No matter where she moved, she wasn't getting away from it. She had an idea.

"Do you like to read, Sylvia?"

"Well, I can't say I've read much, but I guess it's a pastime."

"Great! Why don't you join us?"

"I don't think –"

Velveteen finished the sentence for her. "I think it is a fabulous idea. We are starting a new book. It's the second in the series, but I absolutely know you will love it. I do!"

"Blackwells and Tofts don't usually –"

"Today you are a Price." The next phrase slipped out before Velveteen could stop it – a problem she was having more and more as of late. "Like sisters." She regretted it the minute she said it.

Sylvia's eyes lit up. "*Then* can I give you a makeover?"

Velveteen did not know what that had to do with the book club, but she was determined she could have a part in bringing peace between the women. "Of course, a makeover would be lovely."

Sylvia Toft sauntered into the living room, blinked her elongated false eyelashes at the Blackwell ladies, and sat her bottom down in Granny's armchair. Velveteen opened her mouth to speak, but no words came out.

"The Toft's tooshie sat on Granny," Greer muttered. "Maybe Granny will bite her." A few of the women giggled.

Velveteen gathered herself and cleared her throat. "Ladies, we have a new member. I'd like you to meet Sylvia Toft. We met not long after Gideon's accident."

"I brought Velvy a batch of burgoo and gave her a treatment. We might as well be sisters." Sylvia confidently crossed her legs. "Do I need a book?"

Clover handed the Toft her copy. "It's nice to have you."

"Maybe if she and her family would move back to where they came from we could claim what's rightfully ours." Velveteen couldn't tell which Blackwell had said it; they were all sitting up with their backs straight and exaggerated smiles spread across their faces.

This was a mistake. Velveteen sat back down in her chair across from Sylvia. "Where were we?"

"The attributes." Velveteen knew she could count on Clover to be the sane one of the bunch.

"Yes, the attributes of Melba DuMont, our heroine. As we begin book two, let's keep in mind the type of woman she was and also the woman she became. Does anyone recall what happened at the end of book one?" Velveteen lifted her eyes, half expecting Sylvia to be filing her nails or touching up her garish lipstick. Instead, Sylvia Toft's eyes were glued to Velveteen. "Anyone?"

Clover hesitantly raised her hand. The ladies usually didn't raise their hand to answer. "The sheepherder revealed his identity to Melba and asked her to come live in his palace, but Melba was conflicted – torn between her life on the farm and returning to her station as the heiress of DuMont."

"Aren't you excited?" Velveteen's voice cracked as she forced a squeal, but the ladies did not return her enthusiasm. The awe and anticipation for the new book was gone. The ladies had something else – someone else – on their mind. She had to do something to bring the meeting back.

Sylvia spoke up. "I for one can't wait to read what happens to… What's her name?"

Clover leaned over to her. "Melba."

"Right, Mel-va. You know what? It just occurred to me. I have a great idea!" Sylvia clapped her hands on both sides of her face.

Velveteen tried to speak, to stop the woman from saying whatever it was she was going to say, but Sylvia's tongue was too fast.

"After the meeting, I'd be happy to give you all makeovers. I've got my kit. A few of you could use a bit of fixing up."

Velveteen watched as Moira Blackwell reached for one of the petal pink macarons. Moira turned it over in her wrinkled hands. She raised her eyes toward Sylvia and then looked back at the macaron.

No. Velveteen had worn that look once before.

Sylvia thumbed through the pages. "It's too long for my taste. Velvy, why don't we read something else! Maybe something from the library? You ladies do know there is a library in town, don't you? It's named after my grandfather, Ernest Toft."

Moira nudged another aunt, a near identical, minus seventy pounds or so, version of Granny. She nodded at the macarons. The aunt grinned and reached for one of the pink confections. Velveteen didn't know what to do. She had to stop Sylvia from speaking.

"Clover…" Velveteen's voice cracked again. She shuffled through her notes. This was not going as planned. "Um, will you, um –"

"Yes! Of course! The, um, heiress, Melba, is kind-hearted. She looks past the shortcomings of others…"

Velveteen took back over. "And she would *never* do *anything* to harm another human being…"

By now Greer and Gavina were holding the round sweets.

This isn't happening. Oh God, please don't let them do this!

Moira continued to stare, passing the macaron back and forth from arthritic hand to arthritic hand.

Sylvia Toft reached for a treat.

Velveteen held her breath.

Sylvia took a bite. "My mother makes the best macarons in the town. Everyone says so, even the tourists. She's thinking of opening her own bakery. You can't keep all the business up on the hill."

Of all the places in the world, Velveteen had landed in one obsessed with macarons.

"You know my mother, Nora Toft, don't you Moira?"

Moira didn't answer, but took a deep breath… continuing to turn the sweet cookie over in her hands.

"Oh, I'm sorry." Sylvia leaned in to Moira. "There was a teensy weensy bust-up between the two of you, wasn't there?"

It was the first time Velveteen fully understood how deep the hatred ran between the two families.

"You did a fine job, Velvy. Family recipe?" Sylvia took another bite.

"Yes, it's Granny Blackwell's recipe."

Velveteen had no more than said the name Blackwell, than Sylvia spit the partially chewed bits of macaron out of her mouth and onto the digitally enhanced face of Melba DuMont. "I'll have to have mother come over and show you –" She couldn't finish her taunt because a pink macaron hit her between the eyes.

Sylvia jumped to her feet and tossed her half-eaten cookie into the lap of Moira Blackwell.

Gavina threw back – this time hitting Sylvia on the cheek. In a matter of minutes, puffy pink lemon curd-filled macarons were sailing from one side of the living room to the other.

Oh no! It's happening again!

Charlie Price had news. The Boy Scout badges had sold to a collector in the South. He could have them packaged, shipped, and expect feedback before the week was over. The sale of the badges was nearly as big a victory as the French horn. He planned to pay what needed paying and then give Velveteen some extra for next month's Christmas party. He couldn't wait to tell her.

When Charlie walked in the door to the Toft house, Velveteen was lying on the couch with the second Melba DuMont novel open across her face. The floor was covered in a smattering of badly damaged macarons.

"Sweetheart! What happened? Are you okay?"

Velveteen Price pulled the book off her face and turned toward her husband. "I should have never told them, Charlie. It was *The Rooning* all over again! Not our Rooning, my Rooning! They went to war. First Moira threw one at Sylvia. Then Sylvia –"

"You invited Sylvia Toft to your book club?"

"Not exactly, but sort of. They really can't stand each other, Charlie. I didn't know how to stop it, so I hid under the kitchen table."

"I find it hard to believe Clover was in on this."

"No, she wasn't. I think she might have been under the coffee table."

"How did it end?"

"With a lot of shouting. One of the Blackwells yelled, Heads will roll, Toft! Heads will roll! And then Sylvia: You may have taken the hill, but we took the valley. And one of the Blackwells shouted, We let you stay in the valley! And Sylvia: Lies! Lies! Then the door slammed… several times. Clover found me ten minutes later. She offered to help clean up."

"Why didn't you let her?"

"Well, I didn't think you would believe me, so I left the evidence."

CHAPTER 23

1890

M ungo Blackwell looked down upon the valley. When he was young, his father often spoke of the rolling green pastures that fell between the hills of hickories, oaks, and cedars. *"It's waiting for us Mungo. It's our land. There's a house… More than enough for us all,"* Mumford would say. *"We'll find our way back."*

Mungo knew the tale, how his father had left the country as a young man, using the family trade in hopes of saving his family, while also satisfying his adventurous spirit. Every penny he made he sent back home, but it wasn't enough, so he'd purchased the land, sending instruction that his family could settle there. The family had made the journey across the sea to the new land as Mumford hoped they would. Eventually he felt it time to reunite with them and began the long journey to his new home, only to learn they had all died, leaving Mumford and Mungo the last of the Blackwells.

But the illness had taken Mumford before he could see the land he'd given to his family, and the modest homestead had fallen into disrepair.

All that remained of the Blackwell estate were four stone walls. It wasn't what Mungo had in mind, but it would have to do. He would need more stone, but as the soil was rocky he would have to quarry what he needed from the valley.

Mungo would repair the homestead a section at a time; they could live in it while they raised their first-born – Sarra was with child.

The house would be a long house of sorts, in the fashion of his ancestors; he'd separate their dwelling from the barn and build a workshop to make their shoes. In his travels he had seen the architecture of many homes. He did not need a castle or a sprawling palace, but he did not want the ramshackle house of a pauper either. It would be *their* home, with everything they needed, but above all, he wanted to build for Sarra a reminder of her home far away – an arched doorway.

For four months Mungo hauled stones up the hill, carefully placing each one. On one particular cloudless day as Mungo toted the heavy granite up the hill, his wife called for him.

"Mungo!"

Mungo dropped the stone and raced to his love only to find her surrounded by three men. "Good day, Mr Blackwell."

Mungo nodded.

"We have an issue, you see. You are building your home on our land – Toft land."

"I believe you are mistaken." Mungo crossed his arms across his chest. "This is Blackwell land – belonging to my father, Mumford Blackwell, son of MacDonnell Blackwell."

"It is you who are mistaken, Blackwell. This land has laid unclaimed for more than forty years. It's Toft land now."

Mungo was taken aback. "And how is it you claim it as Toft?"

"Because we took it."

Sarra placed her hand on her husband's shoulder.

Mungo reached in his pocket for his can of beeswax. "This is Blackwell land, Toft – the home of my father. It belongs to me. You are a thief."

"We will give you three months to gather your belongings and leave, Blackwell. After three months, we will take back our land," the Toft snarled.

"So be it." Mungo twisted his mustachio and stroked his red beard.

Three months came and went. Mungo continued to build their home, and Sarra's tummy grew into a large round ball. As a gift and a place to birth their baby, he hand-carved her a huge four-poster bed of walnut. He placed upon it a featherbed filled with down given to him by the commander of the Serbian army – the prince and military leader had been very pleased with his tall boots, particularly the bit of a lift Mungo had added to the heel. Mungo had a wool canopy and blanket shipped over from his Scottish homeland in Sarra's favorite color, green. He had asked the weaver to add in a few strands of black to represent his journeys past and white for their days to come. The result was a remarkable plaid that would usher in the new Blackwell.

However, Sarra would not birth her first child in the ornate bed. As Mungo was tending to the sheep on an early October morning before the fog had given way to the sun, his wife screamed.

"Mungo! They're back!"

"Stay away from the windows!" he yelled as he ran to protect his bride. "I'll hang him up if they step a foot closer to our land!"

Suddenly, Sarra's body writhed in agony as an intense pain gripped her. She clutched her rather large front, fell under the threshold of their arched stone doorway, and yelled, "Mungo, the baby!"

"I'll deliver our child when I return." He kissed her on the forehead. "I will always protect you, my Sarra. No son of mine will be born to face the tyranny of dishonest men!" He grabbed his sword, his weapon of choice, and ran out to face the enemy.

In the distance, the oldest of the Toft brothers charged at Mungo, sword in hand. "Your house is mine, Blackwell! This is my land!"

"No, you lopsided mongrel! I own this land and built the house with my bare hands."

"Mungo!" Sarra called, now lying flat on her back with her knees propped. "The baby! It's coming!"

"Then we will fight for it!" the Toft shouted. He thrust his sword at Mungo, but Mungo calmly slid to his left, avoiding the blade.

"This sword," Mungo said, holding it in his left hand and twisting the tip of his mustachio with the other, "was given to me by the pirate king of the mid-Atlantic. Never a man lived that faced its blade."

"Mungoooooo!" Sarra yelled.

"Never a pirate faced me," the Toft snarled.

The two fought – a parrying of calculated back and forth movements. The swords clashed, and then a strike to Mungo's left arm. Mungo passed the sword from his left hand to his right and swung the blade at the face of the man as his lazy brothers stood by and watched – a clean cut to the chin.

Sarra called out in such pain it echoed down through the valley below.

Suddenly, the Toft thrust his sword toward Mungo. Mungo stumbled back but, unfazed by the strike to his arm, he spun around, and with a furious wail, he swung his sword at the neck of the thief.

The Toft clutched his neck and fell to his knees.

Mungo knelt at his side. "I will not take your life, but I will take back my land. You may settle your families peacefully in the valley, but know all of this will forever belong to the Blackwells. Mungo stood and offered his hand to the Toft, who took it and then hobbled off with his brothers.

"Mungoooo!" Sarra yelled.

Mungo ran to her, his left harm hanging in pain by his side. But one arm was sufficient for him to deliver his son – the first of seven sons to be born in the house of Blackwell.

CHAPTER 24

Charlie Price passed through the arched stone doorway of the Coraloo Flea market as he did every weekend, openly defying the constable's advice and Shug's warning. Even with the most recent sale of the Boy Scout patches – which were going to take them comfortably through Christmas – and the sale of the French horn, which was, to his relief, due to be delivered in the next week, he felt numb to it all. His insides were jittery and his normally compartmentalized thoughts were running amuck. He had stayed up late helping Velveteen pick up the crumbs following her book club debacle. Gideon was sorely disappointed, having missed out on a genuine food fight. He asked if they could do it again sometime, to which Velveteen and Charlie, on hands and knees scraping bits and pieces of smashed macaron from the floor, had both replied in unison, "No!"

The storefronts were festooned with glittery garlands and red bows, and a gigantic Christmas tree stood in the middle of the market, to be lit by Shug on Christmas Eve. The Price family had learned of the event at the passing of Granny Blackwell. Apparently, the children had a special performance planned – one Danger claimed was the most important of them all, but he had sworn Gideon to secrecy, saying it would be a surprise for the elder Prices. Traditionally, Granny provided the cookies, but as the cousins and aunts still held strong that their baking capabilities were not up to par, there would be none this year. The aunt who made the ribbon began bottling mulled wine in September for the occasion, and Stephen read passages from *A Christmas Carol.*

It was a night for the Blackwells, but open to anyone that would come – because of the Prices, this was the first year they actually expected anyone from the bottom of the hill to attend.

"Will you go to the lighting?" Velveteen had asked Charlie on their walk home from the vigil.

"Of course, we'll all go, as a family."

"What about –"

"I can't be afraid of him, Velveteen. Coraloo is where we live, and if this is what they do in Coraloo, then it's what the Prices will do."

"You know the Tofts have a separate tree lighting in town, don't you?"

Charlie had laughed. "I guess we will have to go to both. After all, we do live in a Toft house."

With Velveteen's party only three weeks away, preparations were in full swing. It had taken her months to pull off the feat in the city; in their new, simplified life, Charlie was excited to see how the Price Christmas party would come together. Velveteen hadn't mentioned any trips to the city as of late, but he couldn't put aside his unease. The stories of seeing the acquaintances and medical records – they didn't add up.

The market shops were busier than usual, flooded with gift buyers searching out that final special item on their list. However, the vendors were fewer and less eager to draw in customers, most of them actually sitting in folding chairs behind their tables chatting with one another. Charlie was about to examine the contents of what appeared to be a turn-of-the-century tin hatbox when he noticed the constable and his two plain-clothed volunteer officers walking briskly toward Stephen's shop.

As the competition was slim to none today, he headed in their direction, but made a note to come back and attempt to make an offer before he left. A small crowd had formed around the exterior of the bookshop. Charlie scanned the market for Gideon, forgetting for a moment that he was safely in school. He picked up his pace and shouldered his way through the spectators and into the shop. He could see Stephen speaking calmly to the constable and the officers dusting for fingerprints around the counter. Something had been stolen. Charlie craned his neck to get a better look – the glass case with the wooden frame stood open: the Kipling was gone.

Charlie's heart sank as if his own possession had been taken from him. He moved toward the front. Stephen waved, not looking away from the constable. Charlie returned the greeting. Stephen waved again, this time with an agitated motion that told Charlie to go. He understood; Stephen had a lot to deal with. As Charlie turned to walk back out into the market, he found himself once again facing Shug Blackwell.

"Here's your man, officers!" Shug held up his arm and pointed down at Charlie. Stephen had been trying to warn him.

"Now wait a minute!" Charlie shouted over the commotion caused by the officers running toward him. The constable and Stephen Blackwell were not far behind.

"What's going on?" Stephen stepped between Shug and Charlie.

"Stephen, you told me Price had his eye on it, didn't you?"

"I did, but that was only because –"

"Business has been a little slow for you lately, hasn't it, Price? That book would help things out. Buy your pretty little wife a new dress?" There was a smirk, a grin hidden behind the bushy red beard.

"Hold on, hold on," Charlie squared his chest. He had hit Shug before; he wasn't afraid to do it again.

Stephen stepped between them and held his hands up. "Come on now, Shug. You don't really believe he –"

"Roy, we have prints!" an officer called from the back.

Shug nudged his way back in front of Charlie. "Are we going to find your prints on that case, Price?"

Stephen threw his hands in the air. "Shug, enough of this."

"Are we, Price?" Shug pressed.

"Those prints could be anybody's. A thousand people must have passed through here," sighed Stephen. Charlie stood stock still.

"He doesn't deny it."

Unless Innis had wiped it down, his prints were on the case. "It was weeks ago," Charlie looked to Stephen, "I… I just wanted a proper look at it. I should have told you."

"Sounds to me like you should take him in officers. He admits his prints are on the case."

The officers stepped closer.

"I didn't take the book!"

The constable placed his hand on Charlie's back. "Come on Mr Price – let's go down to the station."

Charlie jerked away. "No! I'm not going anywhere. Are you really going to arrest me for nothing a second time?" He turned to fight his way through the audience, but his anger got the best of him. "And another thing, did you really think I was a spy for the Chinese? Does that make any sense to anyone?"

"All right, Mr Price, calm down. We just want to ask you a few questions."

"I won't calm down! You'll lock me up for something ridiculous. What is it this time, the Russian mafia? Or better yet – "

"Charlie," Stephen tried to calm him, "you need to stop. I know you didn't steal the Kipling. Answer his questions, and you'll be home with Velveteen and Gideon before nightfall."

"Oh! I'm just getting started! What if I'm a hired assassin on the hunt for rogue emissaries from Bermuda?" Charlie shouted as he ducked behind an innocent onlooker and pretended to hold out an imaginary gun. "Or, or what if I'm a ninja! Yes! That's it!

I'm a ninja!" Charlie jumped out and began swinging his arm like a sword at the two officers attempting to corner him.

Charlie slid to the side, escaping their grasp. "Is that all you've got? I could do this all day!"

He took off toward the front door, imagining a stealthy somersault past Shug. But two strong hands to the chest stopped him. The constable stood in front of Charlie with arms outstretched. He was much stronger than Charlie would have guessed. Charlie's heart raced as he attempted to slow his breathing, catching both his breath and his sanity.

"Let's not go frightening the tourists, Mr Price. We have a few questions to help with the investigation and then you will be on your way."

Charlie backed away. "I'm not going with you!"

The constable stepped closer. "Mr Price, under the statutes which prohibit obstructing an officer in an investigation you are under arrest." The officers surrounded Charlie. "You have the right to remain silent." The constable pulled Charlie's hands behind his back and placed him in handcuffs. "Anything you say can and will be used against you in a court of law."

The curious onlookers parted. Charlie had half a mind to bark at the tourist who said, "I believe he's gone bonkers!"

Maybe he was going mental. Maybe he did steal the Kipling… no, he had only wanted a peek, and that was weeks ago. Truthfully, he hadn't even thought about the book since.

Innis Wilkinson pushed her cart of cleaning goods past them – her scissors remained secure around her neck. *What makes a person do such a strange thing?* He laughed, prompting a warning eye from the constable who held tight to his arm. Five minutes ago he had attempted to assassinate Shug with his finger gun and nearly chopped off the heads of the officers with his ninja arm sword. Innis Wilkinson's scissors had nothing on Charlie Price's rant in the bookstore. *I think the Blackwells are rubbing off on me.*

On his way out, he caught a glimpse of the tin hatbox, unmoved and unsold. He doubted he would be back the next day to purchase it. Like all of the other unpurchased items dotting the vendors' tables, there was a time when it represented provision and possibility, a hope for a different life, a simple life, but now, for the first time, he could see it was merely a place to hide from his failure.

"Move along, Mr Price."

Charlie didn't argue this time. He didn't have the fight in him anymore.

"Oh, Charlie!" Velveteen shouted as she pushed through the wooden door of the law enforcement office. She was immediately silenced and asked to have a seat by the front door until they were done processing the prisoner – at the word *prisoner* she ran to a row of chairs designated "Waiting", crying uncontrollably. Charlie wanted to run after her, to tell her everything would be okay – he had told her that all too often in the past year. She would know what had happened soon enough. Not much was a secret in Coraloo. He'd been accused of stealing the one thing he had wanted more than anything else; not only that, he had entered into what most likely appeared to be a schizophrenic battle with the two elderly volunteer officers of the Coraloo police department.

Charlie slouched in the same hard metal chair he had sat in the last time he had been there. Nothing had changed. Portraits of the past seven Coraloo constables hung in a row on the wall. Charlie studied the photographs to find the man in front of him. The constable was slightly older than the man in the photograph – gray hairs, wrinkles above his eyebrows, and added weight around the chin. This man had served more years as constable than Gideon had lived.

Charlie leaned over to watch what the officer was writing, and then glanced over his shoulder to Velveteen, who was putting her sunglasses over her tear-filled eyes. She had hung on this far – made it through the loss of their period townhouse, their fashionable lifestyle, and the lunacy of every day since their move to Coraloo. *Hang on Vee. Don't give up on me yet.*

"Name?" The constable studied Charlie over rectangular spectacles.

"You know my name."

"Name?"

Charlie sighed. "Charlie Price."

"Address?"

"Thirty-one Odenbon, Coraloo."

"Right, old lady Toft's house." The constable scribbled something on the form in front of him. The room was quiet, except for the occasional sniffle from Velveteen. The cells were empty, and the phone did not ring. "Occupation?"

Charlie leaned forward in the chair. "Do we have to go over this again?"

"So you're still at it?"

"Yes."

The constable scribbled some more, set down his pen, and then looked sternly into the tired eyes of Charlie Price. "How's it working out for you?"

"What?"

"Are you doing well? Taking care of Mrs Price? Are you happy?"

What kind of police station is this? The constable's questions sounded more like something he would have gotten from a therapist in the city than a man who had just arrested him. Charlie didn't know which question to answer first. "We do all right. We simplified our life; that makes it easier."

"But are you happy?"

A lump formed in Charlie's throat. He hadn't cried since he was a child, and he didn't plan on doing it today. Behind him,

Velveteen had picked up a very outdated edition of *TV Today*, which she was now flipping through. They never watched television anymore. It was a pastime the two of them partook in nearly every night in the city – in their former life. After they'd said goodnight to Gideon, they would curl up on the couch together. Charlie struggled to remember what they watched; it was more about the time together than the show. Comedies, they liked the comedies – how they laughed at the people who worked in *The Workplace*. If those antics actually took place in an office setting, they would all be fired, but it was funny, and it made her laugh. He missed those nights. And the mornings… Velveteen woke early to see Charlie off to work. She would kiss him goodbye and wave until he was out of sight. Was their old life really so bad?

"Mr Price? Is everything all right?"

"I didn't steal the Kipling."

"Well, somebody did." The constable stood up and filed Charlie's notes in an old wooden filing cabinet behind the desk. Charlie started to stand. "Sit back down. Right now, you're all we've got to go on. Until we run the prints –"

"Mine will be there. I wanted to get a better look. Like I said, it was weeks ago."

"Why didn't you ask Stephen?"

"I don't know… caught up in a moment? But I didn't touch the book – just the case. I wanted to, but I didn't."

The constable positioned himself on the corner of the desk. "Mr Price, I've been at this desk for twenty years. With the exception of a couple of scuffles between the Tofts and the Blackwells, and maybe having to pull a drunken idiot out of the Beaver's Beard, you're the most interesting thing that's happened around here. But, I'm not convinced –"

"Sir, I'm not a thief…" The word made him think of the feud played out between Danger and Gideon in his living room the night Stephen, Clover, and family came over for dinner – an epic battle between a Toft and a Blackwell.

"I'm not finished yet, Mr Price. I'm not convinced you've got yourself together as much as you're letting on." Charlie didn't feel like talking about his personal life anymore. "You're going anti-clockwise, and I believe you know it, don't you?" What was it with this town? The constable was sounding like Granny with all her talk of the right and wrong shoes. "I can't keep you, Mr Price, not without any real piece of evidence. However, I will give you a call if something looks suspicious."

Charlie held up his cuffed hands as far as the bracelets would permit. "So why arrest me?"

"I needed a reason to get you out of there and attacking my two officers didn't do you any favors. Mind you, you've given Everett and Jasper story fodder for at least a year. It's my duty to keep this town and its people safe, Mr Price. Shug would have laid you out. Besides, you needed to cool off. At the rate you're going, you may do more harm to yourself and these people than you realize."

"I don't understand."

"The Blackwells don't normally welcome newcomers, Mr Price. But most of them have taken a liking to you."

"Shug must not have gotten the memo."

"Shug's full of wind. He's not the whole family. They don't need any more loss. Are you following me?"

"Not really."

The constable laughed. "I have a feeling, one way or the other, you will before long." He scooted down from his perch and unlocked the cuffs holding Charlie's hands together. "Stay away from the market for a couple of days, at least until we figure this out."

Charlie offered his hand. The constable shook it. "Thanks."

Upon seeing movement from Charlie, Velveteen rushed to him, wrapped both arms around his neck, and spluttered a series of questions as they walked toward the door.

He stopped and turned back to the constable, unable to shake off a nagging question.

"Excuse me, Constable? Are you a Toft or a Blackwell?"

The Constable peered over his spectacles. "Blackwell. Mr Price…"

Charlie took a step toward him. "Yes?"

"… it's a long way down the hill. If you're pushed, you'll find yourself lying in a pile of yourself at the bottom. But if you choose to walk down it with your head held high, you'll see the possibility in front of you. Hold your head high, Mr Price. The hill hasn't got the best of you yet."

Charlie forced a smile.

Velveteen leaned in to him. "What was that all about?"

"I'm not sure, but I think it was somehow supposed to make me feel better."

"Do you?"

"No."

CHAPTER 25

"Where should I put these?" Charlie stood at the entrance to the kitchen with a tray of cream cheese and ham stuffed mini-Yorkshire puddings in his hands, while Velveteen hurried from one side of the counter to the other, stirring, mixing, and spreading.

"How do I look?" She wiped her hands on her vintage-modern pink and blue apron. In the past month, it had acquired a fair amount of staining. Velveteen called the smudges of grease and splatters of chocolate "badges of honor" – proof she could finally cook.

"Exhausted, but as lovely as ever." He stole a kiss on her cheek as she whisked by him.

"Will you light the candles, Charlie? The timer on the stove should buzz shortly. The glasses are out. The mini-Wellingtons need to be warmed, and the tree! Oh Charlie, please turn on the tree lights!" Velveteen skipped through the Toft cottage arranging and placing.

Charlie's phone beeped. He pulled the handheld device from his pocket and checked the screen. He read the message. The French horn had arrived in one piece; however, the buyer was concerned about its authenticity. Charlie had done extensive research and had even listed in the description that the horn had no papers of identification. He told himself he wasn't worried and would deal with it first thing Monday morning. But a shadow of fear crept over him. What if the buyer wanted a refund?

The little cottage was decorated in an assortment of holly and ivy. Hand-dyed ribbon from Sorcha Blackwell's shop accented the garlands. Velveteen's signature scent for the home was replaced by one of Aunt Moira's homemade clove, orange, and cinnamon candles. Perry Como's "White Christmas" played in the background as tiny puffs of snow fell outside the windows.

"Velveteen, the…" He sniffed the small pieces of bread piled high with turkey, cheese, bacon bits, and some sort of white sauce. "What are these?"

"Baby Hot Browns! Aren't they adorable! Oh, are you still holding those? Set them anywhere for now." She flopped down on the sofa. "I'll find a spot for them in a moment. Let me rest, for just a minute."

Charlie set the tray on the coffee table beside the sweets. "You don't look well. Why don't you go upstairs and rest? We have an hour before the party starts."

"I'm fine, Charlie, really." Velveteen laid the back of her head against the couch and closed her eyes.

He rested his hand on the side of her cheek as she breathed, an inhaling and exhaling of peaceful controlled breaths. Despite her apparent exhaustion she was simply beautiful.

Charlie picked up the tray and relocated it to the kitchen where Velveteen had already lined up a few dips. The timer sounded from the stove. He quickly flipped the switch to shut it off and removed the golden brown baked Brie from the oven. It was a masterpiece.

A copy of the invitation lay beside the stove. On the front she had sketched a picture of their cottage and had it copied onto card stock paper; inside she'd handwritten each invite in detailed scrolling letters:

Please join us for our
Christmas Party
December 22nd at 6:30 PM
31 Odenbon St. Coraloo
Regrets only to
Velveteen

She'd had the foresight to reserve six rooms at the bed and breakfast for the acquaintances making the trip. Charlie didn't know whom to expect. He had invited Stephen and Clover, telling them it would be okay if they brought Danger. Gideon would enjoy having a friend for the first time at one of their Christmas parties. He had also phoned the constable, and not knowing if he was married, encouraged him to bring a guest. He had considered inviting the entire Blackwell clan but feared they would not have enough space to fit everyone. Velveteen said she had only sent out twelve invitations, and while she was disappointed seven of the invitees regretted they had prior engagements, five had accepted. That left one extra room, by Charlie's calculations.

The phone rang. He tried to answer it before it woke Velveteen, but she'd moved from the couch, presumably upstairs "fixing herself up" a bit. Ten minutes ago he could have marched around the living room banging a pot with a wooden spoon and she would not have awakened.

"I've got it!" he called up to her.

"This is Charlie Price." Charlie listened to the masculine voice on the other end. "Who did you say is calling?... You want to speak to my wife?… I'm sorry, could you repeat your name again? Your room?"

"Who is it, Charlie? Please don't tell me someone has cancelled on us?" she called down from the second floor.

Charlie didn't answer her. His heart raced and beads of sweat formed on his brow. "And Mr Walker, what business do you have with my wife?… You can't say… But you are here at the bed and breakfast for the Christmas party, yes? Are you sure she didn't mention a party?" Charlie tried to stop his mind from going where it had gone the first time she had said she was going to the city. Heat rose to his face. "And you know her well?… I see. You have an appointment with her tomorrow? Have her phone you? No, I have a better idea, why don't you talk to her yourself, Mr Walker. Do you have plans tonight? There's this party…" Charlie went into autopilot as he calmly told the mystery man the essential details, then hung up and felt the sickening truth settle in the pit of his stomach.

How could Velveteen do this to him? Was their marriage a facade? Maybe she was waiting for him to lose it completely before she ran off into the arms of Mr Walker.

No. Think on what's true, Charlie, he tried to remind himself. *Velveteen loves you. If she were going to run off with another man, she would have done it long before Coraloo.* But he couldn't stop his thoughts returning once again to her unexplained trips to the city. It was all starting to add up in a way he never could have imagined…

"Charlie, who was that?" she called again.

Guests would be arriving within the hour, along with Mr Walker.

He could not answer her. He could barely speak. He should confront her now and get it over with. "I can't believe it; I just can't believe it," he mumbled.

"Believe what?" Velveteen Price stood at the top of the stairs in a sparkling red party dress looking as lovely as she did on the day he had married her, but he could not look her in the eye.

"It's a surprise." Bitterness welled up inside of him as he plotted to expose his wife's infidelity in front of the acquaintances.

She squealed with joy. He wanted to throw up.

Stephen and Clover were the first to arrive – ten minutes early. Velveteen assumed when Charlie said he wanted to invite guests that he had meant Stephen, but she had not expected Danger to run in after them.

"I hope it's all right." Clover allowed her husband to remove her coat. "Stephen insisted it was okay if we brought him."

"It's perfectly fine." Velveteen didn't tell the whole truth. It wasn't really fine. Her parties were meant to entertain her friends – adults. She would have to find a way to explain to Charlie that if they allowed one child this year, next year they would have to invite the rest of them, and then the Christmas party would turn into a nursery school for the Blackwells, potentially making the other guests uncomfortable. However, at least she wouldn't have to constantly correct Gideon for slouching and moping the entire night. Gideon would never mope around Danger.

The next to arrive were the Lawsons and the Baileys. Velveteen was thrilled they had R.S.V.P.'d. Alice Lawson and Sandra Bailey were not only prominent members of the garden club and historical society but were also charter members of her book club in the city.

Alice leaned in to kiss Velveteen on the cheek. "You look stunning, Velveteen! Absolutely stunning. You're glowing! And let me guess, the dress is couture. You must tell us who you are wearing!"

Velveteen twirled. Charlie frowned.

"A girl must never give away her sources." What Velveteen really did not want to tell them was she had bought it at the market. One of the uncles had given her a great deal on it. The musty smell she had fought with over the past two weeks made her certain that it was vintage, but she was sure Sandra and Alice had never heard of this common brand.

Sandra's eyes examined every inch of visible space. "It's fabulous, Velveteen. I mean the whole place is positively stunning. Such charm and so unassuming."

Velveteen disguised her delight with a bashful smile.

"I can hardly believe you did it," Alice chimed in. "We all said you couldn't do it, but here you are."

Sandra leaned in close to Velveteen. "To be honest, Velveteen, we heard Charlie was struggling… financially."

Velveteen glanced over to where Clover was carrying the cherry trifle in from the kitchen. She was about to tell her where to set it, but Clover carefully and strategically shifted the trays of sweets to set the layered dessert decoratively in the middle.

It's exactly where I would have set it.

"Who did you use? Brookside House and Associates?"

Velveteen had used the talented decorating group to overhaul Gideon's nursery. "Actually, I did it myself."

Both of the ladies gasped as if Velveteen had told them their furs were synthetic. There was another knock on the door.

Velveteen opened the door to find the constable standing with a woman she had never seen before; however, by the look of her make-up, the lady on his arm had been solicited by Sylvia Toft. "Come in, please." Velveteen could not believe Charlie had invited the constable and some woman that nobody knew.

"Glad you could make it," Charlie called, making his way through the party to his guests.

"I'd like to introduce you to my… date, Margarette Toft."

A Toft? That accounted for her choice of cosmetics. But she was certain Charlie had said the constable was a Blackwell. A Blackwell with a Toft? Velveteen briefly considered hiding the desserts, then hugged the lady casually and kissed her on the cheek. The pungent fragrance of rose oil and peppermint nearly knocked her backwards and made her stomach a tad unsettled. "It's a pleasure to meet you, Ms Toft." She passed a concerned glance toward Charlie, but he didn't acknowledge her.

Velveteen tilted her head toward her husband. "Interesting choice in guests, Charlie. Was that my surprise?"

"No." He fought the urge to laugh spitefully and say, *If only you were so lucky!* Here she was flitting around a party he had paid for. He had paid for all of it – the townhouse in the city, her car, jewelry, and expensive clothes. Even in Coraloo, it wasn't any different – he struggled to make it, and she spent it. The doorbell could not ring soon enough. He couldn't wait to get this over with. What would follow he did not know. But he'd already decided he would deal with the fallout of the wrecked marriage as he had dealt with his dismissal from Heritage Financial: he'd regroup and start over. But what about Gideon? Would there be shared custody? He'd call his attorney in the morning and figure out how to pay him another day.

There was laughter and eating as Bing Crosby crooned "I'll Be Home for Christmas" in the background. Velveteen strolled the room in her highest heeled shoes, offering her guests red velvet macarons that perfectly matched her dress. She was in her element, accepting the accolades of the acquaintances and the gratitude of the Blackwells. Her cheeks were flushed from the warmth the fireplace added to the room. Charlie said he had a surprise, but she had one too. It didn't even worry her that Stephen was talking to Mr Bailey. She had already had enough of the acquaintances to last her the rest of her life. It was a mistake; she shouldn't have invited them. Charlie was only half right – it wasn't that they didn't know the acquaintances anymore; they were exactly as she remembered them. It was that the acquaintances no longer knew her.

The doorbell rang. Velveteen sauntered over to answer it, excited to welcome their next guest. She smiled wide and threw open the door.

"Mrs Price." The man in the tan fedora took off his hat as the winter's snow fell on his thin gray hair. She stared at him – dumbstruck by the presence of the man in front of her.

"What are you doing here?"

"Your husband invited me. You decided to tell him early? I thought the three of us were meeting tomorrow. He's oddly collected considering what little you told me about his situation, don't you think? When we first met, you said he would be upset. But he insisted. I brought you –"

Charlie Price, upon seeing who had arrived at the door and that a hushed conversation was taking place between the man and Velveteen, rushed to his side and ushered him across the threshold. "How rude of my *wife* to leave you outside in the cold." He placed an eye-narrowing emphasis upon the word *wife*.

"Charlie, this is –"

"I know who he is, Velveteen. Ladies and gentlemen, may I have your attention!" Charlie made his way to the eight-foot evergreen standing near their fireplace with a glass in his trembling right hand. Velveteen stepped up beside him and prepared for the toast he made every year at their party. His face was solemn, and he could not look at his wife. "Mr Walker, will you join us please?" His voice was sharp and cold. "I have a surprise for you all, an announcement of truth you all should know."

Surely he doesn't know. Velveteen's heart raced. The color drained from under her perfectly applied rouge. This was not how she planned for him to find out. She had rehearsed the speech every day in the mirror from the moment he had agreed to her having the party. At first it had been about the money – she didn't want him to worry, but then Granny had convinced her to tell him, and what a better way than in front of all the people they loved – and a few she was now regretting inviting. Mr Walker would fill in the details the next day so Charlie wouldn't have to make the trip to the city – he wasn't ready to go back.

"My beautiful wife…" Charlie took his glass and threw it into the fire. He glared at Velveteen. "Is having an…" He couldn't say it. The guests were silent, beginning to sense something was very wrong about the scene playing out in front of them. "What do you want, Velveteen?" he snapped. Pent-up frustration from the past two years and his new discovery of her infidelity was like venom on his lips. "Is it the money? Is that it? I'm sure Walker will take good care of you. I didn't think you to be the type that would go for an older man, but I guess if the pockets are big enough –"

"Stop!" She couldn't choke out the words. Tears streamed from her eyes.

"I know, Velveteen! I know all about it! Now everyone else does too!" He continued his rant as if it were only the two of them. "Your trips to the city, the lies, the phone calls. Well, here he is!"

"You spoiled it, Charlie. You spoiled it," she whimpered.

"Are you kidding me? Are you still worried about your stupid party?"

"Charlie, I'm…"

"What? Are you sorry?" He shoved his hands into the pockets of his suit and pushed through the guests.

"I'm pregnant!" she cried.

He stopped. Was she telling him she was carrying another man's baby, or… his mind spun with the possibility. Clover and the now less-mysterious, but most likely highly confused, Mr Walker consoled his wife. The expressions of the guests were a mix of delight and concern.

Velveteen pulled from the arms of Clover. "Don't you remember, Charlie? Mr Walker delivered Gideon. We're having a baby, Charlie. I brought him to Coraloo to see if he could deliver our baby here… So you wouldn't have to go back."

Mr Walker reached inside his black suit coat and removed a small white bottle. He handed it to Velveteen. She took the bottle of prescribed prenatal vitamins and clutched them in her hand. "Your husband insisted I bring them to you. I figured you had told him. Thanks for inviting me to the party, Mr Price, but I think with all the confusion I should be heading back to the bed and breakfast. Mrs Price, I'll talk with Dr Toft and let you know."

Charlie went to Velveteen, but she pushed away. "You spoiled it, Charlie. It was my Christmas gift to you. Happiness, Charlie. It's what I wanted to give you for Christmas. But you spoiled it."

Clover led Velveteen away from the gathering and toward the stairs. Velveteen shivered and shook; her lip quivered – she had never been so humiliated in her entire life. Not even *The Rooning* had left her in such a state, but before they arrived at the second level, Danger appeared on the top step with his arms outstretched and a wide grin spread across his face.

"May I have your attention, please?"

"Now is not the time," Clover hissed.

"It's okay Mom, this is the best part. Grab your coats –"

"Danger Blackwell, go back –"

"And join us in the back garden for the funeral of Gideon Price! Everyone is invited!"

In front of everyone, Velveteen, already sobbing, crumbled into Clover's arms.

"No one told me the child had passed," one of the acquaintances that had shown up fashionably late whispered to Alice Lawson.

"What a tragedy! It all *just* came out: an affair and a baby. I didn't catch who the father was, but it's no wonder Velveteen looks like she has aged ten years."

"She does look awful, doesn't she?"

"Are they having the funeral tonight? That's most odd."

"Maybe it's what they do in the country."

"Excuse me, ladies." Stephen Blackwell, overhearing the gossip developing between the two, stepped in. "Gideon is alive and well. The boys were pretending."

"Pretending!" Sandra Bailey gasped. "How horrid!"

Stephen didn't try to explain. Instead, he reached for a tray of sweets and stuck it in the middle of the acquaintances. "Dessert?"

Charlie Price could only see one thing – the front door, guarded by a winding labyrinth of whispering onlookers casting concerned and questioning glances his way. He took a step. *A baby.* And another. *I humiliated her.*

"Hey old chap!" Howard Lawson stepped directly in front of him. "How is life in the country treating you?"

"I need to step outside, Howard."

"I hear Heritage is in desperate need. Rumor has it they regret letting you go. And with a new one on the way, and by the looks of this place, I'd say you need them like they need you."

"I, um, I really need to step out for a minute, Howard."

"If you're ever looking to come back our way, you should at least see what's available. I heard they're paying high dollar." Howard's words were going in one ear and the other. Charlie loosened his tie. He couldn't breathe.

Right now Charlie Price didn't care about Heritage Financial, high dollars, or anything else for that matter. Velveteen had caught him when he fell from his career. He didn't know who was going to catch him now. Charlie turned the front door handle of the Toft house and stepped out into the snowy night air of Coraloo.

CHAPTER 26

The sign remained: NO DOGS OR TOFTS – GRANNY BITES! Charlie stepped inside the empty market, hardly knowing where he was – or who he was. Granny was gone, but the market had continued on. If he were gone, would life just move on? The thought was morbid, but it wasn't the first time he'd traveled this road. Charlie had felt strained since the day he graduated high school and entered into what everyone said should be the best years of his life. But university exams were harder than anything he'd experienced, the expectations greater – and then it was off into the world... Find a job, get married, have children. *Lose your job, lose your wife, and make a fool out of yourself at a Christmas party.*

The usual aromas of leather and lavender were replaced with the smells of cold stone and pine. It was a Saturday. Open – but closed for the evening. The usually full vendors' area was empty – no sellers, no blanketed tables hiding the next day's profit. *Strange.* Vendors didn't take down until Sunday. *Holiday hours?* Charlie dragged his feet to the bench in front of Stephen's shop. He had been so close, the closest he had been to the Kipling since *The Rooning*, but now it was gone – stolen and most likely sold. *Everything is gone.*

He cradled his head in his hands, his mind awhirl with the events of the past few hours. What had he done? A baby? He laughed into the openness of the market, his voice echoing through the dark rafters, and then he cried. His chest heaved with heavy sobs as tears coursed down his face. He wanted to throw something – no, he wanted to throw *himself* right down a flight of stairs to see if he would land on his feet.

Charlie Price land on his feet? Who was he kidding? Nothing had gone to plan. They were supposed to forget about their old life – and his mistake that had jolted them out of it – and move on to something new and simple. *Simplicity.* He didn't even know what the word meant. All this time he had tried so hard to live differently. Why? He knew why, but he fought the temptation to dwell on it. But the truth was too strong. He wanted it all – the best of both worlds. He wanted the money without the constraining society, the work without the long hours away from his family; he wanted to be successful but not have to sacrifice his life for it. Sure, the Toft house was great; Velveteen had made it…

Velveteen. He could picture her – his beautiful wife standing at the top of the stairs with the red party dress she'd purchased at the market. There were no tears or sunglasses covering her shining eyes.

"Don't you love it?" she asked, holding up the red taffeta dress. "I promise I didn't pay too much. Do you know where I got it?"

Charlie had no idea. "The city?" He was agitated, not really understanding why she kept going back without him.

"Of course not, silly, I bought it at the market! Sorcha insisted I look in the boutique, but you know how I feel about wearing other people's clothing. I went, just to be kind. But don't you know, the clothing is exquisite! Vintage, Charlie… Vintage! Sorcha insisted her brother steams every piece before he puts it out, so I wasn't completely put off trying on the dress. Oh Charlie, it was the perfect fit! So I had to purchase it. Won't it be wonderful for the party?"

There was a lightness about her – a love of things that seemed utterly ridiculous to him, but made her smile. "All you need is a tiara."

He thought about purchasing one for her as a Christmas present, but opted for a blanket she had circled in a catalog he'd found lying on the coffee table.

"Charlie Price, I'm not royalty."

"But don't you have a relative who's a duke?"

She slapped him playfully on the arm, kissed him on the mouth, and said, "Thank you so much for loving me, Charlie Price."

Of course if he'd been in his right mind he would have known Velveteen would never seek out another man, especially not because of money – after all, she'd been the driving force in their quest for simplicity. And now here she was, ecstatic over a second-hand – or *vintage*, as she had described it – dress. Not to mention the fact that she refused to watch soap operas solely because of all the extramarital relations... *"It's tacky, Charlie. I can't keep up with them all. For the love of marriage, pick one!"*

And a baby. How did he not notice...? Maybe he had. He had to admit some of her clothing looked a bit more snug than he remembered, but was that surprising with all of her recent baking and sampling? However, there was the night he had gone to the Beaver's Beard with Stephen and came home to find her mixing chocolate chunk brownie batter. She'd told him to go on to bed. When he woke the following morning, expecting to find a container of brownies, he only found a dirtied mixing bowl in the sink.

"Didn't you make brownies last night?" he asked.

"Just batter."

"Oh, I see. You pre-made the batter for –"
"I ate it all, Charlie."

She hadn't said another word, but went straight to the sink, washed the bowl, and went about planning for the book club.

Charlie Price smiled through his pain at the memory of her. But as he lay down on the bench and closed his eyes, sorrow washed over him. She would never forgive him. His marriage was over. In less than five minutes he had sabotaged over a decade of marriage.

"Get up, Price."

Charlie's head throbbed. He adjusted his eyes to the dim glow produced by the night-time illumination of the storefronts.

"You look like a tramp."

Charlie focused in on the Oakeshott XIV reaching towards him.

Shug's breath smelled of whiskey. "You can't sleep here, Price."

"Sleep?"

"You've been out for about an hour."

Charlie pulled his body upright. "Do you have your cronies keeping an eye on me?"

"I've had my eye on you from the day you stepped into Coraloo, Price."

The red-bearded man towering over him came into focus.

"What are you doing here? Haven't you learned by now –"

"I'm not in the mood, Shug. Let me have a few minutes by myself, and I'll be out of your way."

"Do I need to call the constable, Price? Or are you going to make this easy and get out?"

"I didn't steal the book. And I'm not a spy, and I don't plan on corrupting your market. I just want to –"

"Just want to what? Pick? Good luck, Price. Come Monday, there will be no more of that."

"What did you do? Kick out the vendors?"

"Aw, Price, you don't think I'm that cold-hearted, do you? I gave them a nice little notice and a handful of chocolate doubloons!" The beast of a man chuckled, spewing his rank spittle on Charlie's lap. "You can't mix oil and vinegar, Price. Your type and ours don't belong together. I've got plans, Price, and you're not in them. See you around… but not in my market."

Shug Blackwell walked away, leaving Charlie feeling as if he had been shoved down the hill. It was done – his life had come full circle and was on repeat, but this time he would not be bringing Gideon and Velveteen with him. Velveteen had once said she would go anywhere with him, but not this time; there was nowhere else to go.

Charlie forced himself to stand but stumbled on his own defeat past the bookshop and toward the entrance. *Forgive yourself.* Stephen's words echoed in his mind. *Who do you have faith in?* Hadn't this whole ordeal – packing up Velveteen and Gideon and shoving them into the middle of his great big plan – been some kind of act of faith? A belief in redemption? But where had it gotten him? He couldn't forgive the mess he'd made. There was no future or forgiveness for him here. The town and its flea market no longer had anything to offer Charlie Price. He stumbled across the arched threshold into the icy wind blowing up from the little town. It was time to say goodbye to Coraloo.

He trudged on, feeling weak against the wintery force that fought to hold him back. He wanted to let go, to stop struggling, to give in. He held his arms out and tried to scream, but the rushing blasts of cold air caught his breath and threw him on his back. The stone street beneath him was hard and unforgiving. He could stand if he wanted to, but he didn't.

"Charlie!" Someone called his name, but he didn't respond. He didn't want to be found.

Charlie closed his eyes and envisioned Velveteen sitting at a table outside of Francine's on 5th. It was the day Velveteen had told him she was pregnant for the first time. She had ordered a custom-printed tea bag – the label read, *I'm not TEAsing, we're having a baby!* On the morning she decided to share her news – having waited two weeks after her own discovery and initial visit to Dr Walker – she asked Charlie to meet her for tea, which he found odd considering it was a Saturday, a day they usually spent together anyway, and he didn't usually drink tea.

She wore sunglasses and a pink dress. The summer sun illuminated her golden highlights. She was more giddy than usual – talking all about the townhouse they had looked at the day before.

"Don't you think it might be too big? It's just the two us."

She smiled and glanced at his tea for the third time since he'd sat down. He'd much rather have a coffee, but she'd ordered the Earl Grey before he arrived.

"It's our dream home, and you know you like it more than you're letting on. After all, it does have a study. Can't you imagine the Kipling sitting on the shelf?"

He laughed. "You know exactly what to say, don't you?"

"Charlie Price, don't be rude. How's your tea?"

"Fine?"

She had leaned in curiously, pretending to read what she already knew. "What does that say?"

"Earl Grey."

"You didn't even read it, Charlie!"

He saw the black lettering on the tiny white tag in his mind as clearly as the day he had read it. He had read it twice, thinking, That's a fun way to announce a pregnancy. Then he saw her face, full of delight and hope for the future, and the reality hit.

"You're… no we… a baby? We're having a baby?"

She stood up and flattened out the waistline of her dress. "Do you see my bump?"

He didn't. And he wouldn't for another three months. But he did see her joy, the same joy that was in that moment winning the battle against his practicality – life would have to work differently, and he would have to work harder from now on.

Charlie blinked and pulled the blanket up around his neck. He blinked again and allowed his eyes to focus on the room. He was home. But how did he get here? The last thing he remembered was lying in the cold thinking he never wanted to wake up. He sat up and tried to figure out what was going on. The living room was dark and silent. Remnants of the Christmas party – trays of crumbs, plates of half-eaten tartlets, and the fragrance of burnt wood from a fire, the embers still glowing faintly – occupied the space. But Velveteen didn't believe in *We'll take care of it tomorrow*; she was more of the *Get it done so the house will look spectacular in the morning* mindset.

She wouldn't leave a mess. But he had. The reality of the night before invaded his thoughts – the misunderstandings, the shame, his public humiliation, Velveteen's embarrassment… How could he have been so stupid, so heartless, when all she was trying to do was surprise him – surprise everyone – with a baby?

"Vee!" His voice cracked as he called her name. "Gideon!" No response. He jumped from his bed on the couch and banged his shin on the coffee table, welcoming the shooting pain as confirmation that he was, in fact, still here. He leapt up the stairs, two at a time. "Vee! Gideon!"

They were gone.

Charlie ran back down the stairs – sliding more than stepping – and dove for his phone. His hands shook, his mind constructing the worst possible scenario. He would never see them again. He scrolled through his recent calls and dialed her number. "Pick up, pick up, please pick up."

"*Hello –*"

"Vee!"

"*You've reached me! I am terribly sorry I am unable to speak with you at the moment. Please leave your contact information at the tone. Have a lovely day!*"

"Vee, it's me. I…" Why would she listen? "I… Um… I need… I… I need you." He couldn't let them go. He searched his contacts again.

Charlie paced the floor as he waited for Stephen Blackwell to answer the call. Stephen had been at their party; he would know what happened after Charlie left. "Come on Stephen, come on."

"Hello."

"Stephen! It's Charlie… My family… They're gone. I don't know where they are. I need your help. Have you seen them?"

"Charlie, it's okay; they're at the market. I think you should get here as fast as you can."

Charlie located his shoes from the night before – neatly paired at the end of the sofa but badly scraped, and one of the soles had pulled from the leather. He grabbed his coat and let the door to their Toft house slam behind him. In the distance, through the morning fog, he could see the Coraloo Flea Market at the top of the hill, like a beacon. He paused a moment, took a deep breath, and ran.

CHAPTER 27

1929

Following Mungo Blackwell's epic battle with the pygmies and before the birth of their first son, on a visit of the shoe-cobbling nature to Dokabar, the sheikh had invited Mungo and Sarra to view his collection of exotic birds. One bird in particular caught the eye of Sarra – the Doka bird of Dokabar. The bird's eyes glowed emerald green, and its feathers changed from deep garnet to blackish purple when it became too warm.

While it was its beauty that caught her eye, it was its song that captured her heart. It is said the Doka bird will only sing for love, and this particular bird had yet to sing, as the sheikh of Dokabar was only twelve and still of the mindset that love and kissing and all that stuff was quite disgusting. But when Mungo and Sarra stepped in front of the bird, it opened its beak and sang, *Coralooooo, coralooo.* Each time it sang, the roll of the *r* became stronger, and it held its gentle tune longer.

From that moment on the word became a term of endearment between the two – a gentle whisper in the other's ear – *coraloo*; a playful luring – *coraloo.* When the Blackwell children were small, they would play and sing songs about their parents' funny word. "I Love You, Coraloo" was sung every year at Christmastime. When it became evident the family had grown so large they had formed their own little town on the hill, with the Tofts spreading out in the valley below, and settlers passing through finding it a lovely place to dwell – it was time to give the town a name. And so, it was agreed, a place full of the love of the Blackwells should carry the song of the Doka bird – Coraloo.

Word of the upcoming event had spread far beyond the growing hillside town of Coraloo weeks before the day of Mungo Blackwell's funeral. Mungo had invited the whole town – most of which were his children and his grandchildren, and even a few great grandchildren. Among the guests were the barber who kept Mungo supplied in his favorite brand of beard wax – The Queen's Nomad – the priest he had asked to give the eulogy, the innkeeper and his wife, and the doctor.

The morning of his funeral, Mungo Blackwell woke early. A hint of damp hung in the air from the night's rain. He had hoped for a sunny day, but it was no matter – rain or shine, he would get the answer he needed. In the barn he had built forty years before, a black coffin made from the same walnut from which he had made their bed hung from the ceiling. At one time it had sat on a rafter, but as the children recognized it as a desirable place for hide-and-go-seek, Mungo had moved it to an even less accessible location.

He slowly lowered the coffin, wondering who would have lowered it had he passed before his funeral. He slid off the lid and ran his hand through the yellow wheat berries that filled it. He would send his boys, but not his oldest, for it later. His eldest, Menzies, refused to partake of the event. As the most superstitious of the now thirteen children, he feared God would strike them all down dead for partaking in the funeral of a man who had not yet died. Menzies instead opted to stand guard over the Blackwell estate with the dog.

Mungo stood outside the door of his home and greeted each of his guests. A crowd was forming in the distance – onlookers, he assumed, curious Tofts who wanted to witness the gates of heaven opening up to smite the Blackwells. Mungo would not have it. In the brown leather boots he had cobbled for the day, he marched to the horde of valley dwellers and with a raised fist shouted, "Cowards are the men that won't try what has never been done!" And then he turned to leave.

"You invited all of Coraloo, Blackwell!" A familiar voice emerged from the gathering. As the years had passed the town on the hill and one in the valley had experienced such growth no one was quite sure where the Blackwells began and the Tofts ended.

"Never a Toft stepped foot in the home of a Blackwell."

"And never a Blackwell in the home of a Toft," the old Toft snarled.

"You may listen from outside."

Mungo then entered his funeral, set up in the entertaining quarters of his home, sat on the front row with Sarra, who was fully supportive of his endeavor, and waited for his coffin to arrive. There was a contagion of Toft gasps outside, as two of his sons along with a grandson and a son-in-law arrived carrying the coffin to the front of the room, where they sat it down on a table Mungo had made especially for the occasion.

The boys sat and Mungo stood. He carefully slid the lid off of the coffin and proceeded to distribute a handful of the exotic Moroccan wheat berries to each of his guests. He said five words: "In memory of the day." He thanked everyone for coming and introduced the Baptist preacher, Reverend Ronald M. Smith, whom he and Sarra had met while attending the Barnum and Bailey Greatest Show on Earth. The ringmaster had had a bout with bunions. Hearing from two clown brothers about Mungo's work, the ringmaster sent for the infamous cobbler. Not only had the ringmaster compensated Mungo heavily for his craftsmanship, but he had given Mungo and Sarra ringside seats. It was there Mungo met the preacher and for the first time heard stories of a man who walked on water. Curious about the likes of such a man, Mungo promised the preacher to one day bring him to Coraloo.

Reverend Ronald, a stout man who paced the floor wiping the sweat from his forehead, preached a loud message unlike any the people of Coraloo had ever heard before. Menzies was right, mostly. While God did not strike down the guests of Mungo Blackwell's funeral, Reverend Ronald spewed fire and brimstone across the gatherers in such a way the Tofts swore they felt the heat outside. The women were wide-eyed and the men somber. The innkeeper and his wife tried to sneak out the back, afraid the fiery reverend had gotten wind of their side business and would ask them to openly repent in front of their customers and their spouses.

At one point the reverend walked out on the porch and admonished the Tofts, who had set up small booths of their wares hoping to make a profit off the grand event. They fell on their faces in pools of tears, swearing they would change their ways and give the money back.

Two hours later, when the reverend asked if anyone wanted to be baptized, everyone in the room, including the priest, stood up. In a single-file line, with Mungo in the lead, all of the funeral goers, followed by the Tofts, marched down to the river. One by one, Reverend Ronald submerged them in the name of the Father, the Son, and the Holy Spirit. Born again, the funeral party returned to the house, where Father Ferguson proceeded with the eulogy.

"Cursed at birth," the priest said. The people nodded; they knew this part.

I'm still cursed, Mungo thought. *A man can't go to his grave cursed.* As Mungo heard the great feats of his travels, his soul ached with yearning to carry on to yet-untrodden lands. But he couldn't; this was home. He had fought the urge for forty years, set up shop in his home, and tended to the feet of travelers from all over the world. He listened to their stories, anxious and eager, wondering if there was more. *The curse.* Father Ferguson continued, his voice like aloe to the burn of Reverend Ronald. He spoke of Mungo in terms of his family and his fatherhood. The reverend mentioned the names of places and people all too familiar to the family. They were the tales of Mungo Blackwell – their patriarch and their leader.

Here Mungo sat, partially hearing the words he had written himself, but one word echoed in his ear – *cursed.* The funeral had done what he had intended for it do. He had brought his loved ones together, entertained them, and saved their souls – even though Reverend Ronald was a bit much for his taste, he had gotten a good laugh out of the drama, and found some truths in the preacher's teachings he had never heard before. And, as he had hoped, now the family wouldn't have to fuss over a funeral once he was gone. But it turned out he had also discovered that what his family would remember about him was not the man he wanted to be; he discovered the one thing he had yet to do in life.

Father Ferguson proceeded to read the names of Mungo's family, which traditionally would have been done graveside. But as Mungo said it would be a waste to bury an empty coffin only to unearth it once the ceremony was finished, he asked the priest to read them at the end. The priest's words passed over Mungo. He stood up solemnly. There was one more thing he had to do before he died. He had to find his peace – he had to break the curse.

CHAPTER 28

O nce again, Charlie Price stood outside the arched doorway of the Coraloo Flea Market, struggling to process Shug's words of the previous night: the vendors weren't coming back – Shug had said he had "plans" – so there would be no reason for him to come back either. So why was he here, if only to be humiliated and shamed for his failures? Was it all a sick joke? Were his wife and son really waiting for him inside? And what could he possibly say to them to make up for everything he had done? His *sorry* would never be enough; he had nothing to offer them. Why would they ever forgive him?

He stepped through the door. Constable Roy Blackwell waited for him inside dressed in formal uniform – including a high hat adorned with a silver badge. As if on cue, the rows of Blackwells seated under the chandeliers turned to face him.

"Let's get you fixed up." Roy straightened Charlie's tie with his white gloved hands, smoothed down Charlie's stray hairs, and dusted off the shoulders of the black suit coat Charlie had slept in.

"What is this? Where's my Velveteen?" Charlie scanned the sea of sober-faced Blackwells looking for his wife.

"You're lucky you didn't die out there; but maybe that's what you had in mind."

For a moment he thought maybe he had, but then an absurd idea popped into his head: *If I had, Granny would surely have something to say about it.*

"There's not much we can do about those."

Charlie followed Roy's eyes to his badly scraped shoes.

"We can get you a new pair when it's over."

Realization dawned as Charlie looked at the man before him. "You brought me home," he choked. "I'm not sure that was a good idea."

"We'll see. I tried to warn you." Roy dusted off his shoulders once again. "There. You'll be fine."

"Be fine for what?"

"Go on, Mr Price."

Charlie walked cautiously toward the group. The Blackwells stood – clothed in black from their hats to their shoes.

"One more thing, Mr Price…" Charlie turned back to face the constable, "when you take off the lid, be sure to pass out the wheat berries."

"Wheat berries?"

The constable nudged Charlie Price forward, but stayed close behind him as if Charlie would turn and run the other way.

Charlie walked down the center aisle, flanked on either side by rows of Blackwells. He knew them all by name, but in their suits and gowns he had to study their faces to place them in their shops. There was still no sign of Velveteen or Gideon – Stephen had said they would be here. He looked back at the constable, who stood back now and waved Charlie on.

The Blackwells graced him with gentle smiles and nods. He made his way to the front. Then he saw her, standing by herself on the left.

"Velveteen!" He ran to her and hugged her. "I'm so –"

She held her finger to her lips. "Have a seat, Charlie."

Charlie sat, followed by the Blackwells.

From the front of the market, from the general area of *Granny's*, he could see his son walking toward him slowly, balancing something huge on his shoulder. On the other side was Stephen. He could see Danger and the oldest of Stephen's sons. Between them they were carrying a large black coffin – *his* coffin. Charlie Price was attending his own funeral.

Velveteen placed her hand upon his knee. He rested his shaking hand on hers. She reached for something from the pocket of the black satin dress she had worn to the vigil of Granny Blackwell. Sunglasses. She discreetly placed them over her eyes.

The pallbearers placed the freshly painted coffin on a long table at the front. Gideon sat down beside his father. Stephen and Danger sat behind him. Danger leaned forward. "You need to give out the seeds and say, *Never a Toft* –"

"Sit back Danger." Stephen leaned forward. "The seeds are inside. You don't have to –"

"No, it's okay." Charlie wasn't sure why this was happening or how the event had been orchestrated, but he would go along with it – if only for Velveteen's and Gideon's sake.

Charlie stood up and timidly raised the lid of the coffin – fearful he might discover the remains of Granny Blackwell or some other deceased Blackwell. Inside he found a small box filled with tiny oval seeds – wheat berries. What was it Roy had said? He scanned the crowd for Roy, and spotted him sitting next to his date from the Christmas party. Charlie was shocked they had allowed her – a Toft – to cross into Blackwell territory. What would Shug say? Charlie shuddered at the thought: *Was Shug here?* But he somehow knew he wasn't; he felt a strange sense of peace start to wash over him.

Be sure to pass out the wheat berries. Roy's words came to mind.

Charlie grabbed a handful of the seeds and pulled them close to his body so as not to drop the grains on the floor. He proceeded to give Velveteen one berry, and then one to Gideon.

"Give them some more –" Danger tried to whisper the instructions, but Clover had covered his mouth.

Remembering Danger was an expert on the family, Charlie proceeded to move between the aisles distributing small handfuls of the berries. As soon as Charlie sat back down, in unison, the Blackwells said, "In memory of the day."

"In memory of the day," Charlie tried to repeat. His throat was tight, his eyes heavy, and his voice cracked when he attempted to speak.

A man Charlie had seen once or twice in town, but never in the market, stepped in front of the coffin. "Blackwells, Prices, and friends, welcome to the funeral of Charlie Price."

"That's Pastor Danger Donaldson!" Danger whispered to Gideon excitedly.

Gideon turned around. "He's the traveling preacher who delivered you!"

"Right about where you're sitting. Took me right out of mom's womb. Fife said the tip boot was overflowing with money that day! Pastor Donaldson doesn't stay around here most of the time; he usually shows up around Christmas. And he doesn't do the funerals, but you're in luck he was here, Mr Price, or we would have had to pretend someone else was the preacher. Fife makes a good preacher."

Stephen passed a stern glance to his son. "That's enough, Danger. You don't have to narrate."

Charlie barely heard Danger's words, his attention focused solely on the woman next to him and their son. What now? If this was his funeral, then was this the end – the end of life as he knew it, the end of his marriage, his family?

Danger leaned forward again. "This is the part where we would all get baptized, but Mom says we only need to be baptized once if we mean it. When Finella was baptized, the river was frozen too, so we did it in the bathtub. Pastor Donaldson says the Lord doesn't care. I asked Father Milligan, just to be sure. But my dad says we're not doing it today. Must be 'cause you're too big for the bathtub."

With what Charlie could comprehend between his own scattered thoughts and Danger's interjections, the pastor spoke on love and forgiveness. The pastor said, "Amen." Charlie didn't even know they had been praying.

Stephen approached the coffin as the pastor sat down. "Thank you, Pastor Donaldson. Usually Father Milligan would give the eulogy." Stephen nodded to the man seated on the other side of the aisle in liturgical garments. "However, your wife has asked if she could do it. Would that be okay with you, Charlie?"

Before he could even think to respond, Velveteen was on her feet. He was at a loss for words. She unfolded a sheet of the monogrammed stationery he had given her two years ago as part of her Christmas present, along with a box of gold sealing wax and a sealer embossed with a scrolling letter "P". She used the paper sparingly following *The Rooning* – withholding it for special correspondence.

"I met Charles Edward Price when I was a sophomore in design school." Her voice broke. She wiped an escaping tear away from the bottom rim of her sunglasses. "He liked the model of my nursery. Um…" She cleared her throat and started again. "I met Charles Edward Price when I was a sophomore…" She glanced down at her paper and then over to her husband. She shook her head. "I can't do this…"

Charlie stood up. He wanted to be by her side, to hold her hand, to tell her how brave and strong she was, but she motioned for him to sit. *Please don't tell me goodbye.*

Velveteen carefully folded the cream linen paper into a square and removed her sunglasses. Her waterproof mascara was doing its job even though the tears did not stop. "Do you know why I quit design school, Charlie?"

Did he really know? She had said life had so much more to offer her. She was good, and he had never quite understood it. He had even tried to convince her to keep at it, subscribed her to five different interior design magazines, and bought her a new laptop for online designs before Gideon was born.

"I didn't love it anymore. My professors told me they could see the potential, my eye for color, the depth of my contrast. And the more they said it, the more I wanted it. And I designed more of what *they* wanted." She paused and gathered her breath. "I think that's how my life has been for a long time. It's been about the *they* and not about the me." She locked eyes with Charlie, no longer trying to dry her tears. "But it didn't make me happy. So, one day I designed what I wanted – a nursery." She laughed. "My professor hated it. He said the color scheme was all wrong. He said the concept was outdated and void of life. But then you walked by – because you said you had never been in the university gallery before, and you were curious what might be inside. You've always been curious. You said it was the most beautiful room you had ever seen. You said you liked the painting, the one I put over the bassinet. We both know what you were up to, Charlie Price." She covered her mouth and giggled. The tears had stopped and a smile formed on her ruby lips. "Then you fell through my portrait and put a hole in my face."

The Blackwells laughed. Charlie remembered, completely swept up in her vulnerability. He had passed her every Tuesday en route to his Finance and Investment Banking course. And every Tuesday, he would imagine where she was going. So, one day, he turned and followed her into the gallery.

Realizing where he was, Charlie suddenly developed an interest in interior design. He made his way over to her, slowly, pretending to carefully scrutinize each of the model rooms until he was close enough to her he could smell the faint hint of sweet citrus that wafted past him every Tuesday morning and see a remnant of green paint on her chin.

"It's the most beautiful room I've ever seen."

"Excuse me," she said. "Do I know you?"

"No... Did you do this? Pick it all out, I mean."

"I did." She eyed him suspiciously, more than aware of his flattery.

"The details…" He had stepped into the model room as if to inspect the bedding on the bassinet. "And the painting… Did you do this too?"

She nodded.

"It's incredible." He placed his hand on the bed, leaning in to get a better look at the piece of art. "Vee? Is that you?" he asked, pointing to the signature in the corner.

"It's short, for Velveteen."

"And the woman in the painting?"

She didn't have time to answer. The throw rug in front of the bassinet slid, pulling his back leg with it.

Velveteen turned the folded stationery over and over in her hands. "Did you really think my artwork was good, Charlie?"

"Yes… It was the most beautiful part of the whole room." He meant it. He had been in such awe that the gorgeous university student he had dreamed about for months could produce something so lifelike that he leaned in that day to touch it, to make sure it was real. He'd had the same sensation the night she gave birth to their son.

"I should paint more. I enjoyed it once. I think I will, Charlie. I'm going to paint more. I shouldn't have given up on it just because somebody said what made me happy wasn't good. Design school didn't make me happy, but painting did. Do you understand, Charlie? It was kind of like that when we lived in the city. It was pretend. A game we played to make everyone happy and a lot of times it was fun. It was so much fun. But it didn't really make *us* happy, because when we lost the game, we didn't want to play it anymore. But since we've been here there have been glimpses of happiness, true happiness. So let's find what makes us *both* happy. We'll live in a camper van if we have to.

If I can make the Toft house home, I can make anywhere home. Please don't give up, Charlie."

"That's not a eulogy!" Danger stood up with his hands on his hips. Clover pulled him back down to his seat. "Mom, I don't think she knows what to do! She's saying it wrong. This is all sappy and stuff. It's not how we do it."

Clover put her arm around her son. "It's okay this time."

Suddenly Charlie Price saw what had been staring him in the face all this time: his happiness, standing there, tear-streaked and beautiful. And next to him, the gift of their love, his son, who never doubted him, who had not only accepted their new lifestyle but thrived in it, making friends and embracing all Coraloo had to offer. Charlie had fallen from the pinnacle of success down a hill into a depression and then had tried to hide under the guise of a quest for simplicity. But what he needed, that one thing missing from his life, was contentment with what he already had, a freedom – a release from the bondage of self-doubt, failure, and the pressure to provide – that only self-forgiveness could provide.

He embraced his wife, never wanting to let her go. "I'm sorry. I'm so, so sorry. How could you –"

"I love you too, Charlie Price."

He kissed her on the mouth as all the Blackwell children broke out in a series of overexaggerated *ewwws* and gagging noises. The rest of the Blackwells stood and applauded.

"I think he figured it out, Mom," Danger whispered loud enough for Charlie to hear. "Even if her eulogy was all wrong."

Charlie leaned into his wife. "What do I do now?"

She rested her hand on his cheek. "Whatever you want."

"I don't know… I want you and Gideon and the baby… We're having a baby!" He picked her up off her feet and swung her around. "A baby! I'll need to find work. We'll start over, go back to the city if that's what it takes." He meant it. He'd do it for her;

he'd do it for them. "We'll start small, I'll work my way to the top, and whatever happens, happens. We'll make it work."

"Do you really want to live in the city, Charlie?"

"Well, no. Do you?"

"I like it here… in Coraloo."

"You do?"

She smiled.

"Okay then; we'll stay. I can drive back and forth – it's not too far."

"You can't drive back and forth, Charlie." She laughed. "It's much too far."

"Then maybe I'll look at the purse factory. It's what everyone in the valley does."

"But it's not what you do. We'll figure it out," she patted her belly, "the four of us."

He stopped and grabbed her hands. Even though he had nothing, she still wanted him. She said they'd figure it out… together. All this time he had believed a lie. In truth, she didn't care where he worked, how much he made or what kind of house they lived in – ramshackle, rented or a high-paid renovation. No matter what happened, he understood. It was a small glimpse of the faith Stephen had talked about, the knowing that something far greater than himself was at work. And that something was to do with love: he saw it in Velveteen's capacity to love him despite the fact his actions hurt her; in how she loved him even though she knew he was flawed; and in how she had forgiven him. Perhaps he too could forgive himself.

Charlie suddenly knew what he wanted. They would be okay. "I'm happy here too, but I'm not happy doing this!" He motioned to the market. "I need something more, not more money, or a bigger house, I want more for me… for you, for Gideon and for… our daughter, wait, is it a girl? I'm okay with a girl… or a boy."

"It's too early to tell." Velveteen moved his hand to the small bump on her belly. He hadn't even noticed... actually he had noticed, but he'd convinced himself it was the brownie batter.

"Aunt Sorcha told me how to tell!" Danger stood up on his seat and pulled his shirt up. "You take a string and tie it on your finger, then you swing it like this." He swung his hips around in a circle and pretended to draw a circle with his finger.

"Not now, Danger." Clover tried to pull him down, but Aunt Sorcha was climbing up on the casket to lie down.

"No, no! You do it like this!" The old woman was about to pull up her dress and demonstrate the proper technique to reveal the gender of the unborn baby, but Stephen jumped over the bench in front of him and threw himself in front of the soon to be half-naked woman.

"You really want this?" Charlie asked.

"I really do. It's what Melba would do." Velveteen winked at her husband.

Charlie kissed her on the forehead. "I am sorry I forgot myself, Vee."

"I think we both did. So, by all means, Charlie Price, let's remember."

CHAPTER 29

"Please be careful. Call me as soon as you get there?" Velveteen straightened his tie and pulled her wool coat around her emerging belly. She shivered in the frigid January air.

"You should go back in. I can't have my favorite girls getting sick."

Velveteen plopped her hands on her hips.

"Too soon?"

"Three weeks and then we'll find out. Dr Walker says any sooner and there is a fifty-fifty chance he'll get the sex wrong. Can you imagine, Charlie? Clover throws me a fabulous shower in the market, all the ladies attend –"

"Sylvia Toft, too?"

"Don't be ridiculous, Charlie Price! There will be a cake, maybe even macarons. We are not having a third *Rooning* – not at my own baby shower! As I was saying, if Dr Walker gets it wrong and all the ladies lavish me with blue sleepers and blue blankets and funny little cars that make honking noises and books about pooing in the potty, and then we have a girl? What then?"

"Girls don't poo in the potty?" He laughed. She hit him playfully on the shoulder. "Okay, okay, okay. I'll be patient. I should be going."

"Are you nervous? Are you sure this is what you want? Maybe there is something else you could do from home?"

He pulled her to him and kissed her. "Yes, very. No, I'm not sure. And if there was a better option, I would take it."

"What about that one thing, oh you know… What was his name? He came by the house. It was something about restaurants." In the past month her memory lapses had been a cause of frustration for both of them. Dr Walker said it wasn't uncommon for pregnant woman to feel a little off balance from time to time.

Charlie laughed at the memory of their annoying visitor. "It wasn't restaurants. It was rest homes… for dogs."

"That's it! He said he would put you at the top."

"Yes, if I found three people to put under me, and they each found three people, and they found three people –"

"Right. I remember now. Call me as soon as you know something."

"I'm sure they won't tell me right away. It will be a couple of days and possibly another interview or two before they make their final decision."

She looked into the face of her husband. "I am so proud of you, Charlie Price."

"I know." He kissed her forehead and climbed into their car.

"Oh Charlie, wait!" She ran inside the Toft house and returned with a small box. "I made these for you – in case you need a snack."

Charlie took the box and started the car. He glanced out the window as he backed out of the gravel driveway. She had sworn she would not leave until he was out of sight. With one hand she attempted to hold the periwinkle coat closed around her round tummy; with the other she blew him kisses. On her feet she wore shiny black rain boots. He had never seen her wear them before and thought they were front door décor like the coat rack or umbrella stand. Most of the time she preferred to be barefoot, claiming she hadn't found her shoes yet.

He blew a kiss back. A nervous excitement overcame him. He had to catch his breath. Since his funeral he experienced this often: a heightened awareness that the moment he was living might not have been had the constable not found him the night of the Christmas Party.

They had come a long way since *The Rooning*. On the outside, Velveteen was the same woman who had passed out at the sight of the dahlia-patterned wall covering, but on the inside, she was someone else. She had developed a confidence Charlie had not seen in her before, even finding the courage to ask the Blackwells if they would let her sell her paintings in the market. And the cooking and the baking – Charlie was gaining weight right alongside her. She smiled more, laughed more, and one day, as she was putting the finishing touches on a homemade lemon tart, proclaimed, "From this point, I will have no further correspondence with the acquaintances." He hadn't asked her why, but he already had a good idea.

As for Charlie, he still didn't know what he wanted to be when he grew up, but he knew what he didn't want – no more hiding from his past and pretending to be something he was not. He could be happy and content with life the way it was. Their house was big enough, though they would have to convert the attic space into Gideon's room so the baby could take residence among the cowboys. He loved the simplicity they had found, the life they had forged together, but he still needed to earn a living – and picking wasn't the answer. He knew what he needed; his funeral had shown him that. Charlie hoped he would find the contentment he sought at the end of the long drive.

Charlie watched the miles of limestone walls and horse farms blur past as he neared the city. He had to give Velveteen credit for this trip. The night Howard Lawson had told him about the opening at Heritage Financial, he hadn't heard a word, but lucky for him, Alice Lawson had mentioned it to Velveteen. At the time, Velveteen said she laughed it off, thinking Charlie would never dare return to the place of his demise.

But the day after Charlie's funeral she hesitantly brought it up. He didn't blame her; there would be another mouth to feed soon enough. And at this point, he was out of options for employment.

"I have an idea, Charlie. It's not ideal, but hear me out before you say 'no'. At the party Alice Lawson –" at the party and Alice Lawson; she wasn't off to a good start – *"mentioned Heritage has not been able to fill your position permanently. It's been almost a year, Charlie. Well, you know how the Lawsons are friends with the Rogers… Mary Beth told Alice that Carl should have taken over from you. In fact, he was counting on it – which makes me dislike the Rogers even more – but Ralph Walsh hired someone from the outside. Seems the lady they hired was all well and good until Carl went digging online and discovered the woman had three husbands… three, Charlie! She was living three different lives – it was such a scandal they let her go. Now, I know I can't believe a word Mary Beth says, but apparently she said Carl tried for the position again, and they still refused. Do you want to know why, Charlie?"*

Charlie had not really wanted to know why. He couldn't care less about the interworking of Heritage Financial, but at the time, Velveteen was on the edge of her seat, clearly excited to tell him.

"Okay, why?"
    "This is what Alice told me. She said Ralph Walsh said… they're friends with the Walshes too. Did I tell you that already? Anyway, she said Ralph Walsh could not find anyone as good as you to fill the position, and until he did, he didn't plan to hire anybody! Charlie, do you know what this means?"

"Heritage Financial is one card short of a full deck?"

"A full deck? Are you trying to say they are crazy? Anyway, it means you should apply for the job! If you want... only if you want. You could suggest you work remotely. Tell them you want to work from home. People do that all the time, Charlie."

"They fired me. Why would they take me back?"

"Well, Alice also said –"

He cut her off. "I'll call and see if there is an opening. I doubt they will give me my old job back... and let me work almost three hours away, but I guess it wouldn't hurt." What other option did he have? They needed the money. Even though they both knew it was a long shot, they had spent the night dreaming about a life where Charlie would work from home and they would stay in Coraloo.

In a matter of minutes, Charlie Price would take his first step into the city since he had lost his job. Knowing Robert Walsh took both the week before and after Christmas off to spend time with his family, Charlie had waited to call. The conversation had been casual at first, catching up on the past year – Walsh's grandchildren and Velveteen's pregnancy. Walsh had heard the Prices had moved to Coraloo and wanted to know all about it, so Charlie told him about everything from the Toft house to his visits to the constable's office. Walsh had cackled so hard Charlie was sure he had forgotten he was even on the phone.

"And you want to come back?"

"Yes, sir. I made a mistake. I'm not proud of it, and I don't have any excuse or detailed explanation for it. It was careless and sir –"

"How about you come in on Wednesday? I can't make any promises. You know the board will have the final say."

"Thank you, sir. It means a lot."

"Oh and Price, you've got to tell me about this Mangoo Blackwell fellow. Sounds like a man after my own heart."

Charlie almost corrected Walsh's pronunciation of the Blackwell legend, but immediately caught himself. Correcting the man who had agreed to interview him might not play out in his favor.

Velveteen had made a batch of macarons, though Charlie had been quick to remind her there was nothing to celebrate. Even if he was offered the job, and he could work from home, is this what they wanted? Did he really want to go back to hours spent writing reports, worrying about deadlines, and making small talk with prospective clients? But he would be foolish to let the opportunity pass him by without at least giving it his best shot.

They could live off the sale of the French horn for about two more months. Charlie had contacted the buyer, fearing the Australian would demand his money back over the horn's questionable authenticity. But the buyer had laughed and said he had already sold it on, pocketing a five hundred dollar profit.

"Can he do that, Charlie? Is it legal?" Velveteen had asked.

He recalled staring at her for a minute. Did she not know what he had been doing in Coraloo? To avoid confusion, he simply answered, *yes.*

A giant wreath with an oversized red bow – leftover decorations from Christmas – hung over the entrance to the Heritage Financial building. Velveteen had insisted their home decorations come down right after New Year's Day. Charlie paused a moment, remembering the excitement of their first Christmas in Coraloo. In the weeks leading up to it Charlie had been anxious about having enough money to buy gifts for Velveteen and Gideon. In past years he had not spared any expense, always buying his family one special – and usually very expensive – gift.

This year things were different. Charlie had traded a vintage stethoscope – a poorly calculated purchase during his early days of picking – to Roy Blackwell for a bicycle. Seemed the constable had a whole shed full of them, which he refurbished in his spare time. Roy had lovingly transformed a worn-looking mountain bike into a one-of-a-kind *Pirates of the Cosmos* original, complete with pirate flag and handlebar ray gun. Charlie had never seen Gideon so excited about a gift, another clear indication that their previous, pretend existence hadn't been as rewarding as what they now had. Velveteen had made them pancakes – cinnamon with a spiced whipped cream, and they'd spent the morning as a family, just the three of them, knowing that this time next year, there would be four. In the evening they went to the market to see the Blackwells. Clover had called ahead to warn Velveteen not to eat the plum pudding. Apparently the aunts had argued over a few notes on Granny's recipe, resulting in a beautiful yet boozy laxative bomb with a sprig of holly stuck on top.

Gathering himself, Charlie opened the door and stepped onto the marble floor. The building moved with hurried employees, racing from destination to destination. It smelled of bleach and pine-scented wood cleaners.

Charlie walked up to the circular desk in the center of the lobby. He didn't recognize the receptionist – she must be new. "Good morning. I have an appointment with Robert Walsh?"

"Name?" The girl could have easily been one of the Blackwell children with her red hair flowing down in ringlets to her shoulders. He wanted to ask if she knew them.

"Charlie –"

"One moment. Heritage Financial, how may I direct your call?" The girl rolled her eyes, sighed, and rolled her eyes again. "One moment, please." She then looked at Charlie as if he were forgetting to do something. "Your name?"

"Oh, Charlie. Charlie Price."

It might as well have been the first day of middle school all over again. He was nervous, uncomfortable, and even though he had spent most of his adult life walking in and out of this very building, he was the new kid.

"Take the elevator to the top floor."

"Does he know I'm coming?"

"Um, yes. One moment. Heritage Financial, how may I… No ma'am…"

Charlie didn't wait for her call to end. He proceeded to the elevator, boarded with five other suits – three women and two men he had never seen before – and waited for the elevator to carry him to the top. His mind wandered back to Coraloo, to Gideon, and to Velveteen. He paid no attention to the other employees coming and going as the peaceful commerce taking place at Coraloo captivated his memory. What were the vendors doing since their eviction from Coraloo? He had taken for granted he would always see them and had never said goodbye.

"Are you getting off?"

"I'm sorry, what?"

A woman with black hair twisted into a braided bun on the back of her head held the door open for him. "This is the last stop, or you're going back to the lobby, unless you've just been along for the ride."

Charlie glanced up at the woman, and then glanced again at what he thought was a birthmark in the shape of a star on the bridge of her nose. "Ipunistat?"

"Excuse me?"

Charlie rubbed his eyes and took a second look at the woman. He had seen the birth of the Blackwell patriarch to the native princess played out in front of him over a dozen times and the star was imprinted on his memory.

"Is something wrong?"

"No, no this is my stop." He glanced back at the woman, but the elevator door had shut. *Get it together, Charlie.* He inhaled deeply as he walked onto the executive floor of Heritage Financial.

He stepped up to a man who he assumed was sitting behind the desk. But he was standing, though he must have been a good two feet shorter than Charlie. "A pygmy," Charlie mumbled.

The man furrowed his brow, but thankfully had not caught Charlie's utterance. "Name?"

"Charlie Price. I'm here to see Robert Walsh."

"Have a seat." The man motioned for Charlie to sit in a small waiting area to the left where one other person sat reading through a magazine with the picture of a pirate on the front.

Charlie's throat constricted. He loosened his tie for fear of suffocation. He watched the man in front of him flip through the pages. The vintage wall clock ticked away the seconds. Charlie checked his watch; he was early. Images of Velveteen in the Toft house scurried through his brain, as he envisioned her baking under the stained-glass bumblebee – which she had come to claim as her favorite item in the home – swinging over her head casting shadows across the room.

Gideon would be in school dreaming up ways to persuade Velveteen to homeschool him, and the Blackwells… would of course be at the market – where they were every day. Stephen had expressed concern as January and February were their slowest months, and with the loss of income brought in by the vendors, he feared the market would not make it through the summer. Charlie could not get his head around it: what would Coraloo be without the market? Although he was in no hurry to go picking again, he missed the market, and hadn't been back in over two weeks. They had attended the tree lighting and partaken in all of the Blackwell festivities, including the mulled wine. The children had re-enacted the year's final tribute to Mungo in a demonstration that involved Danger shouting, *I am your blood,* and seconds later five of the Blackwell children, along with Gideon, dumping buckets of water on Danger.

Charlie checked his watch again. He breathed in slowly and then exhaled. He couldn't sit still any longer. He would have to get used to desk life again – even if it was from the kitchen table – assuming all went well. Charlie stood up and walked to the floor to ceiling window overlooking the street below. He put his hands in his pockets and stared down at the row of food trucks – chicken burgers, wraps, and… He placed his face against the glass, squinted, and tried to read the farthest truck on the end – Kuru's Curry? He turned his head away and then back again. The truck clearly read "Kale and Corn".

> *"They can't blame you for poor immune systems. Besides, God never intended for us to eat from a truck."* Velveteen's words rang in his head.
> *"What about the truffle truck or the cupcake truck on 7th?"* he'd said.
> *"Dessert is always an exception, Charlie."*

On that day, he would have never imagined over a year later he would be waiting to interview for the same position that had been stripped from him. *So you're sacrificing me?* The dismissal played over in his mind. *No, Son. We're firing you.*

The toes of Charlie's new brown leather dress shoes peeked out from the hem of his trousers. He liked the shoes – he liked them a lot, in fact – but not where they were standing. Who was he kidding? This wasn't what he wanted. He saluted the row of trucks, removed his tie, and made his way toward the elevator. *Cowards are men that won't try what has never been done.* There had to be another way, and Charlie was going to find it.

Charlie pushed the button on the elevator and watched as the digital number at the top climbed from three, to four, as the elevator shot up toward him. For the first time since *The Rooning*, he didn't see himself as a failure. Velveteen was happy, Gideon was happy, he was happy – that's all that mattered. He would figure out the rest of it.

"Charlie Price?" Charlie turned at the sound of his name. "Mr Walsh will see you now."

The elevator door opened. Without looking back, Charlie stepped inside.

"Mr Price," the man at the desk repeated, "Mr Walsh will see you now."

The elevator doors slowly pushed closer together. Then a familiar voice made his blood run cold. Charlie stuck out his hand to stop the closing doors. On the other side, he could see Robert Walsh shaking the hand of Shug Blackwell.

"Mr Price? Charlie Price?" the man at the desk called again.

Charlie stepped out of the elevator and glared into the cold eyes of Shug Blackwell. "I'm Charlie Price."

CHAPTER 30

1929 and ½

Mungo Blackwell stepped boldly into the camp of the Na-rts natives, just as his father Mumford had done over seventy years ago. Mungo missed his bride and his thirteen children, but he could not live the remainder of his years as a man cursed with a restless soul. It had been a difficult life for him and for Sarra. After the birth of their firstborn, so many years ago, he had dragged his young family around the world, unintentionally forcing Sarra to give birth to their second child in a cave off the coast of Nova Scotia. It was the second time a child of theirs had not been born in the bed he had made for her. That was when he realized his family needed to be home. Somehow he needed to find contentment at home. And now, following his funeral, it was time to end the curse where it had all begun.

"Halt!" Mungo stopped in front of the dark-skinned man. The man, scantily dressed with the exception of the work boots on his feet, motioned for Mungo to follow.

"I must see your chief," Mungo said.

The native nodded and motioned for Mungo to follow. The native led Mungo to a triangular tent made of sticks, where inside Mungo found a man, much older than he, lying on a bed of feathers surrounded by five women who were dripping oils from large bowls on his forehead and chest.

"He is leaving us for the after," the native said to Mungo.

A sense of urgency faced Mungo. He must have the man undo what was done so he could live the remainder of his life in peace.

Mungo leaned over the dying chief.

"What does he trade?" the chief asked.

"I have nothing to trade."

"Do you have shoes?"

"I do." Mungo removed the bench-made leather boots from his feet and handed them to one of the women. The woman examined the boot, looked down at her own ladies' patent leather dress shoe with a Cuban heel, and nodded her approval of the trade. She then tossed the boot over her shoulder to where it landed in a pile of other shoes. Mungo surveyed the camp, contemplating the loin cloths and flimsy wrappings each of the natives wore along with elaborate shoes of one kind or another.

The chief motioned for Mungo to speak.

"Seventy-three years ago you cursed me to wander the earth, to never be satisfied to live in one place. I want you to remove the curse, so I might live in peace with my family."

"I cannot."

"But you must!"

"I cannot."

"You put the curse upon me, so you must remove it. I traveled many miles to find you!"

"I cannot remove what I have not given."

"You are the chief, are you not?"

"I am."

"Then you must take this curse from me! I need to live! It's all I have left to do!"

"I cannot give you what you seek." The chief choked and coughed. The woman continued to drip oils down his face.

One of the natives placed his hand on Mungo's back. "You must go."

"No! I have come too far. I cannot finish my life like this. It is all I have left to do." The native raised his spear and ushered him back. "Please!" Mungo yelled to the chief, "I've seen it! I know! You must speak it away from me! Do you know who I am? I am your blood! I am the son of the star, Ipunistat!"

"Stop!"

Mungo froze and looked into the face of his ancient grandfather.

"I hoped you would return one day, my only male heir."

Mungo knelt down by the old man's side. "But you cursed me."

In his last breaths the old chief laughed. "Are you saying all this time you thought you were cursed because of the angry words of an old man?"

"It is what I was told."

"Then you, my grandson, cursed yourself." The chief's eyes slowly fell closed as he passed from the earth. The women broke into wails. The native dropped his spear. Mungo was left hopeless and defeated.

"You are the chief," the native said. "He named you."

"I am not the chief."

Suddenly Mungo found himself wrapped in an animal hide robe and a crown of feathers set upon his head. His curse wanted him to stay and live among the natives as one of them, but for the first time, his heart told him it was time to go. Mungo removed the crown and the robe and walked sock-footed from the camp.

He walked morning and night without stopping; he would not give in to his urge to roam, to go and seek out his next adventure. He followed the stars across the desert and over the mountains until he reached the ocean's edge. Upon his arrival, a large storm cloud distorted the horizon line. Mungo watched as the lightning lit the sky, but he did not move. He had come seeking peace and instead he found a storm.

Mungo faced the storm head on. He let the rain wash over him. He fought to stand tall in the wind, but over and over it knocked him down. The thunder echoed in his ears. He begged the mover of the storm to free him of the curse. At that moment a wave swept over him and pulled him into the sea. When he woke, he was lying in the sand on the other side of the ocean.

Mungo wrung the water from his wool socks and stood to his feet. He gazed back on the sea, always moving, never stopping to rest. Ahead of him, several days' journey from the coast, lay the still green hills of his homeland. He reached in his pocket for his can of beeswax – a little damp, but it would do the trick. He twisted the edges of his mustachio into tiny hooks, placed the tin can back in his pocket, and set his course for home with no desire for anything more than what he had waiting for him.

CHAPTER 31

Charlie Price stood outside the front door of the Toft cottage in the crisp snowy air. He grinned. He had called Velveteen earlier in the day to let her know the interview had taken a turn and was going to last much longer than either of them had expected – four hours longer in fact.

Charlie went over the events of the meeting in his mind. Robert Walsh, without hesitation, had offered him his job back, but Charlie had lifted his chin and said, "Robert, I must decline."

Charlie turned the doorknob and stepped inside his home. The cushions were fluffed, the mantel dusted, a fire crackled, and one dozen red velvet macarons sat ready to celebrate Charlie's successful interview at Heritage Financial. It was clear there was no doubt in Velveteen's mind that Heritage had asked Charlie to once again lead the team of bankers – especially when he told her over the phone the interview was prolonged, and he had news involving her. Gideon sat at the kitchen table doing homework, and Velveteen, in full make-up and heels – she had dressed up for the evening – greeted him with a calm, "Hello, sweetheart."

"How are you feeling?"

"Swollen, exhausted, and perfectly pregnant!"

Charlie considered asking her to sit down, but decided to tease her first. She had probably gone over all possible scenarios for the last six and a half hours, but he was certain she would never see coming what he was about to tell her. He wandered over to the coffee table and picked up a macaron. She had become quite good at baking the colorful treats. The red velvet was his favorite.

He entered the kitchen and leaned over Gideon's shoulder. "What are you working on?"

"Geography."

"I'll come back later when it's time for literature."

Gideon offered up a courtesy laugh.

"How was your day at school?"

"Okay. Did you know the number of children who are educated at home by a parent is rising every year? And, homeschooled children are just as likely to attend university as children who are educated in a traditional classroom setting?"

"Talk to your mother."

"I did."

"And…"

"She said when the Tofts and the Blackwells learn to get along, then she will consider it."

"So, it's a no."

"It's a no."

Charlie leaned over and whispered in Gideon's ear. "Between us, I have it on good authority there could be a Blackwell–Toft marriage this spring. We may have a truce yet."

From the corner of his eye, he could see Velveteen straightening the cushions once again and carefully laying the blanket he had gotten her for Christmas over the arm of the sofa before she moved on to lining up her acrylics in neat little rows on a table she had set beside the easel she'd found in the attic. He wondered how long she would last until she asked him about the interview. When she went back and straightened the cushions for the third time, he couldn't stand it.

"Stop, stop, stop." He laughed. "I'll tell you!"

"Charlie Price, you drive me crazy!" She calmly sat down on the sofa, but placed one of the cushions behind her back for extra support. "So, how did it go?"

Charlie sat down beside his wife and took her hands in his. "I have something to tell you."

He proceeded to tell her how he had seen the food trucks, how he had almost walked away, and how the sight of Shug Blackwell had stopped him.

Velveteen gasped. "Shug Blackwell! Oh Charlie, you're lucky to be alive! What was he doing at Heritage Financial? Oh no! Was he applying for *your* job?"

"No, turns out he was looking for an investor."

"For the market?"

"Robert Walsh was more than happy to tell me about it." He had her attention.

Charlie had stepped out of the elevator more out of curiosity than an interest in fulfilling his appointment with Robert Walsh. He boldly strode up to the two men.

"Robert!" Charlie stepped in front of Shug and shook the hand of his former employer. "Good to see you, old friend."

"Price," Shug growled, "what are you doing here?"

Charlie hadn't planned what to say in response; he was thankful Robert answered for him.

"We go way back! Not surprised you two know each other. What was the name of the town?"

"Coraloo," Charlie and Shug replied in unison.

"Right, like the market."

"The market?" Mention of the market was enough to keep Charlie around longer.

"Mr Blackwell is looking for a buyer, and I have to say, we're very interested. Old Charlie's the one I should run this by. He had his own share of success with assessing small businesses in his day."

Shug crossed his arms across his chest, exposing the tip of the Oakeshott blade on his forearm. "I believe I read about that in the paper. Was it a food truck, Price?" He spat the words.

Again, Robert took the lead. Charlie had forgotten how much the man liked to talk. "One deal gone south won't kill a man."

Charlie stood tall; he wasn't going to let Shug Blackwell win the day – one deal had almost killed him, but the one forming in his brain was about to give him life.

"It was good to see you, Shug. Let's catch up back at the market." With that, Charlie Price ushered Robert Walsh back into his corner office, leaving Shug with his mouth open.

Velveteen stared at Charlie with eager eyes as he recounted the day's events. "So what did he do?"

"Who?"

"Shug Blackwell! After you left him out in the hall?"

"I don't really know. He probably left."

Velveteen fell back against her neatly organized cushions. "I can't believe he's trying to sell the market, Charlie. It's been in the Blackwell family for years."

"He's not trying; the market is as good as sold. Walsh said it's a solid investment."

"Does Stephen know about this?"

"He does now."

"You told him! Oh, Charlie, if Shug finds out you were the one who told… Should we purchase a gun? Or maybe we can put up some of that pokey wire around the house –"

"Barbed wire?"

"Yes! That's it… We'll hire someone to deliver our groceries, and I guess I'll be forced to homeschool Gideon. Oh I wish Shug would just go ahead and get it over with!"

"Get what over with?"

"Skinning us alive!"

"I doubt he will try to skin us from jail."

"Jail!"

"It's temporary. Roy Blackwell is holding him until he cools down a bit. Walsh and I had a nice long talk. I had already told him most of our story, so I filled in a few of the missing pieces – the history of the Blackwells, the vendors, *Granny's*. Told him he would be an idiot if he didn't buy the market."

"So, now they'll all be coming after us? It's just like Melba all over again when the count's men tried to storm the palace!"

Charlie squeezed her hand. "I called Stephen from the office. I wanted his permission before I ran the numbers. Walsh wanted me to look the deal over since I had so much *experience* at the market, and I wasn't part of the family. I could never make sense of the fact the market was always inches from shutting down or work out why Shug was so hot to have the vendors leave."

Velveteen sat up. "Shug didn't want the market to survive, did he?"

Charlie loved how she, in her own unique way, was always a step ahead of him. "That's my guess. From what I could see, a portion of the market's profits filters into an account marked *repairs*… except there is no record of the money being spent on repairs. Whatever he was up to, it put the market in the red – they would need an act of God to keep it up."

"He was stealing! Granny Blackwell is probably rolling over in her grave, Charlie. How could her son do this to the family?"

"I don't know – yet. I'm going to let Roy and his officers get it out of him."

"Oh, Charlie, Heritage must be thrilled to have you back! Will they let you work from home? Or maybe you could open a branch here, in Coraloo. I have the best idea for a remodel – we'll go for a masculine flea market meets industrial chic!"

"Vee…"

"Yes, Charlie?"

"I turned it down." He didn't want her to worry for even a second, so he went straight for the point. "I can't do it again; I can't have that life. I've seen the other side. I've seen the freedom of being with you and Gideon. I want to be my own boss. I want to set my own hours. I know it's different, but I don't want to drive to the city once a month to sit around a big table with a bunch of hotheads spouting numbers, and I don't want to wear a suit. Granny said the shoes fit. She's right – I'm a businessman, and I'm good at it, but not in the city. I want to be here. So… that's what I told Robert Walsh."

"You told him you didn't want to wear a suit?"

"Along with the rest of it. You see, I remembered something. Walsh is a family guy. I must have heard a hundred times how Heritage was founded by his great-great-great-whatever. I told him Coraloo had to stay in the hands of the Blackwells. I told him about all the crazy stories –"

"It's history, Dad!" Gideon yelled from the other room.

"You didn't tell him about the funeral, did you?" Velveteen asked, her hand covering her mouth in shock.

"I did! He loved it! He loved all of it! So just like that, I had an idea. I said, 'Robert, I have a proposal for you.' And he said, 'All right, what is it, Charlie?'" Charlie's heart pounded and his face hurt from the permanent grin. "I said, 'You buy it, I'll run it. I know the market, and I know the industry.'" And with that Charlie triumphantly grabbed a macaron and shoved the whole thing in his mouth.

Velveteen was on her feet now. "What did he say? What did he say?"

Charlie started to speak, but Velveteen couldn't make out a word he was saying.

"Chew, Charlie, chew!" She moved her mouth up and down as if to show him the proper method.

Charlie swallowed the bite. "These are so good, Vee." He reached for another one – knowing his smile already said it all. She playfully smacked his hand away.

"Charlie Price, if you don't tell me what he said, so help me I will start throwing these macarons at your face… And you know I will, Price! You know I will! It wouldn't be a Toft house first either!" She fought to withhold her laughter.

"Do it Mom!" Gideon called from the kitchen.

Charlie clutched his stomach and fell back down on the sofa. He laughed so hard his side began to cramp. Velveteen picked up a macaron and flipped it from one hand to the other. "Heads will roll, Price! Heads will roll!"

Charlie pulled her down onto his lap. "Walsh wants me to oversee the transition. Then, Heritage will be hands off. I'll work from the market… marketing, managing, branding, all of it. Heritage will make a percent, but the rest goes back to the family. I ran it by Stephen and he thought it was a great idea… it should keep anyone else in the family from getting too greedy. We discussed a salary. What the market will pay me is more than fair. Walsh's team is projecting the market and the town to be the state's next big tourist draw, but we won't make any major changes without consulting the family."

Velveteen covered her eyes with both hands as happy tears threatened to overcome her.

He pulled her hands and polished nails away from her face, revealing two beautiful watery eyes. "My first point of business is to get one of the market's key attractions back up and running. It's going to need someone to take it over."

"Do you mean *Granny's*? Who do you have in mind?"

"Well, it would have to be someone with a great mind for artistic detail. Someone who is creative, loves her co-workers…" He brushed a loose strand of hair away from her face as earnestly she nodded along, "Vee – Stephen, Clover, and I think you should run *Granny's*."

"I couldn't Charlie. I could never…"

"Apparently, Granny thought you could, or she wouldn't have spent so much time with you."

"Really?" She paused, openly astounded. "But what about the others? I mean, so many of the Blackwell ladies could do it."

"They have their own businesses to attend to. What do you say, partner? Want to try something new?"

"What does it pay?" Velveteen asked, slowly smiling, "Would it be enough for this partner to get her hair done, at an actual salon? I'm not very good at it; I tried. I really did. And I love our home, but you know the water shuts off occasionally, and if I'm stuck again with Cocoa Blanket in my hair –"

"Then you call the Blackwells."

"Charlie!"

"Of course you can get your hair done. I'm sure Sylvia Toft will be more than thrilled –"

Velveteen reached over and grabbed the tray of macarons, then paused. "I haven't worked since before we were married. What if I burn down the market?"

"Then we help to rebuild it."

"What if the customers don't like me?"

"They won't like you; they'll love you."

"What if I fail, Charlie?"

He had asked the same question of himself on the drive home. "We try again."

"Can I make macarons?"

Charlie picked up one of the treats from the center of the tray she was holding. "As long as you promise not to throw them at anybody."

CHAPTER 32

One month later, Charlie Price called a meeting of the Blackwells. Despite Charlie and Shug's public disdain for one another, Charlie tried to be as gentle as possible. Shug was family. With Stephen by his side, he explained that Shug had had big plans for the market – he wanted to turn it into a bustling tourist attraction complete with a food court, go-carts, and slew of kitschy souvenir shops that bled down into the town. It was his idea of improving the market.

But Shug's bad decisions had caught up with him. Apparently, after selling replicas of eighteenth-century weaponry to overseas buyers, they'd discovered his deceit. Mix that with the interest rising on an unpaid gambling debt, and Shug was forced to change his plan. His new plan: to sell the market and move south. Charlie knew all too well that money had a way of shifting a man's motivations. With the profit, Shug would be able to pay his debts and make some extra on the side.

His plans discovered, Shug was currently serving fourteen years in prison – seven for the swords and seven for skimming off the top.

After the initial shock of Shug's betrayal, the family was ready to talk about the future of the Coraloo Flea Market. For three hours the Blackwells asked questions and made suggestions. Ralph Walsh answered and responded to every single one of them. He told the family the acquisition of the Coraloo Flea Market was more personal than business. He believed in family and proceeded with the speech Charlie could now recite from memory: "You see, Heritage Financial has been in my family for nearly one hundred years…"

As was the Blackwell tradition for voting, they cast their shoes into the center of the meeting – a left for no, and a right for yes. By unanimous decision, the Blackwells agreed to support Charlie Price. Ralph Walsh took both his shoes off and tossed them into the pile because he wanted a reason to walk around barefoot as Charlie and Stephen gave him a tour of the market.

Charlie spent the next month at the market planning, contacting vendors, and casting his vision. With the grand re-opening of the market only weeks away, and Shug's shop locked up, Charlie felt it was time to repurpose the space or find someone else to tend to it. The police had gone over the shop when Shug was arrested. As well as confiscating files, they uncovered the stolen Kipling – another of Shug's attempts to rid the market of the one man he feared would uncover the financial damage done to the Blackwell legacy: Charlie Price.

Charlie waited for Innis Wilkinson to unlock the door and then stepped inside *Shug's*. Stacks of antique china, a vintage wedding dress, oil lamps, chandeliers, military uniforms, and tools welcomed him. He felt a twinge of regret as he recalled the days of picking, finding, and researching his treasures, only to turn around and sell them for a higher value.

He had been in this part of the market twice – both times Shug had asked him to leave. Charlie sat down in a nineteenth-century antique French carved armchair, a basket filled with wooden shoe forms on the floor beside it. He picked one up and ran his hand over the smooth wood.

Charlie closed his eyes and allowed himself to be transported back to a time when the building hummed and bustled as a newly mechanized shoe factory – and before, as the children told, the home of Mungo Blackwell himself. But as with most things, something bigger, better, and faster had come along, wiping out the old and, for a brief moment, becoming the new, until the cycle repeated itself. Charlie opened his eyes, surrounded by Shug's den of antiquities. The history, the memories – it was the one part of the market he and Shug had in common. It would be sad to see it all go. He turned the shoe form over. Engraved in the wood was the name *M. Blackwell*. Charlie had an idea.

Charlie, Velveteen, Gideon, and the entire Blackwell family stood outside the arched stone doorway of the Coraloo Flea Market. A red ribbon tied into a bow at the center held back the tourists and vendors. Mr and Mrs Wilkinson waited at the ready for any custodial mishaps. A columnist from *Wayfaring* magazine stood by with a camera in hand asking Velveteen a series of questions regarding the new management and what patrons could expect from the bakery. Having succumbed to the belly-freeing freedom of maternity fashion, she looked like a celebrity, waving at a bundle of Tofts who said they had ventured up the hill for the event to make sure the Blackwells didn't do anything illegal.

"It's perfectly quaint! It will rival anything you find in the city. You have my guarantee, sir." Velveteen pulled the purple scarf around her shoulders.

The reporter jotted a few words on a piece of paper as Velveteen stood on tiptoes to see what he was writing. "And the shotgun?"

"I beg your pardon?"

"The shotgun, ma'am. Rumor has it Granny kept a shotgun behind the counter in case a feud broke out."

A slow smile formed on Velveteen's face. "Let's just say, some things at the Coraloo will never change." She winked.

The reporter scribbled.

"Ladies and gentlemen." Charlie's voice echoed across the crowd. "Welcome to the grand reopening of the Coraloo Flea Market. Stephen, would you do the honors?"

Stephen Blackwell stepped up to the door. "This building has been in my family a long time. It's a part of our history; it's who we are. We are artisans and collectors. Our ways may be peculiar and our stories –"

"*History*, Dad," Danger interrupted.

"Our *history* somewhat strange, but it is the way we love one another that keeps us going. However, sometimes, you need a little help." Stephen reached over and shook Charlie's hand. "Sometimes, you need help from the outside to get back on your feet. Thank you all for being here today. If it weren't for you, well, we'd have a lot of stuff piling up inside. Thank you for believing in us." Stephen smiled and scanned the crowd. "Innis, would you join me please?"

Innis Wilkinson stepped up to the ribbon, removed the large pair of scissors she wore around her neck, and uttered, "I've been keeping them safe for a long time, Mr Blackwell."

It was as though this was how it was meant to be all along. Charlie was a little surprised that it wasn't one of the Blackwells who would ceremoniously usher in the new era in the family history, but he had an inkling there was more to the Wilkinson couple than meets the eye. As part of the transition, Charlie had stumbled across a handwritten note from someone named Smith, naming Mr and Mrs Wilkinson the official custodial staff of the Coraloo Flea Market. That was it. There was no background check or employment application, just a note. Charlie had started an investigation of sorts to learn more about the strange couple, but nobody could remember a time when they weren't there. Curious, Charlie did the best he could to research the scissors Innis wore around her neck but, not finding any connection between the hand-forged iron scissors he found online and Innis's, he'd decided one day to ask her outright why she wore them. Her response was simple but suitably cryptic: "To protect them from the morticians." Charlie didn't ask any more questions.

Stephen nodded. "Thank you, Innis."

Innis pried open the partially rusted scissors and then snapped them shut, slicing the ribbon in two. Stephen broke a bottle of mulled wine on the side of the archway. The attendees cheered and poured through the entrance as Charlie handed them a map and brochure of the market. On the back he had carefully, with the help of Danger, the self-proclaimed family historian, written the history of the Coraloo Flea Market.

Inside, soft white canopies accented by streamers of Aunt Sorcha's hand-dyed ribbon provided mini-shelters for the vendors to display their treasures. It was Velveteen's idea – a way to make the hodgepodge of finds look a little less disorganized and more visually appealing. Not much changed in the shops – Charlie said they were perfect the way they were. Aunt Moira had suggested she have a security guard stationed out front of her shop to make sure Sylvia Toft and her mother didn't try to sneak in. Charlie said it wouldn't be necessary and had to convince her, as well as a few other Blackwells, that the Tofts should be allowed to shop the market.

"Thieves and liars!" an uncle had shouted at a meeting called for the sole purpose of voting on the Toft dilemma.

"They stole our land!" another had added.

"That Sylvia is a piece of work." Moira and Sorcha had sat through the meeting with their arms crossed and their backs turned, refusing to turn around unless Charlie did something about the Toft problem.

"The whole lot of them is trouble makers. Who sells their goods at a funeral? Tofts. That's who!"

Charlie looked to Stephen for help, but he could see by the distant expression on his face that the custom of hating the Tofts was as ingrained in him as it was in the rest of the clan.

"Excuse me, Charlie. May I ask a question?" The ruckus of Toft-bashing came to a halt at the sight of the raised hand

of Velveteen Price. "I do not claim to know much about business, but if the Tofts are buying your items, are you not also taking their money? I was once an avid shopper before our days in Coraloo, as some of you know, and I have to say, I gave quite a lot of our money to many a boutique in the city –"

"Let the Tofts in!" someone shouted. "We'll take their money."

Other than the proposal that the market implement a special identification process and tax on the Tofts, which Charlie promptly shut down, the right shoes prevailed in the vote to allow the Tofts to shop the market. However, the sign out front would remain.

"Oh Velvy! Look what you've done with the place. Isn't it just darling!" Sylvia Toft squatted down in front of the rows of colorful treats lined up in the case. "I didn't tell Mother where you got the recipe. She'd rather die than eat something Granny Blackwell had a hand in."

Velveteen knew right away what she wanted to sell at *Granny's*. From the moment Charlie had asked her to take over the counter, Velveteen had set to work deciphering – with the permission of the Blackwells who were thankful they weren't the ones in the kitchen – Granny's handwritten recipes. Finella and Fiona, who had begun to wear their hair like Velveteen's and begged Clover to buy them high-heeled shoes, were thrilled to work alongside her in the kitchen.

Velveteen made an attempt to put on a pair of heels for the market's reopening, but her feet had nearly doubled in size and forcing them on made her feel like she was playing pretend with the acquaintances. They looked good but didn't feel quite right. She tried flats, sandals, sneakers, rain boots – she liked them all, but none of them were as comfortable or as lovely as her heels had been. She told herself she would give the heels another try after the baby was born; until then, with the weather warming, she'd just go barefoot. But when she entered Granny's she found a pair of handcrafted leather sandals. On the sole was stamped *F. Blackwell*. The sandals, crafted especially to fit her larger than normal feet, fit perfectly. She had her first customer before she could track down and thank the gifted party.

"How will I ever choose? Oh, aren't you a clever one – did you paint them? Are they safe to eat? It's no matter. I trust you Velvy; after all we are practically *sisters*, you know. What's in a Melba-roon?"

Finella pulled the dark red macaron from the case and handed it to Sylvia. Velveteen wiped her hands on the new apron Clover had made for her. "It's cherry and black tea."

"Oh… maybe the Velva-roon instead? You can't go wrong with orange!"

"It's bergamot with a lavender filling."

"I see." Sylvia frowned at the treat and flung her arms up in the air. "Well, I guess I don't have to eat them. I'll take one of each."

Velveteen laughed. "So you're purchasing them, but not going to eat them?"

"Velvy, sisters support each other. It's what sisters do, right? Should I make you an appointment at my shop? It looks like you're due to get those roots touched up."

Charlie Price walked the market watching the shoppers moving in and out of the shops with their bags full of the Blackwell wares. The vendors were busy too. Charlie recognized a picker by how he stepped away from the booth, checked his phone, and then went back in for the offer. He watched as the picker walked away with a 1951 Peter Pan record player. Charlie shook his head. This guy was new.

"I see you finally sold the Peter Pan." Charlie sorted through the vendor's collection of old records.

"It's good to see you, Charlie. I hear this is your doing? It looks nice."

"Thank you. I think it turned out all right."

"How did you convince Shug Blackwell to let us back in?"

"The inside of a prison cell can change a man's heart real quick." Charlie didn't really want to talk about Shug. Part of him had compassion for the man, but the other part was relieved to not have him breathing over his shoulder all the time. "I see you still have the hat boxes, Curt."

"I'll give you both of them for a good price."

"My wife would think I've gone mad." Charlie had sold nearly everything he had picked, and what remained he'd moved to his office.

"How about for old times' sake?"

"What do you want for them?"

"Twenty-five."

Charlie laughed. "Are you trying to give them to me?"

"A way to say thank you, and because I like you, Price."

Charlie pulled twenty-five out of his wallet and took the circular tin box. In the distance, the dialogue of the children performing under the grand chandelier induced a round of laughter.

The tip boot will be full today.

"Cursed!" one of them shouted.

Charlie overheard the children practicing so many times, he could practically recite their lines from memory.

The crowd applauded.

He shuffled through the busyness of the market to Shug's shop. A sign hung above the door – *Mungo's*.

Danger Blackwell ran through the door before it had time to shut. "I'm all finished up, Mr Price."

"How's it going, Danger?"

"Great! Three tours already."

"Sounds like Gideon is wrapping it up. Why don't you take a break and grab a macaron? Tell Mrs Price it's on me."

"Thanks, Mr Price."

Black and white photographs of factory workers seated at long tables inside the Coraloo adorned the walls. Shoe forms, a cobbler's anvil, and leather-working tools filled wood-framed glass cases – each with a typed description containing the date and purpose. Charlie had learned many of the antiques in Shug's shop were family heirlooms Shug had discovered in the factory's loft storage space – one of Shug's many efforts to pay off his debt.

Shug's had become *Mungo's* – a tribute to the history of the market and the Blackwell legacy. In what free time he had, Charlie searched online, digging for anything the family could add to the museum. In the back, he had made his office.

Charlie set the tin box on his desk and carefully opened the lid. He reached inside and removed a furry black nineteenth-century Royal Scots Fusiliers busby hat with a white plume and gold medallion on the front. Instinctively, he checked its value online – he could easily triple his money. He spun around in his chair and placed the hat on the bookshelf between Shelley and Stevenson. His collection of classic literature was finally free of their boxes and acid free paper holdings. Charlie stood to return to the market, accidentally knocking a small package – brown paper tied with twine – to the floor. He hadn't noticed that one before. On top of the package was a note that read: "Thank you, friend. S. Blackwell." And below, a quote Charlie new well: *For the strength of the pack is the wolf, and the strength of the wolf is the pack. R. Kipling.*

Charlie carefully pulled back the paper. He could see the blue peeking through. He tossed the parchment aside and stared at the elusive Kipling. This was it – *The Jungle Book* – the book his father had read to him every night as a child.

"Charlie, are you in here?" Velveteen Price was not thrilled her husband had chosen Shug's shop as his office – it smelled like rum and cigars and needed a bit more work than she wanted to take on at eight months pregnant. "Isn't it wonderful, Charlie! The whole day has been absolutely fabulous. The market closes in a few, and I thought we –" She stopped in front of his desk upon seeing the book. "Oh no, you didn't! Did you, Charlie?"

Charlie could barely speak. He shook his head and handed her the note, which activated her prenatal hormones, causing a flood of tears. He moved from behind the desk and held her in his arms until the lights went out on the Coraloo Flea Market.

CHAPTER 33

1937

It is not often that a man is born of a native princess and cursed to wander the world in search of something he can only find within himself. Nor that he would live to witness his own funeral. Mungo may have battled the pygmies of the South Seas and traveled with pirates, but it was neither the thrill nor the adventure that moved him closer to his death. Every day he lived, as all men do, he inched closer to his end. A friend to kings and an enemy to neighbors, Mungo Blackwell died in his sleep in the four-poster bed on a quiet morning surrounded by his children. A son, a cobbler, a husband, and a father, Mungo Blackwell died having accomplished everything he set out to do in his life – he even found contentment.

His sons attempted to bury him on the hill overlooking the town of Coraloo, his beloved having gone on before him. His home he had asked be converted into a factory for making shoes – as the talents of a single cobbler were no longer of use in a world obsessed with industrialization. He believed the space would one day employ the town.

But, as with Mungo's life, his burial was anything but ordinary. The sons had no more than put the coffin in the ground than the eldest son remembered they had forgotten to put shoes on their father.

When the sons returned to the home, they discovered all of his clothing and footwear had been donated to the town parish, as their father had instructed. Unwilling to bury their father without shoes – especially as Menzies was deathly afraid that burying his beloved father in bare feet would bring a turn of bad luck that would send the family into sudden poverty – the two brothers went to the priest to ask for a pair of shoes.

The priest would have been happy to return Mungo's shoes had they not already been distributed to the needy. The boys, weary and nervous their father would not be buried before dark, walked the town looking for at least one person who might know the whereabouts of a pair of Blackwell shoes.

As it turned out, their trek did not take them far, for in the Beaver's Beard sat Jonathan Toft with his arms crossed and his feet propped up on a table. The boys recognized their father's boots immediately and demanded the thief of a Toft give them back, but the Toft refused. Menzies swung first. Other Tofts in town got wind of the brawl and joined in. Soon the Beaver's Beard was overflowing with Tofts and Blackwells engaged in an epic war Mungo Blackwell could not have planned better himself.

In the end, Menzies held the Toft down, clamped a hand over his mouth, and wrested the shoes off his thieving feet. When the Toft wrestled himself free, he stood up and shouted, "You may have taken the hill, but we took the valley!"

"For now, you dirty Toft – you have the valley, but we have the shoes! They didn't fit you anyway!"

That night – Menzies, with a black eye, and his brother, with a busted lip – buried their father under a full moon overlooking the town of Coraloo. The next day, surrounded by the love of family and friends, they celebrated in a vigil the life and death of Mungo Blackwell.

Acknowledgments

Every time I sat down to write, I invited the Lord to sit down and write with me, to be beside me while I set out to forge a lovely place to dwell. I kept inviting until I realized that I just needed to recognize that He is always with me. Then, somewhere among the words, I found myself. I also found that He has a great sense of humor. I'm so very thankful for His company, creativity, forgiveness, unstoppable love, and endless grace.

Jamie, thank you for letting me tell our story, even if I did blow it way out of proportion and toss in a bit of weird family history. You're my Charlie Price and I will forever be proud of you. I love you twenty. Kensi and Jack, thank you for your grace and patience and total acceptance of my frantic-quirkiness. I'm crazy blessed to call you mine. Mom, you're my biggest cheerleader. I'm quite certain you would brag about me even if I wrote the most ridiculous story ever told – oh wait… I did and you did. Thank you. Jordan and the rest of my Crawford clan, you inspired me to twist and tell our tales and encouraged me to press onward – you keep me safe with your strength. Julie Gwinn, you told me once that you believed in me; thank you for never stopping and for telling me to write this story six years before I had planned. Jessica Gladwell, thank you for taking a chance on me. I couldn't imagine my *Mungo* in better hands. The publishing team at Lion Hudson, you've worked so hard to help me bring this to life – thank you for loving on me from so far away. Julie Frederick, I feel we became fast friends. Thank you for making *Mungo* shine. Duty calls! Sarah J. Coleman, you got it perfectly right! Thank you. And the many others: Gigi, for your constant prayers, my writing gals – Valeria, Melissa, and Keely – for all the calls, coffee shop meet-ups and conversations, my Realmies, my nacho mommas (you know who you are), my Shanan family and all my young writers, my friends, Larry and Shirley, my Brandenburg family, and every single one of you who have listened to me go on and on about this tale… Thank you from every inch of me!

Reader's Guide

1. This book is called *The Death of Mungo Blackwell*. Why do you think the author chose this title?

2. The Blackwells hold a funeral for each family member before they die. Do you think this is a good idea? Does it make you think about what might be missing in your life?

3. Charlie and Velveteen set out on a quest for simplicity, but find what they really need is contentment. What do you perceive to be the difference between simplicity and contentment? Do you think the characters find what they are looking for?

4. Discuss Velveteen, her upbringing, playing "pretend" with the acquaintances, her fascination with Melba DuMont, and her relationship to Granny Blackwell. Do you relate to her character at all?

5. Discuss Charlie's life before and after *The Rooning*. What do you feel was ultimately driving him to seek success in both the city and in Coraloo?

6. What parts of the novel did you find most humorous or relatable?

7. Velveteen tries to find her shoes but in the end is given a pair of sandals custom-made for her by a member of the Blackwell family. Discuss the importance of "shoes" throughout the novel and the significance of Velveteen finding comfort in a pair of Blackwell shoes.

8. Did you like how the author handled the resolution of the story? Is there anything you would add or change for either Charlie or Velveteen?

9. "The feelings of defeat and fear surrounding Charlie in the days after the food truck debacle were now replaced by a sense of purpose – a mission – and a new family motto: 'Simplicity.'" Do you have a motto that you live by? Do you think this was a good motto for the Price family? How would a different motto have affected their move to Coraloo?

10. Stephen Blackwell says, "We Blackwells have always been about two things: faith and family... I was willing to take the risk." Would you be willing to currently leave the life you have to try something new? What would that new thing be? Would you imagine it would be an act of faith or an act of survival?

Author Interview

What first inspired you to write *The Death of Mungo Blackwell*?
A piece of history my dad passed on to me about a family member, who actually had his funeral before he died. Seriously! No wonder I'm so quirky. When I first heard this, I knew I had to write a character who would be bold enough to do that. The rest of the story is loosely based on my family's own "Rooning" – we experienced financial loss during 2008. There was always a story there; it just so happened I was able to blend the two family narratives.

Do you have a particular writing routine?
Not particularly. I do my best to get up before my kiddos, especially when I am in the middle of edits. Other than that, I take advantage of any free time I can to write, whether that's in a coffee shop while my daughter is doing her martial arts or at the dining room table while my son is studying. In the car, on the back porch, in the waiting room of the dentist's office – when there's time, I write. But family is important, so time with them comes first.

What is the writing habit that you rely on to get you through a first draft?
I have to remember that it is the first draft. It's going to be ugly, awful, and I just have to get the words on the paper. I usually have my chapters roughly outlined before I begin, but let's be honest, it never looks the same when I'm done. I never stop when I feel stuck – I'm afraid I won't want to come back

to it. So, I keep going until I know I will be excited to write more the next day.

How much of you is there in your characters?

There is quite a bit of my heart in Velveteen. We're both short, but I wouldn't consider myself as glamorous or as high maintenance by any means. Her thought process is much like my own – a bit scattered, truly crazy about her husband, but trying to figure out her own path to contentment.

Are there any scenes in your novel that you would consider "loosely based" on your own experience?

During our "Rooning" I decided to color my hair, and when I went to rinse it out we had no water. My daughter had to run jugs of bottled water up the stairs and help me pour them over my hair! The worst part was that I had a photographer on her way to take my first professional headshots. Let's just say my hair was really dark. Oh, and when the foreclosure agent showed up at our door, I was hosting a ladies event for our church. I totally played it off and the ladies had no idea what was going on (I didn't throw macarons!).

If you could have dinner with any of your characters who would it be?

Granny! Can you imagine the stories she could tell? I love dinner conversations where I laugh a lot, and I know she would have had me doubled up in a pile of myself laughing so hard. And her food! I would have been happy to dine on her pastries any day. I'd just have to make sure it didn't get too boozy – the woman likes a good splash of bourbon in her confectionery!

Who is your favourite literary character?

I adore Jo March in *Little Women*. She is such a strong female character; so willing to do whatever it takes for her family. And she is a writer! I always wanted to be Jo when I was a little girl. She was kind of the leader of the bunch. I liked that.

Did any of the characters in your book surprise you while writing?
Definitely Velveteen. She's a lot stronger than I originally thought she would be.

What is the worst job you've done?
Oh my goodness! This takes me back to high school. I worked as a dressing room attendant for a clothing outlet. It was horrible! I'd have to clean out the dressing rooms after each person used it, fold the clothes, and then put them away – All. Day. Long. And some people had a smell that just stayed in the dressing room and would stick to the clothes. And if there was no one in the dressing rooms, I had to walk around straightening all the clothes racks… even if they were already tidy. Most boring job ever!

What is the most important lesson life has taught you?
To dwell on what is true and lovely. It's from a scripture in the book of Philippians: *Finally, brethren, whatever is true, whatever is honorable, whatever is right, whatever is pure, whatever is lovely, whatever is of good repute, if there is any excellence and if anything worthy of praise, dwell on these things.* Thinking on what is true avoids a lot of unnecessary worry and conflict. And dwelling on what it lovely just makes life, well, more lovely.

Which book do you suspect most people claim to have read, but haven't?
The Bible. You can't just read a scripture or two and say you've read it. You have to really read it, study it – what comes before and after – to understand what it says.

How do you feel about physical books versus eBooks?
I almost always prefer a physical book. My dad bought me a hardbound copy of *Little Women* when I was ten. It was the first chapter book that I could actually call my own. I still have it. Occasionally I will download an e-book or a free sample to get an idea of the writing before I purchase the physical book.

Do you have any advice for an aspiring author?
Be prepared and be professional. Study the craft of writing, listen to podcasts, buy the books, attend a writers' conference, and surround yourself with other like-minded writers. Read both in and out of your genre. Professionals know their market and understand the whole process is a lot of hard work!

For more information please visit:
www.LaurenHBrandenburg.com

Return to Coraloo for

Publishing May 2020

It is said that something magical happens during the festival season in Coraloo, something unexplainable. People tend to be a little crazier, reckless. Maybe it's because it coincides the full moon, but Coraloo's constable, Roy Blackwell, is beginning to think it's something else.

That said, Roy has other things on his mind, like marrying Margarette Toft. A controversial decision as the Toft and the Blackwell families have a hatred for one another that is older than the town itself. Tradition collides with superstition as the feuding families compete to organize the events surrounding the most talked about wedding in the history of Coraloo.

Despite the array of minor catastrophes that ensue, Roy and Margarette hold fast and declare they will do whatever it takes to wed.

That is until Roy unearths a town secret – a murder involving a pair of scissors, an actor with a severe case of kleptomania, and the mysterious marriage of Innis Wilkinson. Can good come out of unearthing the past – or will only heartbreak follow?

ISBN: 978 1 78264 299 2 | eISBN: 978 1 78264 300 5